Leeram in Fordlandia

Leeram in Fordlandia

Buell Hollister

Merrimack Media
Cambridge, Massachusetts

Library of Congress Control Number: 2013955539

ISBN: print: 978-1-939166-60-9
ISBN: ebook: 978-1-939166-60-9

Published by Merrimack Media, Cambridge, Massachusetts
January, 2015

To my wife, Margaret

Acknowledgements and Introduction

I suppose it belabors the obvious to insist this is a piece of fiction, but the reader should know that all of the details regarding the town of Brookline and the first class public university system in the Commonwealth of Massachusetts in this book are completely made up. I had fun writing this book, letting my alter ego run about like a diminutive mad man. I can only caution the reader not to try this stuff at home.

I credit Ann Colette, a literary agent, for giving me – whether she knew it or not – the energy to start this book and Gabe Robinson, whose editing skills and encouragement were essential for me to finish it.

The command (well, let's say fervent hope) that the reader suspends disbelief after the first few pages, is assumed. Anyone who takes all this seriously is welcome to join the ranks of tabloid readers in supermarket checkout lines, who believe that Bat Boy really exists. To

them I say: Leeram knows all about you. Keep one eye
open at night.

Chapter 1

The shrunken head had the feel of an old, dog-chewed baseball as I lifted it out of its wooden box. Its owner, a friend who was also my dentist, poured us both another dollop of Jim Beam. "I got it from a guy years ago when I was in South America," he said. "He was down on his luck and needed twenty bucks. He told me he won it in a poker game." A voyeurish thrill—almost like a feeling I knew I shouldn't have—teased me as I looked at it. Its eyes were sewn shut and beaded sisal strings dangled from its lips. Its features were at the same time very human and very distorted. The eyes and mouth were closed, of course, but the cheeks and forehead were out of proportion—much smaller than the nose and mouth, which were protuberant. The hair was luxurious and closely bunched, tied in the back into a little black ponytail that would never, ever, get gray. I could almost imagine what he looked like in life when I looked at it from one angle and then lost the link when I looked from another. "Too bad they don't leave teeth in those heads when they shrink them," my friend said. He put the head away and changed the subject.

My friend died a while ago. I was helping his widow get his effects in order. She wanted to move to a smaller house and was getting rid of most of the artifacts he had collected over the years. There was a lot of it and no children to pass things on to, and the head was one thing she had absolutely no—*nada, zero*—desire to keep. I wondered if the native who it once was had made contact with my friend, now that they were on the same plane of existence. Perhaps they had a conversation: "You know what we do with dentists?" the head could have asked. "We have a big pot."

"Wait a minute," my friend might have said. "Not my fault what happened to you."

The reply might have been: "Well, you got me for almost nothing from a guy down on his luck and he just got lucky once in a card game. It was insulting enough to be killed and shrunk, and to be sold for a knife and a bamboo pan flute, but to be tossed around like a poker chip really puts a twist in my breechclout." And yet he might not have said anything like that at all.

"I thought about selling it," the widow said, "but I have no idea if that's illegal and, anyway, I don't think I could go through with the process. I was told that these things can go for thirty thousand dollars on eBay if they're real."

I looked at it again. Its skin was hard and chalky. I

sniffed. It was mostly odorless, yet was that a hint of decay? Just in my mind, I decided. An imitation? Not a chance! The words were out of my mouth almost before I was aware that I said them: "I'll take it if you don't want it."

"Oh, thank you," she said, as though I had scraped something really unpleasant off her shoe. "I really don't care what it's worth, I just want to get it out of my house."

A few days later I was looking at the head again. It was a little less repulsive now; its *ickiness* had begun to subside. I named him Little Red Man because he looked vaguely like the head on the chewing tobacco can. After a few weeks, I realized that I was fond of him. He was the perfect roommate—not messy at all and didn't eat things in the fridge that I had been saving for later, or drink my liquor. Did I mention that I was not married and living alone?

Eventually, I drifted into collapsing his initials to Leeram—it was just easier to say. I fantasized that Leeram preferred to stay in my dresser drawer at first, but after a while I put him on the bookshelf, a totem of my solitude. A quiet soul, I remarked to myself, like me. He had no objection at all. He pretty much liked my apartment; at least he didn't complain or roll his eyes behind all those stitches. When I put Art Tatum on, he seemed to enjoy it. I amused myself by imagining that our tastes in music were serendipitously alike. I made myself sense his approval of Joe Venuti, Lena Horne, the Ink Spots, and Fats Waller. Occasionally, if I was in another kind of mood, one of the old chorale performances would make us smile (me anyway), especially Brahms. I knew that Leeram's brain had been replaced with hot sand during the process of pocket-sizing his head, but amputees can still feel their missing limbs, I had read. During one evening of solitary drinking, I amused myself by surmising that perhaps Leeram could still feel his own missing brain.

After I graduated from college twenty years ago (a famous, old southern institution that cultivated the image of a Virginia gentleman—and more lately Virginia ladies), I had been on a kind of random, unfocused walk through life. At first, I worked as a reporter for a small town weekly in Connecticut, then a wire service. That company went out of business. Afterward, I got a job in a public relations company where I made more money, but came home every night just to get half drunk, eat, and sleep. I met and married a woman whose biological clock evidently had overwhelmed her common sense. (I thought I had just gotten lucky.) My pheromones linked into her mental receptors like the couplers on a railroad car. Unfortunately, my sperm cells didn't do the same thing with her eggs. Eventually we separated anticlimactically and I found myself, now in my early forties, living in a small apartment near Boston. My ex-wife had tenure in a local university with a secure, if modest, salary so there was no question of my paying alimony, and aside from all the sex, I didn't miss her that much.

I eventually got a job at a local coffee shop, and even toyed with a mild inspiration to someday run one myself.

By now, though, I had to admit that my entrepreneurial drive lacked the horsepower to ever reach such a goal. I don't mind being on my feet and the place just smelled good, so eventually I went there every morning just to hang out and make a little money doing it. You might say I was lazy and lacked ambition, but each to his own, and it's none of your business anyway. One great advantage of working in a place like that is that I got to take some really choice products back home with me. I had an elaborate grinding machine and a special oven just for roasting the beans, and eventually my apartment took on the same aroma as the coffee shop itself. It reminded me of the way a tropical plant greenhouse feels in February, without the interesting people, of course. I did not really have any close friends and actually preferred it that way; I could get all the conversation and human connection that anyone could want at work, then when I came home, I could just turn it all off. It was a beautifully perfect arrangement. My apartment was my castle, and I was the monarch of all I surveyed. It was a perfect, fragrant little world.

A few months went by and I discovered that I had begun to think of my new roommate as less of a piece of bric-a-brac and more of, well, a Leeram. To be honest, I don't think of myself as being especially credulous or open to the twilight zone, and I am not an obsessive Stephen King reader; I take things as they come, as I did Leeram. I even took him to work one day in a man purse, the only thing I could think of to carry him in. He was pretty much unnoticeable as I walked around, serving customers and chatting with them. As it happened, the house was featuring "rain forest dark roast" that day. My customers were unusually friendly as I poured small, medium, and large paper cups with misleading names. It was almost as though I had a larger presence, as though the customers were inspired to buy more than they had in the past. The ones who normally ordered smalls now ordered mediums and so on. The customers would retreat to their usual tables with their MacBooks and type away at (it seemed to me) a much faster rate, as though their brains had been hooked up to invisible jumper cables. Had this anything to do with Leeram, I let the idle, wondering thought slip by. Of course not. I batted the thought away as though it were a fat housefly, glistening from its latest meal. I am, I repeat, a realist. It's a mistake to anthropomorphize things. I certainly knew better than to imagine that the wooden table in front of me was a living tree, or that the BLT I had for lunch had any notion of distress about being compressed between two slices of bread and eaten.

Yet, when I got home that evening, took off my coat, took Leeram out of the man purse, and put him back on the shelf, I thought that I noticed just the faintest sliver of something shining between the stitches in his eyelids. It wasn't there when I looked again, so I opened the fridge and poured a glass of wine, sat on my sofa, put my feet on the coffee table, and flipped on the PBS News Hour. The announcers, as they always did, reminded me of one of my grade school teachers—simultaneously comforting and boring. The old familiar French horns went boop de doop de doop doop, and the sponsoring company that somehow has a finger in everything we eat, drink, and wear announced that as long as we were in their hands, the world would be just wonderful. They read the headlines of the moment, then went on (more French horns here) to announce the featured topic of the day: deforestation in the Amazon.

I began to doze off, as I always do during the "snooze hour," my head on the back of the couch. I began to dream that I was in a rain forest and I was standing next to a small brown man, nearly naked, dressed in a breechclout and holding a bow. "You are a strange people," he said.

"No stranger than you," I replied, a little annoyed. He looked very familiar.

"Next time you take me to work, you should introduce me around."

I had to admit that I had not been very polite. "It never occurred to me," I said. "Anyway, you are just partly in my possession. I only have your head."

"This will have to do—the rest of me was eaten long ago."

If I was having a nightmare, it was curiously not at all scary. "So what do you want from me?"

"I'll tell you what, Mr. El Giganto, first, I want you to lose your ignorance. I do not look anything like the guy on the tobacco can. He's a distant northern cousin and our lines separated thousands of years ago. When I was alive, I was one of the best medicine men in Brazil. My enemies killed and ate me to get my skills—those dumb fucks . They were all worked to death by the *capatazes* in sugar cane plantations right after."

"I had no idea," I said. "I'm terribly sorry. Is there something I can do?"

"We're going to have to work on that. Wake the hell up and we'll get started."

Suddenly I was hearing French horns again and it was seven o'clock. I took my feet off the table and stood up. I felt a little dizzy, a little disoriented. It had started to rain outside, the water loud against the window. I was hungry and the half-empty glass of California chardonnay was warm.

As I pawed through the freezer for something quick to microwave from my weekly trip to Trader Joe's, I thought about my dream. I must have, I decided, an imagination that was more vivid than I had thought—maybe I shouldn't have had that glass of wine; too buttery, too oaky. Leeram was perched on his usual shelf. I went over and turned him around to face the wall. Public television can only be bad for a shrunken head. Later, after eating supper and watching another couple of hours of TV, I went to bed, wondering if I was going to be able to sleep. Well, I did and it was dreamless.

The next morning, which began with sunlight evaporating the remnants of last night's storm and leaving a distinct whiff of ozone, I left the house on my normal commute but stopped in the driveway. Maybe, I thought, I should take Leeram with me again. Yesterday had been quite productive (although I doubted he had much to do with that). I went back, unlocked the front door, went in and retrieved the head, put it in the man purse, and slung it over my shoulder.

At the coffee shop, I changed into my uniform, a black nylon shirt with my name, Gilbert Greenbush, and rank ("Associate") on the pocket and went to the cash register, bulging purse at my waist. "What's that?" asked the manager.

"A man purse."

"No, I mean what's in it."

"A shrunken head."

"Yeah, sure," he said and turned away. "You're late today—again! Get with the program or look for another job," he tossed at me over his shoulder. So much for the friendly ambience the place advertised. It was going to be a hot day and the barest hint of sweaty saddlebags was already apparent around his armpits.

It was like a second shift for the customers, coming in around mid-morning with their laptops. They were beginning to fill all the available seats vacated by breakfasters. The new crowd would begin their usual routine, hunched over the keyboards, rattling away with an extra-large cardboard cup of java at close reach. It was the time each day when the coffee shop turned into an office or library, the wireless router in the back room almost smoking under the load. Novels under construction everywhere. Occasionally someone would come in for a cup and have to take it out with him when even the window benches were full. Management hated that, but the place had a reputation in the neighborhood and they felt it was worth the lost business. I always wondered about that, but then I was just a worker bee around there. Sort of a worker bee, anyway.

One customer, who never took off his beret as though it was the only thing that kept all his thoughts together, had been nursing the same cup of coffee for almost an hour while he worked. My boss looked at him, then looked at me. I knew what I had to do. I walked over to him and asked if he would like some more coffee.

"Would you *please* leave me alone!" He glared at me.

"I'm sorry, sir, but there are customers waiting to use this table. If you don't want anything else, you'll have to move."

"Get lost," he muttered and went back to his work.

"What a dick!" I heard somebody say. I turned around but everyone was pecking away like geese in a cornfield. "You ought to dump that coffee on his head, or at least on that thing he is poking at!"

Again, I looked around. Unless one of the customers was a ventriloquist, nobody within earshot could have spoken. I felt a small movement at my waist. Nah, it couldn't be, I said to myself. Feeling really stupid, I whispered, "Is that you, Leeram?"

"It sure as hell isn't your Aunt Priscilla."

I suppose I shouldn't have been surprised, given the events of the past few days.

"My Aunt Priscilla wouldn't have been so harsh," I sotto voced, trying not to look like a lunatic talking to himself.

"I'm not harsh, just pissed off at you. Grow a pair!"

I was speechless. I not only had a shrunken head, but it was giving me a hard time. All I had done was to help the widow of a friend simplify her life and now I had Yosemite Sam on my case.

"Look," I said. "If I throw that guy out, I will probably lose my job."

"Yes, you probably would."

It was a revelation, a dawn breaking, a synaptic collusion of everything in the back of my brain. I went into the storeroom, took off the store's shirt, and threw it on the floor. Then I went over to Mr. Beret, closed his laptop with a snap, and walked out the front door with it under my arm. He sat there, stunned for a moment, then was outside the door in front of me in an instant.

"What are you trying to do? Gimme that!"

I tossed it to him and he barely caught it before it hit the ground, then I walked to my car. "Thanks, Leeram." I heard a chuckle from the man purse. "Now tell me more about the rain forest."

"Guess what: I'm not in the rain forest anymore."

Chapter 2

A person with a weakness for metaphors (not me, of course) might have said that the locomotive of my life had gone into a roundhouse and was slowly turning toward an unknown track. I was not in a big rush to find another job immediately; I had some savings and was able to sell a few pieces of valuable furniture that I had inherited from an elderly aunt—Priscilla, as I suppose you might have guessed by now. Leeram and I were in a period that might have been called a honeymoon; we were getting used to sharing my space. I am not a nosy person, but the fact that I was having conversations with a formerly human head did give me pause, to say the least. I have always been a little reticent about asking personal questions of anybody; Leeram's leathery attitude did not make it any easier for me to ask them of him. One day, I couldn't resist any longer. It was making me crazy. "How is it that you can talk to me, anyway?" I asked.

Leeram was silent for such a long time that I began to

think he hadn't heard me. I was about to ask him again, when he said, "The Universe is a lot wilder and woollier than you can imagine. Everyone wants to live forever and they've told each other a lot of fairytales to make them feel better about dying. Also to keep them in line by scaring them with stories about hell and damnation." Leeram sighed, then went on, "There was only one person who came anywhere close about the afterlife—your guy, Homer. He tells about it in the Odyssey when Odysseus—or Ulysses—goes down through a cave into Hades and meets his mom and a bunch of his old fighting buddies who are very concerned about their reputations in the world of the living."

"You know about Homer?" I asked.

"Look, big guy, once you're on this end, everybody knows about Homer. He's kind of like your Columbus to us. Some of us think he actually created the place we live in. Ulysses actually made a two-way trip through a wormhole into this universe—the one where I live and everyone else who used to be in yours. I'll tell you later how improbable that is. Hades is infinitely expandable—the laws of physics are different. Other planets probably have their own Hades too, but that's just my guess." I asked Leeram what it was like where he was. "Not too bad," he said, "but it is pretty lethargic. The weather is constantly like it is on earth just before a big thunderstorm—little wind, humid, and the clouds are close. It never rains, though. To tell the truth, it's a little boring for most people even though it's not all that uncomfortable. I live in a rain forest here, so it doesn't bother me much."

"Don't people try to escape?" I asked.

"Almost everyone thinks about it, but those wormholes are pretty much a one-way street. Every now and then someone gets desperate enough to try to get back but it is very, very dangerous. You really don't know where you'll come out the other end, because the hole squirms around so much. Chances are you will step out onto one of Saturn's moons or even on an asteroid, where things will be many times worse than they were at the place you left. To make it back successfully in one piece takes more luck and determination than most people have. I'm lucky—you have my head so I can link up with you and not be in any danger. Why should I even try to come back?

"Like I said, I have always existed, but until you actually picked me up out of that box and felt and smelled me—hell, I thought you were going to lick my cheek—I didn't have much contact with your universe, my old one. When you included me, viscerally, in your world, you opened a channel to me, not a wormhole, just a channel. That's how we can talk."

It was still a little mysterious to me but I went along with it. Leeram's vocabulary kept surprising me. It was a little larger than I expected. Anthropomorphizing may not have been such a silly concept after all.

"Don't worry," he said, "you can't talk with a stone or a

dandelion, even the infinite quantum universe won't allow that, or I don't think, anyway. But I live through you, and because of that I can communicate not only with you, but anyone you know. I can even give you some of my lesser skills."

"Did you ever talk to my dentist friend?" I asked.

"He rarely ever took me out of that box. He was afraid of me."

"Can't understand why," I replied.

***

One morning a few weeks later, I was reading a newspaper article about urban farming and told Leeram about it. "A lot of people are growing food in the city—on rooftops and vacant lots," I said. "It's kind of the old Victory Garden concept, only everywhere." Restaurants had begun planting lettuce on their roofs—any large flat surface away from the sidewalk would do. Architects were designing roof gardens in concept drawings to impress local planning boards. Even the managers of my apartment complex set aside a stretch of open land between parking lots for vegetables. Maybe it was the subliminal effect of my surname, but I was drawn to the idea and had even put in a row of radishes and carrots that spring.

Leeram was noncommittal, which is how I took it when he did not respond.

A few months later, I was pulling some of the carrots up,

fully grown. Leeram was at my side. I got the feeling that he was giving me the old hairy eyeball.

"What?" I said.

"You know how dumb you look?"

"This isn't dumb! This is good! These carrots are going to taste much better than ones from the grocery store."

"Uh huh," he said warily, and please don't ask how I knew a shrunken head could respond to anything warily, but he did. I continued until I had them all in a paper bag. I brought them back to my apartment, washed them, and bit into one. It tasted pretty much like any other carrot I had ever eaten.

"Hope some dog didn't pee on it," said Leeram. I put the rest of the carrot down on the counter, then put them all back in the sink and started to scrub them all over again.

"Thanks, you little bastard," I said. I sensed a grin from him and it made me mad. The newspaper's editors must have become fixated on locavores, because they would return to the topic of local food sources every few weeks. Just a few days later, in fact, an article appeared about a group of people who went around doing what they called Urban Foraging and I told Leeram about it (I should have known better). "This woman goes all over the city looking for things like dandelion leaves and nettles," I said. "She cooks them and makes salads and pesto, maybe even wine!"

"Nettle wine?" he snorted. "Sounds like a punishment.

These idiots should be looking for magic mushrooms, not salad greens."

"If it was up to me," Leeram went on, "I'd go urban foraging for some of those geese that crap everywhere. They may have even crapped on your vegetables." I took the whole bundle of carrots and threw them away.

"Why did I ever take you into my home in the first place?" I said.

"Buddy, you will never know how lucky you were." I was the silent responder this time.

It was now October. My food all came from the supermarket. Leeram and I had resumed our comfortable Oddest Couple life, occasionally quarrelling, occasionally laughing. One day, a rafter of wild turkeys came walking right down the median strip of Beacon Street in Brookline along the trolley tracks like they owned the damned place. I was on the sidewalk and watched, fascinated. The biggest one, it seemed about four feet tall, was aggressively out in front, and as we were looking, it lunged at a stout lady waiting at the Coolidge Corner trolley station. She swung her handbag at it, then turned around and trotted away as quickly as she could while trying to maintain a shred of respectability. The bird, now looking more like an avian dinosaur, followed, pecking at her ample behind.

"You were talking about urban foraging," Leeram said. "Why not forage one of them?" I had to admit, there was some inescapable logic there. Nettles on the one hand and roast turkey on the other. No contest on which one tastes better.

"You can't shoot a firearm in the city," I said. "It's against the law and besides, there are too many people who would raise holy hell if they ever saw someone do it."

"Listen, Greenbush, don't forget I'm a hunter. We don't need a gun."

I was not repelled, but dismissive, and I told him so.

"We need to find out where they live," he said. "And I will show you how to use an atlatl."

"A what?"

"An atlatl. Sounds like rattle-rattle. I used to be able to put a spear through a coconut at one hundred feet with one, and it doesn't make any noise." Leeram described it: basically a stick about the length of an arm with a cup on the end, a little stirrup to support the spear, or dart, that was about twice its length. It had a carved grip on the other end to keep it from flying out of your hand. The cup held the back of the dart and acted like a throwing extension of your arm. "We got tired of throwing stones in a sling," Leeram said. He said he would show me how to make one and to use it. I was intrigued. Leeram's influence on me had been gradual but not unwelcome—a process that I must admit I had not resisted.

A quick Google search turned up the interesting fact that atlatls had made a comeback among a subset of the hunting and fishing crowd in America and could actually be bought from select sporting goods stores. I told Leeram that I didn't actually have to make one, I could buy it.

"I kind of like this world," Leeram said. "Maybe you're not as civilized as you seem."

A couple of weeks later, a UPS package arrived from Amazon; it contained the device and a dozen spear-darts, along with illustrated instructions. It wasn't expensive—a good thing as I had been living on a tight budget ever since I left the coffee shop. Leeram and I went out to a wooded state reservation to try it out. Throwing things, I found to my pleasure, was a talent I never knew I had, never having been much interested in school sports when I was a kid. The darts, about five feet long, were surprisingly easy to handle and after a few days of practice, I found that I was pretty accurate with them. Leeram helped, I must admit, but whether he was doing it by remote control or just by giving me confidence was not clear. When I asked him about it, he shrugged (picture a blob of ectoplasm raising two little bumps, or not, if the image is too disturbing).

After I felt competent enough, we were ready for the hunt. I told Leeram that I was going to get a hunting license with a turkey permit. The season went for two weeks, ending on November 2, just a few weeks away. "A turkey permit?" Leeram was incredulous. "What in the name of Quetzalcoatl is that?"

"Here in Massachusetts, you can get put in jail for hunting without a permit."

"Every time I begin to admire your civilization, I suddenly wonder what I was thinking."

The process was pretty easy, and in a couple of days, I was a licensed wild turkey predator. With my atlatl and darts hidden in a big guitar case at my back and Leeram's man purse next to it, we set out late one afternoon. The big birds would go to their nesting hideouts at dusk and we wanted to follow them; after dark it would be a lot harder. I finally convinced Leeram that to "harvest" a turkey in plain view of a typical Brookline citizen would be calamitous. Looking like an older Berklee music student on his way to a gig, I started around the Cleveland Circle reservoir and headed toward south Brookline. I had heard about rampant wild turkeys harassing local residents in the Fisher Hill area, a place with big houses and vast house lots, largely wooded. It was the kind of place where nervous residents peek through curtains and call the police when oddly dressed strangers are seen on the sidewalks instead of behind the wheel of a BMW. I did my best to walk along with my head up and my shoulders straight, as though I had been invited to someone's house for drinks and dinner. I was wearing a corduroy jacket with lapels and leather patches on the elbows.

We had been looking for a couple of hours when, just before dark, Leeram said, "Stop! Be very quiet. I think I hear something."

I froze, trying to breathe without making a sound. We had wandered all the way down to the Frederick Law

Olmstead estate, a vast, beautifully landscaped parcel covered with many trees, glens, and dells. It was bordered at the sidewalk with a dry stone wall about shoulder height. Slowly turning to peer over it, I saw three of our hulky, feathered targets walking in a line toward a thicket. It was getting dark and no one was in sight. I carefully climbed over the wall and started, as silently as I could, in pursuit. "Slowly, more slowly," Leeram whispered, although I had no idea why he needed to; I was obviously the only one who could hear him. When we were out of sight of the road, I put the guitar case on the ground, soundlessly opened it, and took out the weapon. I notched a spear/dart in the atlatl's cup, holding it in the middle with my index finger, and gathered a few more projectiles in my other hand. By the time I was ready, I had lost sight of the turkeys but had a pretty good idea of where they had gone, and carefully tracked toward them. I was as alive and attuned to the world around me as I had ever been in my life. Every sense I possessed, including Leeram's, which seemed to be somehow linked to mine, was in harmonic vibration with the leaves, insects, small animals, and, yes, birds within spear-throwing distance. "Over there," Leeram whispered. Suddenly I saw them, almost invisible in the dusk. They were huddled together in a small clump of bushes, puffing and deflating, preparing for the night. Had Leeram not pointed them out, I could have passed within five feet and never had a clue.

With the very last of the evening light, I aimed at the

biggest one, the Tom, in the middle, cleared my mind of thought entirely, and threw the dart as hard as I could. An explosion of shrieks and squawks instantly followed. The big Tom ran around in circles then collapsed in a pile of feathers and the other two disappeared almost instantly, leaving a trail of gobbling cacophony. When I reached the dead bird, I could see the fletching of the dart, a few inches of it, still sticking out of its chest. There was very little blood. It must have gone right through its heart; a clean kill. "Congratulations, my friend," Leeram said excitedly. "You are now one of my tribe!" I felt real affection from him for the first time.

It only took a moment for reality to raise its ugly presence. I had two problems: the first being that everyone within a half mile must have heard the racket, and the second, how was I going to get this very large, extremely dead bird back to my apartment? The road back was, to say the least, going to be strewn with obstacles. First, I tried to fit the turkey into the guitar case, a procedure I knew instinctively to be impossible, but I tried anyway. This bird was big enough to star on Sesame Street. I picked it up by the legs, pulling them over my shoulders but its head was still touching the ground; the thought of dragging it along behind me, possibly leaving a trail of blood, was uncontemplatable.

"Sorry, bud, but I can't help you take it out of here," Leeram said. "Why don't you go get something to put it in?"

That was, I had to admit, the only solution. Why hadn't I planned for such an obvious outcome? I covered it with some branches and leaves, put the now-bloodied atlatl back in the guitar case, and crept back to the stone wall, terrified that I would be jailed not only for trespassing, but committing a morally reprehensible act in the eyes of the local citizenry. Relieved wasn't the right word for how I felt; getting out of there unseen was the most delicious sensation I had ever experienced. I could go home now, a free man! Any thought of going back was over. So over.

"I thought you were one of us," said Leeram, "but now I'm disappointed in you. You're just a *franco americano* after all." My elation collapsed. "You just took a life," he said. "You have to respect the life you took. You owe that turkey the right to be cooked and eaten. More than that, you have to make up for the lack of respect you have shown for all the animals that became your cheeseburgers and chicken nuggets over the years. You can't leave that turkey there." I had never heard Leeram sound so serious or say so much; I had never thought about my food that way. The knots in my chest began weaving themselves back together again.

I knew I had to make a dangerous choice, to do something that would very likely get me into trouble with no foreseeable ending or to take the easy way out and just go home. In the end, I didn't really have a choice at all—not with this nun on my case, this cross between a nun and a cannibal. I had seen a convenience store open nearby, so I went in, bought a box of large contractor trash bags, and went back, resigned that there was no way on earth I would ever return to my perfect, fragrant little world without visiting a police station first. Back over the wall, through the Olmstead land, and standing over the cooling bird, I paused for a moment, hardly believing that I had gotten that far twice without being seen. Had everybody been rendered suddenly deaf? I wrestled the turkey, still slightly warm, into one of the bags, put the rest of the bags in the guitar case with the atlatl, threw the now heavy sack over my shoulder, and made my way back toward the sidewalk for the second time, certain as I took each step that I would hear someone shout. My creeping progress was interminable. I had to stop twice to wipe sweat out of my eyes when they stung so much I couldn't see my way at all. When I finally climbed back over the wall one more time and stood back on the sidewalk, gasping, and realized that no one had seen what I had just done, I was almost too exhausted to think. A half hour later, with an aching back, sore shoulders, and in a state of near catatonic shock, I was in my apartment, unapprehended. I poured a water glass full of Jim Beam, put my feet up on the coffee table, and let my mind go blank.

"You did a good job, Gilbert," said Leeram.

I won't go into great detail about the next two hours of plucking and drawing that great creature, after a Leeramic browbeating about having to do it now instead of waiting for tomorrow. When it was done, my little abode that once smelled of coffee had turned into an abattoir with feathers everywhere and the stench of guts and blood in my hands, hair, clothes, and everywhere else. Nearly in a coma, I made it into my bed at 4:00 a.m., after cleaning the last feather, the last bit of offal. I did most of the work in the kitchen and put the carcass into the fridge after removing just about everything else to make room for it.

"All that food you buy in the stores has to be disassembled by somebody," Leeram said. "Now you know what it's like."

Thank you, old Mr. Gobbler, I thought, just before going to sleep. I will honor you now.

Chapter 3

I decided, a few days after the hunt, that if there was a vegetarian gene, I did not have it. The memory of the smell and the blood faded when I took the turkey out of the fridge. It looked just like a turkey from the store, pale and knobbly, with skin like my grandmother's. After reading some online instructions, I stuffed it with raw vegetables, placed strips of bacon over it, and put it in the oven, set low, and let it cook slowly all day. Before long, the kitchen began to fill with deliciousness. That night, alone except for Leeram, I sat down with a bottle of full-bodied white Bordeaux, and ate—my primitive self and Leeram, who I placed on the table across from me. Macabre? Perhaps, but it didn't seem so to me. It was more like a little celebration of freedom. I had passed a test and Leeram approved. I raised a glass, "To you, Thomas the Turkey."

A week or so later, I was walking down the street minding my own business—or should I say Leeram and I were engaged in this self-absorbed process—when I noticed a crowd down the block. As we got nearer, we realized that it contained one, two, no, about a dozen naked women, most of whom were not at all hard to look at, led by one who looked like an Amazon. A real Amazon—large boned and tall, yet attractive. The women were holding signs that seemed to equate the wearing of fur with moral decadence.

"Better to be naked than wear fur," the signs read. This sentiment, I thought, might be a little over the top, especially where we were, well north of the equator, but the weather was warm for the season. "A gentleman does not stare," I reminded myself with my mother's words, which is not to say that a gentleman is unaware of his surroundings.

"Wait a minute!" Leeram interrupted, injecting his slightly accented, ectoplasmic voice directly into my brain. "They have fur. Liars!"

"That's not fur," I said.

This wasn't the first time that Leeram had begun to sound a little salacious.

"Well," I explained, "they invest animals with human sensibilities, so to eat one or wear its fur is an act of murder."

"Tell me about murder," he said. "I think I know a little bit more about it than you do."

"They call themselves PETA," I told Leeram. One of them even had painted PETA in large brush strokes beginning at her right shoulder and sloping down to the left side of her waist. Her navel punctuated the space between the E and the T, while the middle bar of the E looked more like a tilde. I explained to Leeram that PETA meant People for the Ethical Treatment of Animals.

"If you ever tried to get people to do that where I come from," Leeram said, "they would put you in a lion trap for bait."

By then, we were in front of the crowd. I resisted but Leeram wanted to get closer to the action. Suddenly I realized that one of the protesters was looking directly at me. "Someone had to kill an animal so you can walk around in those shoes and wear that belt, and carry that silly looking leather bag!" she said, pointing at Leeram's abode. All of a sudden I felt naked too, even though I was fully dressed. I even felt myself blushing.

"What crap," Leeram said. "What makes her think she's such a saint? She wouldn't be alive right now if animals hadn't died to save her." This was a deep thought, as deep thoughts go. The little beanbag had been influencing me to a greater and greater extent and I was not sure that I liked it all that much, but I had to admit it was kind of like having my own instant speechwriter at times when I would normally have been simply dumbfounded.

"Hey, wait a minute," I said, "You probably wouldn't be alive right now if animals hadn't died for you."

She looked at me angrily and said, "Hah," then turned away.

"How do you think modern medicine is developed?" I added, giving Leeram a mental fist bump.

"Medicine?" she asked, turning back my way.

"Yes, medicine. You must have taken medicine sometimes that was tested on animals."

"I only use herbs."

"Ask her when she gets off work," Leeram said. "This might be interesting."

"Do PETAs drink wine?" I asked her.

She smiled. "Only with people who don't wear fur."

"Tell her that you promise never to eat, wear, or even think bad things about animals," Leeram prompted me. "Give her a smile," he said. What came out was more like a gentleman's leer; that is, a broad smile below nervous eyes.

At that moment the police arrived, covered the protesters with blankets (none too clean, it appeared), and escorted them into a paddy wagon.

It was on the evening news a little later, after the announcer gravely warned the audience that the upcoming story may be inappropriate viewing for some. Religious fundamentalists and their offspring were urged to go into another room until the all-clear was sounded with the advent of the next commercial. Leeram and I watched the protesters, digitally blurred in strategic places, marching around with their signs.

"PETA!" Leeram snorted.

A few weeks went by and I found myself in a local flower shop to buy something to wire for my sister's birthday. A pretty young woman behind the counter looked up as I came in, and I suddenly realized that she was the one who had picked me out in the crowd and made such a cutting remark about my man purse. She recognized me at the same time and it was her turn to blush.

"Listen, I'm really sorry I sounded like that out there," she said. "It's just that, well, when you're doing something like that, you get kind of carried away. It's just too important."

"Oh, don't worry about it," I said. Leeram was suspiciously silent. "I didn't take it personally. Is this where you normally work?"

"Yeah. I used to love it but I'm looking for something else now. The flower trade isn't all so cool; most of them are harvested in South America by really low-wage workers and then they are air-freighted up here. They have an enormous carbon footprint for such beautiful things."

I heard Leeram muttering, "There's a cost to everything, lady."

"Maybe it just isn't possible to be human and not damage something," I said. "Is there a good place to hang out around here?" I asked, changing the subject and taking a real flyer. She was even more attractive than I remembered. Leeram had become my wingman in a subtle way and somehow turned my clumsy words into something else. It worked.

"Yeah, there's a pretty decent place over there on

Newbury Street," she said. "We go there now and then after work."

Her name was Lisa LePage. I held out my hand and said, "Hi, I'm Gilbert Greenbush." We met a couple of hours later at her watering hole. "I can't stay late," she said, when she saw me at a table. She was wearing artfully distressed jeans and a clinging green blouse. She sat down across from me, hands in her lap, firmly encased in guarded body language, which clashed oddly with her clothes. She asked for a glass of Vouvray, and I ordered a Tiger beer, prominent on the list of native brews.

"How long have you been active in PETA?" I was finding it a little difficult to connect this woman with the one in the street a few weeks ago.

"Not very long. I got talked into it by Suxie Redbone."

"Redbone? I think I read about her. Isn't she the Amazon?"

Leeram stirred. "Amazon?" he said (to me).

"Well, that's what she calls herself," Lisa said. "The press gets a little obsessed with that. I think she likes the image."

"I knew it," Leeram said. "She gave me a big boner." I said nothing.

"Suxie, well, she kind of takes over sometimes," Lisa said. "She says she is descended from real Amazon women and that she's traced her family back to northern Brazil and even had her DNA analyzed to prove it."

Leeram twitched inside his leather purse.

"Your bag just moved!" Lisa said. "What DO you have in there?" She pushed her chair back a bit.

"Well..." I couldn't think of what to say. "I must have moved it myself by accident." It was in my lap.

"No, I saw it move. I'm not kidding."

"Why don't you introduce us?" Leeram said to me.

"Oh, Jesus Christ!" I said out loud.

"What?" said Lisa.

"Listen, this is a little hard to explain."

"I'm out of here," Lisa said, rising from the chair.

"Lisa!" I called, but she was out the door without even turning around, her shapely back a slap in my face.

"Goddamn it, Leeram! You've really fucked me up now." Too late, I realized that I had shouted out loud yet again. People turned to look at me. I paid the bill and left. "I'm going to throw you into the first dumpster I see," I said, this time silently.

"Look, Chief, I'm really sorry. If I had a tongue, I would cut it out. I really would."

"You're missing quite a few things, but sometimes I think you forget."

"Well, yeah. You should have seen me when I was alive. Hung like a donkey—the women just wouldn't leave me alone."

"No wonder you got your head shrunk. Was it somebody's husband?" My anger was beginning to fade. Just a bit.

"Tell you what," Leeram said, "Let's think of a way to fix

this thing with her. Give me some time and I'll come up with something."

Back in my apartment, I put Leeram on the shelf with his face to the wall, poured a drink, and sat down in front of the TV to watch the news. Ads for this, ads for that, then a familiar face appeared: it was a fully dressed, grim-faced Suxie. The anchorwoman introduced her. Protecting animals, it seemed, was not her only concern—plastic pollution was another. Styrofoam cups, water bottles, containers for useless crap. "You know," I said to Leeram, "she's not entirely wrong about that." I was still nursing a finger cut that I got trying to get batteries out of some bulletproof packaging.

"If we keep producing trash at the rate we do," Suxie said to the lady on TV, "we will bury ourselves in it." Suxie smiled grimly. I looked over at my trash bin, overflowing with plastic bottles. I began to feel bad. She then announced that she was going to organize a big trash pickup day in a couple of weeks and was looking for volunteers.

"Why don't you go out and help her?" Leeram asked. "Bet Lisa will be there."

I'm not the volunteering type, especially when asked to do so by people who think very highly of themselves. For every recycled plastic bottle, two more will be tossed out of some slob's car window. I am pessimistic about the environment, but the little bastard on the shelf had a point. "Don't forget to take me too," he said quickly.

"OK," I said. Leeram high-fived me in a way that I can't even begin to describe.

Two weeks later, we were standing in front of the local food co-op in a large crowd of Birkenstocks and tie-dyed T-shirts. Suxie climbed on top of a wooden packing crate and began forming us into teams.

"OK, you guys over there," she boomed, pointing at a group nearby. "I want you to go down Huntington Avenue and pick up anything you can find. You people (pointing at another bunch), you cover the Muddy River, start at the Landmark Center and go all the way to Jamaica Pond. She turned and gestured at me: "You two," she said, "Come with me, I want you to help me man the pickup center." Instinctively I thought she was referring to Leeram and me, but I looked around and Lisa was just to my left! My peripheral vision, and hers too, must have been momentarily short-circuited. We looked at each other then she glanced away and shrugged. "Just keep that thing away from me," she said. I do not know how it was possible, but I felt Leeram smile. We followed Suxie to a dump truck in the parking lot and were told to wait there until the volunteers began to show up.

Up close, the Amazon simply overwhelmed. She was a large, female version of General "Stormin' Norman" Schwarzkopf, who could look you in the eye and make you stand at attention without saying a word. Even Leeram did it (I think). Lisa's description of Suxie back in the bar was inadequate—she was more than "a little overwhelming," she was a human avalanche.

"What do you have in that thing?" she bellowed, pointing at the man purse. I looked helplessly at Lisa and opened it up. The silence that followed was like the silence that must occur at the moment of the End of the World. Suxie Redbone looked into the little satchel at Leeram, his eyes and mouth sewn shut with sisal cords fancily knotted in dangling strings, his features so human and yet so oddly misshapen, his hair black and strikingly handsome. The silence lasted, and then lasted some more.

Then a large tear formed in her left eye. She seemed to melt, to physically shrink. She went down on one knee. Against my will, I took Leeram out of the purse and handed him over to her. Lisa made a small, fearful cry and Suxie took him gently in both hands, then held him against her cheek, weeping softly.

"Easy, easy, lady," Leeram said to her. "This ain't the Second Coming." He turned his attention to me and said, "Look, buddy, don't worry, I'll be back. I just need to take a little vacation."

Lisa put her arm around my waist. In his leaving, Leeram had given me a present.

Chapter 4

A couple of weeks passed by—slowly. I had become more dependent on Leeram's crusty little presence than I thought. When he was in his man purse, dangling from my right shoulder and occasionally bumping against my hip, I felt assured, comfortable. Without him, sometimes it was like putting down a half-empty cup of coffee and then forgetting where it was. When that happens, a kind of mental flailing about takes over, driven by a desperate need for another sip, aggravated by annoyance. In this case, though, I had willingly handed Leeram over, not entirely of my own free will. I had to admit, he had a way of getting around, even though he had no visible means of support.

I made peace with Lisa after the trash pickup day. She knew I didn't have Leeram anymore and she said she felt much better knowing that Suxie Redbone did, and also that Suxie loved him. Lisa trusted Suxie and because of that, knew that Leeram couldn't be all bad.

"You just have to give him a little time," I said. "He grows on you."

"Grows on you?" she said. "A lot of things grow on you and you need a doctor to get rid of them."

I didn't reply. I missed Leeram and his little silent hints—the perfect retort at the perfect time. He was like a prompter in a little box invisible to the audience, a box that only I could see. Lisa did make up for some of that sense of loss, though, even though I didn't have Leeram to come up with just the right retort when I needed it the most. I think, though, that most of all I missed the sense of occasionally being absolutely alive with hypertuned senses when he was at my side, the way I felt on the turkey hunt.

"I think I like you better when he's not around," she said. "You're different. Not so snooty."

"Leeram makes me snooty?"

"Yeah, I don't know, kind of like you know it all."

I thought about that, and then, out of some deep well of male lust, replied, "I feel a little lost without him, but I'd rather be with you." She put her arm around mine, looked up and gave me a smile. Leeram wasn't there to say, "Bullshit."

"Let's get a cup of coffee, Mr. Barista!" she said, and pulled me toward a Starbucks kiosk. We ordered two *grandes* and sat down on a nearby bench. "What really is it that you see in that thing?"

"It's not what I see in him," I protested. "I don't know

what I see in him...I just..." I was groping for ways to explain that he had become a weird but genuine friend, and I missed him. We got up and walked for a while longer, then made plans to have dinner in a couple of days. I would have gone out with her that night, but she said she had a date with somebody else. I was frustrated. Leeram would have known how to handle it, and come to the rescue. I needed Amazonian help. I decided to negotiate with Suxie.

The trouble was, I didn't quite know how to approach her. Suxie Redbone did not have an office or even a home address; she just was Suxie and seemed to appear without clothes at unexpected moments, although she was fully dressed when I last saw her. I went home that night, habitually turned on the evening news, dispensed my daily pour, flopped on the couch with my feet on the coffee table, and let the usual force of gravity pull down my eyelids while the usual talking heads went on sagely. The only unusual thing was that the place on the shelf normally taken up by Leeram was empty.

Just as I was drifting off, I heard a voice that sounded like it was coming from a short-wave radio, passing in and out of ethereal static, clear for a second, then not. "Hey buddy," it said. "Wake up! You've got to get me outta here!"

"Get you out of where?"

"I'm in a shrine. There are candles all around me and

they stink. It's her bedroom and I can't take it anymore. She worships me like I was a saint."

I was overwhelmed. Leeram needed me! "Don't worry, I'll find you as soon as I can." Then I thought about Lisa and what she had said about liking me better without him.

"Whaddya mean?" Leeram shouted. "Are you going to choose that ditsy girl over me?" I had forgotten that nothing in my head was private with him around.

"No, no," I said. "I like you too. Just let me try to handle this, will you?"

The next morning, I put my search for Leeram into high gear. Lisa had no idea where Suxie lived. "She just calls me now and then when she wants to do something spectacular. I've never been to her house." Google was clueless; it was as though she existed off the grid. I only came up with rib joints and chophouses.

I tried to retrace steps I had taken over the last few weeks. The town parks department had been in charge of the cleanup day, so I went there first. The clerk at the window looked at me the way a chimpanzee might look at the thousandth visitor passing its cage that day. I asked her if she knew where Suxie lived.

"No idea," she said. Behind her, the neon ceiling lights gave harsh illumination to a half-dozen steel desks, a calendar on the wall celebrating multicultural efforts in getting along with others, the light pea-green walls, and three other people who worked there, all face-lit in front of their computers. I thought I saw a game of Solitaire reflected off the glasses of one of them.

It seemed odd that the town would not have a way of getting in touch with her. "Didn't you have to coordinate the trash day with her?" I asked. "Somebody must have talked with her."

"Must have been the local branch of the Sierra Club, or maybe the Rotary."

I asked her if she had their phone numbers. "Nope," she said. "Go look in the phone book."

I began to realize that the road ahead might not exactly resemble a superhighway. I ran into dead-ends at Rotary, Sierra, the Lions Club, and even the Odd Fellows. Nobody at any of them had a clue.

I finally decided that the only way to reach her was to get her to come to me. I decided to bait a trap. I put an ad in the local alternative weekly newspaper and backed it up with a Craigslist entry. "Expedition to be formed to help Awa people fight land developers along the Amazon River. Volunteers needed." Etc. I had to look up the name of a plausible indigenous tribe. Nothing happened for a week, then one morning my phone rang.

"Is this Gilbert Greenbush?" a woman asked. Her voice was unmistakable, even when not projected through a bullhorn. It was softer than the last time I heard it.

"This is Gilbert speaking."

"My name is Suxie Redbone," she said, "and I want to talk to you about this expedition."

Paydirt! "Yes," I said.

"Can you tell me anything about it on the phone?"

"I can," I replied, "but it would be easier if we were to get together and I could give you more details. Where do you live?"

"I'll meet you somewhere else." Damn.

We finally agreed to meet the next day at the Fern Bar. She walked in, a gigantic lodestone magnet that swiveled every head in the room toward her as though they all had noses full of iron filings. She sat down across from me. She was attractive, I had to admit, even though she cowed the living daylights out of me. The fact that I was making it up as I went along suddenly made me nervous. I felt like a lion tamer winging it with a big new cat recently caught and not sure yet if humans were meal tickets or just meals. Actually, I was scared shitless.

"We are raising money to send sustainable farming experts up the Amazon to give the natives a better choice of livelihoods and to try to save the rain forest that still exists," I said. It sounded plausible, if stilted.

"Do you have any qualifications to do this?"

That stopped me for a moment, but I went on because I could not do what I really wanted to do at that instant, which was to run out of the shop like a terrified lapin.

"Well...I have never done anything like this before, but these poor natives are being screwed by the big beef and timber companies, and I want to do anything I can to help." She looked at me as though I was an idiot. "And I do have a background in the coffee industry," I added.

"Do you have any partners or qualified advisors?" she asked in a level voice, her head back and her eyes looking down at me.

"Not really," I said. "I am just trying to get this off the ground."

She sat, silently, for about an hour. Or maybe it was just a minute. "I'll think about it," she said and got up to go. I felt my chance slipping away.

"Ask Leeram!" I said. I had nothing else left.

Suxie stopped in midrise from her chair, then slowly swiveled back down. The chair gave an ominous creak. "Leeram," she said, "is my business and my business only."

Later, after she had walked out of the place, pulling all those heads back to where they had been when she walked in, I collected my thoughts. It looked as though I was back at the starting gate.

That night, Lisa and I met for our first dinner date. We met at a restaurant of her choice, one that, needless to say, had a great, echoing void in the meat department. I had frozen the last of my turkey and planned on going back to it later, so I dutifully ordered the veggie burger and covered it with as many spices as I could find on or near our table. The wine helped also.

I told her everything about trying to get Leeram back from Suxie and her dismissal of the very idea. I was risking a lot, I knew, but there was such a tangle in front of me that

I could only approach it head-on. Lisa listened carefully and, to my huge relief, didn't make a disparaging comment about my foreshortened friend. "Why don't you actually go up the Amazon?" she asked.

The thought was new to me. "Actually go up the Amazon?"

"Yes, if you actually do go up the Amazon, Suxie will go with you. I promise."

"Where will I get the money?"

"Look, I know her. If she thinks you are really going to do this, don't worry about the money." She reached out and put her hand over mine on the table. She looked at me levelly. "I like you, Gilbert; I haven't known you for a long time, but I like you a lot and I think I misjudged you at first. I know you miss Leeram. I don't know everything about Suxie, but I do know a few things. She does have money, for one."

I sat back in the chair and thought about it for a moment. "Where do I begin?" I asked, mostly to myself. This was a whole new waxy sphere indeed.

"How about the state agricultural school?" she said thoughtfully. Well, I had to admit, the Commonwealth Center for Agriculture and Research was better than nothing. It was in the UMass campus in Amherst, about an hour and a half away.

The next day I called the school's local extension office and spoke to one of the assistant deans. "Would you people be interested in this project?" I asked, after describing it to him.

"Let me bring it up with my boss," he said. "As it turns out, we are looking for a proactive outreach program." I made an appointment with his boss in Amherst for the next afternoon.

When I arrived, Dean Elizabeth Knotwell was sitting at her desk in a new building, as nicely designed and homey as brutalistically poured cement architecture can get. Her gray hair was piled in a Kathryn Hepburnish bun, giving her a grandmotherly look, although her dark suit belied it somewhat. Her eyes were much younger than her face. "Sit down," she said, gesturing to a pair of leather chairs in the corner. They were just this side of being comfortable. She got up from the desk and gingerly sat down next to me.

"I understand you are interested in the rain forest."

"Well, yes, but even more interested in helping out the Awa tribe (I Googled that one). They live in the Amazon River area and are being destroyed by the big agribusinesses that are clear-cutting the forest around them to raise beef and soybeans. Also the big mining companies are in the mix. They are also harvesting all the old-growth tropical hardwood they can find." I had done my homework.

Dean Knotwell nodded. "This has been a concern of mine also," she said. "But what do you propose to do about it?"

"Well, I was thinking that if we could develop some

kind of sustainable agriculture for them, it might allow them to stay on their land. You might be able to help in this."

"You do realize that even if we could manage to develop the kind of agriculture you speak of, you still have to deal with those big companies; they even have their own private armies."

She did not know about Leeram, or about Suxie. "I have some ideas," I said. "If you can give me something real to propose, I might be able to come up with a way to deal with them." She looked at me for a considerable moment, then shook her head.

"I just don't see how."

"Just give me an idea of what to do, nothing that would involve much investment on your part," I said to her, "and I'll work on the rest of it." I realized that I had crossed a line of some kind, from the side that existed because I had a desperate need of a subterfuge, and over to the side that held out the very slim possibility that I might actually go through with this thing. I realized that if I did, Leeram was as good as hanging from my shoulder again.

She looked at me with a wry smile. "You are going to need a lot more than you can imagine." I got to my feet and thanked her for her time. If Leeram had been with me, I would have known exactly what to say. As I turned to leave, she hesitated, then said, "Give me a couple of days—I have to do a little research. I don't think I can help, but I can try."

Later, driving back east on the Massachusetts Turnpike as it undulated its way between and over the Berkshire hills, the northern part of the Appalachian chain, also known as the oldest mountain range on earth, I mused about Leeram's universe. Anything, I thought, is possible. I determined to ask him more about it, despite the fact that he had always changed the topic when I did so earlier. My thoughts shifted. I called Lisa and made a date for dinner that evening. Life in the fast lane from this moment on, I thought. Time to break some rules. I knew, when I finally got a chance to talk with him again, that Leeram would approve.

Chapter 5

I explained everything to Lisa that night at dinner. She looked at me with a raised eyebrow. "I mean the dean didn't promise any money or even that she would get the Ag School involved, but I got the feeling that she might get back to me with some ideas." Until now, putting such a Rube Goldbergian plot together was a means to an end: getting my occasionally insufferable friend back. I had not really given much thought to anything beyond that. Sometimes things acquire their own momentum, though, as I discovered the next morning when I opened my email.

"A friend and colleague of mine who lives in Ann Arbor, Michigan," wrote Dean Knotwell, "is an anthropologist and amateur historian who knows quite a lot about the Amazon. When I told him about your idea, he was excited. With your permission, I will give him your email address." I instantly replied yes.

The next day, his email was on the top of my inbox:

"Dear Gilbert," he began in a formal way. I liked that

immediately, as I am a little put off by the word "Hi" from someone I have never met. "My name is Pericles Xerxes Pangloss. I teach at the University of Michigan. Liz Knotwell told me about you and your project and it stirred my interest. Perhaps we could talk about it in greater detail."

I immediately called him on the telephone number he gave. When he answered, I told him about the Project (as I was now beginning to refer to it), and that Dean Knotwell thought he might be helpful. What the hell, I thought, this is fun—nothing will ever come of it, but why not see how it plays out.

"Liz is right about the historian part of it," he said. "I am a nineteenth century kind of guy and the big South American rivers have always got me going—the Amazon and the Orinoco. H.G. Wells and Teddy Roosevelt are two of my heroes; they both were obsessed with them and now, so am I. You definitely have my ear," he said. I described my idea.

"You speak of big agribusiness," he went on. "Unfortunately, large corporations have a long history in those regions, almost always to the detriment of the local population, and their motives aren't, well, immediately apparent. Have you ever heard of Fordlandia?" I had to admit I hadn't.

He replied that a lot of people who grew up around Detroit, as he did, knew about Fordlandia because it was just so typical of Henry Ford. Detroiters, he said, like quite a lot of Michiganites, were proud of their local Titan of Industry. Mr. Ford, according to Pericles, wanted a cheap and constant source of rubber for his tires, so in 1928 he sent a delegation of Ford management people into the rain forest to hire natives and set up a rubber plantation in the middle of the jungle on the banks of the Tapajos River, a tributary to the Amazon River. His managers hired thousands of local workers and built processing plants, a big lumber mill, little cottages, apartments, schools, a hospital, and everything else that might be needed. The whole thing was overseen by a Norwegian ship captain who knew about as much about carrying out such a project as he did about knitting little cozies for a ladies' tea party, Pericles said. Old Henry might have had many talents, but his hiring skills fell short in this case. Also, Pericles added, he never once set foot in his Brazilian creation, running the whole thing through proxies.

"It was essentially a collision between a particular set of Midwestern American values and the realities of South American life," Pericles said. "The Ford people assumed that they simply knew best—our values, they thought, surpassed any other values, especially South American ones. They started the plantation without knowing anything about growing rubber, the right time of year to start and even the right land to do it on. I felt like a student in his classroom, almost reaching for a pad to take notes. He went on: "Labor and supply problems led to riots and disease. Finally they had to pull up stakes and move the whole plantation miles away downriver to a place called Belterra and start again. "By the early 1940's, artificial latex was invented and it was all over," he said. "It was abandoned completely by 1945." Fordlandia became a ghost town, still there even now, he added, its little cottages occupied by bats and occasional squatters. A few of them had actually worked for Ford in the old days. We finished our dinner and left, agreeing that we would talk again soon.

***

Fordlandia. The idea began to wiggle its way in my brain like a hookworm. A perfect little Midwestern town in the middle of the Amazon rain forest. That's where I would go! Unlike Henry Ford, through Leeram I had access to local knowledge and, by God, I would use it. The next day I asked both Dean Knotwell and Pericles if the Brazilian government would approve of us going down there to start a noninvasive agricultural program, and would there possibly be some grant money around to pay for it all? Their responses were identical: yes. They agreed to write the grant request and a proposal to set up an NGO in Brazil, under the auspices of the Ag School, to the US Food and Agriculture Department.

"There are many species that grow well there, including Acai palms," the dean said. "They produce berries that are a staple food for the natives. Other things that would work are strawberry guavas and aguaje. The aguaje grows very well near water. All of these plants are very nutritious."

They both told me that the grant request process would be glacially slow and not to expect anything to happen for months, which was a little frustrating to say the least. I needed Leeram back!

"What are you trying to do?" said, or demanded, the voice on the phone. I had just returned to my apartment to hear it ringing as I opened the door. It was unmistakably Suxie Redbone.

I stammered, "Do what?"

"You seem to have gotten some very influential people interested in your crazy ideas," she said. I had no idea of how word of what I had been doing reached her, but it obviously had.

"Is there something wrong?" I asked. "I am just trying to help the Awas."

"I thought you were full of it when you first told me about your plans, but, listen, you might be onto something here. I take back what I said before." I was so surprised that I had no reply. "I want to talk to you," she said, without waiting for me to answer. "Meet me at my place tomorrow." I said I would and she gave me an address. At first I was confused; the address was in a local shopping mall. It was the location of a craft shop called Mambo Mama's. I told her I would meet her there at noon the next day.

"How did you find..." I started to say, but she didn't let me finish.

"We'll talk tomorrow," she said abruptly and hung up.

Mambo Mama's was at the end of a long side corridor in the mall—a mall that featured Payless shoes and workmen's clothes and a coin-operated amusement parlor. A fried dough outlet was by the front door and the whole place smelled of morbid obesity. Mambo's shop window, out of the direct glare of overhead fluorescent lighting, was a jumble of wood-carved masks, candles, and one of those holographic images of Christ that opened and closed its eyes depending on which angle you looked at it from. I had gone by it a long time ago but since I don't have a need for dream catchers and lumpy pottery, and I hate the smell of patchouli, I had never gone in. Now, I entered and walked up to a Goth-looking young woman behind the counter. "My name is Gilbert Greenbush," I said to her. "Suxie wants to see me."

Without saying a word to me, the woman punched a button on an intercom. "Guy wants to see you."

A moment later, the room was filled with Suxie. "Wondered when you would get here," she said in a slightly annoyed tone. "Come in." She led the way into the back office.

"How did..." I started to say.

"Find out about you and Fordlandia?" she finished my sentence. "I have a lot of connections. Did you know my ancestors came from the region around Aveiro in Brazil, the same area where Fordlandia was built? My grandfather worked there in the rubber plantation from its start to its finish, and I have always kept in touch with people who know anything about it. Pericles is an old friend of mine and he told me about your project as soon as he heard about it. I think I misjudged you," she said. "For that, I apologize."

"Do you mean you want to help me?"

"I'm in, you very unlikely little guy." I didn't know exactly how to take that, but I did in the best way possible. I am not exactly short, around five foot ten, but she still looked down on me. I thanked her, standing up a little straighter.

"There is one thing that I need to do before anything else," I said. She looked at me sharply. "I need to talk to Leeram."

"Something told me you were going to say that," she said warily.

"Please, it is essential that I talk with him. He's the key to everything. I know how you feel about him, but if you keep him to yourself, we may never get this project off the ground." Suxie was silent for a while. It was the first time I had ever seen her appear undecided, and I was suddenly excited. Is there a hidden door through that exoskeleton, I wondered. I should have known, of course, exactly where it was.

"I'll ask him and get back to you." As soon as she said that, I knew I had won, although in the winning, I might have thrown my entire life into a jumble with no predictable outcome that I could imagine. Goodbye comfortable couch, goodbye News Hour.

Early the next morning, my telephone rang. "I want you to come over to this address; write it down," she said, then gave me the location of an upscale condominium in Chestnut Hill, an expensive section of town. "Ask the concierge for Ms. Gaia Galore." I was there in a half hour, my empty man purse over my shoulder. I even skipped my habitual cup of coffee and was still half-awake. The concierge gave me Suxie's, or Gaia's, room number and in a few minutes I was at her door with my finger on the bell. It opened before I had a chance to push the button and Suxie filled the doorway, but seemed indefinably smaller. Her eyes were puffy and moist. She motioned me in, turning as she did, and led me across an elegant foyer into a living room with a spectacular view of the city. The walls were covered with colorful weavings and hand-carved furniture that seemed very appropriately matched. An original nineteenth century map of the Amazon River had a commanding position on the wall opposite the picture window, and the floor was covered with a quilt-like rug of woven cloth. Suxie was barefooted and it made me want to take my shoes off, too. "Go ahead," she said, looking at my feet. The rug felt really good when I kicked them off.

"Who is Gaia Galore?" I asked. "Are you related?"

"I am Gaia Galore, just as I am Mambo Mama and Suxie Redbone," she said softly. "I have a need for privacy. The store gives me an identity that can be very helpful at times. Here, as Gaia, I can live a comfortable life away from my public one as Suxie Redbone, which is close to my real name, which is mine to know only. I'll tell you more in a little while, but now there is someone who wants to see you." Bingo! She turned and I followed her through a door. The room beyond was dark and my eyes took a few moments to adjust. Leeram was high on a shelf, surrounded by some spooky knick-knacks and painted rays of yellow and red on the wall emanating from his head in all directions. There was a faint scent of cocoa beans and not a hint of patchouli.

"Good to see you, buddy. What took you so long?" A subliminal flash seemed to wink from his closed eyelids. His tassels shook slightly. It was the closest thing to a broad grin that he was capable of. If he had any, he might as well have thrown his arms around me in a bear hug.

Suxie, now behind me, took a sudden deep breath.

"Hey, Greenbush," Leeram said, "don't worry. I had a long talk with her a little while ago and she knows she has to give me back to you." I was overwhelmed. This great big woman who had done nothing but strike trepidation into my heart ever since I met her was suddenly vulnerable. I reached over and instinctively put my arm around her shoulders.

"It's good to have you back, Leeram," I said, then turned to Suxie. "Don't worry," I said, "he will never be far from you." For the first time I felt a small, unexpected smudge of affection for her.

"And now get me the hell out of here!" he barked.

I picked him up off the shelf and the three of us went back out into the sunlit living room. Suxie motioned to the sofa and sat down nearby. I put Leeram on the coffee table and sat down myself. We were silent for a long time.

To say that Leeram broke the silence was odd, since the actual silence was not broken, but he did so in his own way. "OK, tell me about this wacky idea of yours." The command startled me. "Suxie says you want to go up the Amazon River," he continued. I explained the whole, convoluted scheme to him, adding that I was waiting to hear about a grant to finance it.

"Don't worry about the money," Suxie said.

"I have to worry about it; I am living off some savings right now, but that's not going to get us much farther than to the next state south."

"I said, don't worry about the money; I have it. Remember when I told you that my grandfather worked at Fordlandia? Even though he was uneducated, he was very intelligent; he paid attention and didn't take long to learn a lot about the big country in the north, where the Ford Company came from. He was promoted to foreman and went from there to become a liaison between top American management and the native workers. From the Americans, he learned that big companies could be owned in little pieces, called shares, by anyone. At first, he wanted to use his salary, not much by American standards, to buy stock in the Ford Company, but they said there was no such thing because old Henry owned the whole damned thing by himself. So my grandfather did the next best thing and went to a stockbroker in Manaus who advised him to buy General Motors shares. That company, he was told, could be even bigger than Ford. Of course, he kept this all to himself because he thought no one would understand and would call him an idiot, but he spent most of his paycheck each week for years buying GM shares. Well, he died suddenly, before he told anyone what he had been doing. My parents found a suitcase full of stock certificates, which they thought were just curiosities and almost threw them out. Just before they did, they thought I might be amused by them, so they gave them to me instead. That's how I paid for my college education and was able to support them in their old age. Over the years, they just got more and more valuable, splitting and doubling and tripling the way good stocks do, until they were worth thousands of times more than they were when he bought them. My worth, thanks to my grandfather's intuition, is very substantial." It was the most I had heard her say all at once, and I sat back, amazed.

"Pericles." She spoke the name suddenly as the track of her thinking shifted. "We were classmates at the University of Southern Illinois in Carbondale." I had never heard of it. "It was an amazing place—Buckminster Fuller taught there," she said. My understanding of this woman was being altered by the moment. "Pericles and I are in constant contact; he told me about you at the same time he told you about Fordlandia. After that, I knew I had to get in touch with you."

"Your grandfather must have been an unusual man," I said.

"He was an Amazon! And so am I." Any softening effects that Leeram had brought about in her seemed to fade away.

Things were happening almost too quickly for me to keep up. I had the sensation of being inside a papier-mâché dragon on Chinese New Year's day and suddenly finding that it was a real, living beast, breathing fire. "OK," I said shakily. "I'm ready to get started." Ready, that is, as a child mounting a two-wheeled bicycle for the first time. I said I would go home and begin preparations.

"You're going to need help," she said. "Pericles will help too."

Back in my apartment, I was still dazed. I sat down at my desk and began making a list.

1. Talk to Dean Knotwell
2. Find out what actually can grow on the banks of the Amazon
3. Figure out a budget
4. Forget about the whole damn thing, change my name, and move out of town

I pushed away from the desk. I didn't have the foggiest idea of what to do next. What in the hell, I asked myself, have I gotten into? A budget? To do what? I was about to give up and pour a drink when the phone rang. Pericles's voice was getting familiar. "I have a sabbatical coming up," he said, "and I have plans to come east for a conference. Let's get together for dinner and we can talk." Providential, I thought. The list can wait. The chain of events had left the station and was picking up momentum.

A week later, I was sitting at a table at the Copley Plaza Hotel across from a middle-aged, bear-like man with dark-rimmed spectacles that were surrounded by a heavy shock of black hair and a full, bushy beard. His eyes behind the lenses were piercing and humorous. Pericles had just bustled in a few minutes after I sat down, looking around the crowd of diners until he saw me. We recognized each other in the way that strangers often do when planning to meet in a public place. Mental telepathy? "I've been looking forward to this," he said, reaching out to shake my hand as I stood up. "I hope you don't mind," he said, "but I saw Suxie earlier today and she wants to meet with us tomorrow." He paused, then looked down. "Is that your...your ah, companion?" he asked.

I had become so used to having Leeram back in his man purse that I actually forgot that he was with me. "Yes, it is," I said. Leeram had no comment.

"I don't really know much about it," he said, "but Suxie says that it is alive."

"If a beanbag can live and even have a gender, he is alive," I said. I told Pericles that it was a very complicated thing and that he would understand eventually. It was, I knew, entirely up to Leeram. "I don't want to go into that right now," I said. "Let's talk about the Amazon."

"As I mentioned before, I am obsessed with the Amazon, and your proposal has intrigued me in a way that I haven't been moved for years," he said. "If you want to go there, I would be very happy to take as much time as might be needed and go with you. I have a lot to offer and could be of great use to you." The concept that I, Gilbert Greenbush, would be given such an offer was unsettling; a part of me wanted to get up, say that I was going to the men's room, and walk out the door, never to return again.

"I would like that very much," I replied. Then I immediately said to myself, there is no fucking way that I will do this thing.

Chapter 6

The rest of the dinner with Pericles at the Oak Room—we both had the Kobe beef and a bottle of good burgundy—passed in general, but interesting, conversation. My end consisted largely of nodding and saying, "Really." We had many common interests, it turned out. He went on about the Amazon region.

"It's the largest river system in the world," he said. "Can you believe it contains about 20 percent of all the world's fresh surface water? Annual rainfall is about nine feet, all of it gathered into about 1100 tributaries, which in turn empty into the Amazon River. Fordlandia is on the banks of one of them, the Rio Tapajos. Scientists think that over half of the world's species live in Amazonia, many of them, if not most, are still unknown to us. We humans are eating it up like metastasized cancer, driving out indigenous tribes, and every square mile of clear-cut rain forest shrinks opportunities to discover medicines hidden within."

Finally back in my apartment that night, I put Leeram on the kitchen table and said, "I don't know about you, but I'm beginning to think that I may be going through a goddamned looking glass."

"I don't know what the hell you mean about a looking glass," he said, "but when I was alive, they would have called you a lunatic. I told you once before that this is not the rain forest anymore. Why would any sane person want to go there?"

I was in a daze. Intellectually, in the front parlor of my brain, I knew he was right. This loony business had somehow developed momentum, but it really hadn't yet become a reality in the back rooms. Looking back on this moment, I now recognize that I, a man in his early forties, was taking the first baby steps toward maturity. I needed to talk with Lisa as soon as possible. "I really need your help," I said. Over a table in a nearby restaurant the next day, I reached out and took her hand. "I think I've gotten myself into a real jam." For many years, I had carefully built a locked room in that house, where I stored my most introspective thoughts—feelings that might have leaped about like mad things and smashed my carefully constructed world if I let them out. The first thing that went through my mind was a conviction that at that particular moment I needed her more than anything in the world, even more than Leeram, and I told her. I told her about the dinner with Pericles, and the feeling that somehow events were completely out of control. I really just wanted to go on living an uncomplicated life. "What's wrong with that?" I said. She looked at me for a long time.

"Do you really want to double-cross Suxie?" she asked. I hadn't expected that.

"No...I don't want to double-cross anyone," I said. "It's just that I'm not crazy. This is a completely impossible idea. This is something that governments and NGOs do, not individuals. What do you think I can do? I'm completely in over my head. It just got way, way ahead of me."

"You want to back out now, don't you?" she said, pushing her chair back. "I'll never talk to you again." She got up, took her purse, and turned to go. I stood so quickly that my own chair fell over with a loud noise and the other diners all looked at me.

"Wait a minute," I said to her loudly; now we really had an audience. "I'll do it, goddamn it. I just wanted to say that it is so weird, I needed to process it somehow." My mind had been made up—and not by me.

***

I didn't sleep at all well that night. I told Leeram that I thought I had really painted myself into a corner. "It's your paintbrush, buddy," he said. "I think you just let your dick make a decision."

"You're a fucking moron," I shouted. "To start with, she's just a friend. I've never slept with her."

"I don't think I'll ever understand your world," he said.

"Where I used to live, we didn't let things like that get in our way."

Pericles called me the next afternoon, telling me that he had contacted the Department of Indigenous Affairs in Brasilia. He was passable in Portuguese and was able to get through to a midlevel *burocrata* who, according to Pericles, was a little matter-of-fact about the whole thing.

"The big outfits, the mining, grain farming, and cattle companies, all pay fees, taxes, and outright baksheesh to the government," he told me. "The Department really doesn't care what you do as long as it doesn't interfere with the arrangements they have with the companies." We—Pericles, Suxie Redbone and Dean Knotwell—were in a conference room, paneled with Home Depot Luann plywood and accessorized by a big, green USDA poster framed on one wall.

"What if we made Fordlandia into a big farming co-op?" Suxie suggested. "The indigenous population could earn a lot of money and get to keep it."

"Depends on what the Brazilians want to do with it," said Pericles.

I thought about that. "Why don't we go down and talk to them ourselves?" I asked. "Don't forget we have a secret weapon." I felt Leeram quiver slightly. He had been still as, well, a stone ever since the meeting began. I decided to take him out of the man purse and put him on the table.

"It's about goddamn time!" he said. When I looked around the table, I knew they all had heard him too.

Pericles's eyes were wide open and Dean Knotwell dropped the pen she had been making notes with. "I've been listening to you all jabber on like a bunch of frangos," he said. "Only chickens make more sense than you do." Dean Knotwell stood up quickly, her hand over her mouth. Only Suxie was unfazed.

"What do you think, then," I asked.

"Look. I know the people in those tribes, the people you call 'indigenous.' I was one of them, and we called you indigenous, or at least a word we had like that. We were not indigenous, we were the world; you were the others."

"I know, I know," Pericles said, "but how do we proceed with this thing? Can you help us?" After a long pause, Leeram gave what was as close to an audible sigh that a wad of sand wrapped in leather can make.

"I thought I was done with that part of the world," he said, "but, OK, I'll give you a hand." I refrained from comment. Leeram was not long on body parts or human compassion, but we must have struck a chord somewhere. I also thought that his command of American English had improved greatly in the past few weeks. He had a way of collecting language from everyone around him. Sometimes I thought he must have been in the back of a New York taxicab, lost behind the seat for a year or two.

"Dean Knotwell, this is Leeram," I said. "I'm sorry if I hadn't described him more fully, but he is a former ind...a former native of the Brazilian rain forest. As you can see, despite his size, he is, well, formidable. Please don't be afraid. Leeram will be very helpful to us, won't you, Leeram?" He didn't reply, but I could tell he was not uninterested.

"Don't worry," I said to the dean and to Pericles together, "I was just as startled as you are when I first met him. You'll get used to him once you get to know him. He's really a pussyc..."

"Be *very* careful what you say about me."

"What I meant was," I continued, "Leeram is on our side. He can be helpful in ways that we can't even imagine right now."

Suxie had been mostly silent until now. "I'm sorry if I was too possessive of you, Leeram, but you and I share something that these others don't have. When you were with me, I was in the arms of my ancestors. One of these days, I might ask if I could get a sample of your DNA to see if you actually are one of them. That is your hair, isn't it?" I told Leeram that I would explain all that later. Suxie went on, "I have to apologize to you, Gilbert, for my attitude toward you earlier, but after you introduced us, I couldn't stand the thought of sharing him with anyone. I went a little crazy, and I apologize to everyone."

I asked her, a little warily, if she was OK with my having him back. "Don't worry about it," she replied. "I know you now and I'm happy with you and Leeram. Anything that pleases him pleases me."

It was the way she said it that dropped the last tumbler into the locking cylinder of my brain, the tumbler that allowed the cylinder to turn its key, opening up the reality of the trip we were about to make. It was the most insane thing I could imagine, but I was now committed to actually carrying out this weird venture. The course of my life had just fundamentally changed. I could not go back to my old existence, drifting through events any more than I could invent a time machine using stuff in the trunk of my car. No more unexamined life, no more drifting. I had been born again into a larger existence. Having Leeram back was a good thing, but his repossession was no longer driving me. A sense of pure adventure was behind the wheel now.

Suxie, Pericles, and I decided to fly down to Brasilia, the nation's capital, to talk with the proper authorities, then get to Fordlandia via Manaus, where we would buy enough equipment to get started. The only way to our destination with all that gear from Manaus would be on a riverboat down the Amazon, then onto the Tapajos River, a tributary, that led to our destination. "We can wait for the grant money later," Suxie said. "In the meantime, I'll front enough cash to get us started. Can't wait forever, and we can hold on until the grant does come through." Dean Knotwell would remain behind to act as our home base.

"What about Lisa?" I asked. "This whole thing would never have happened without her."

"Who?" asked Pericles and the Dean. I was about to say "my girlfriend" but stopped, as we had never gone that far.

"Oh, Lisa!" Suxie said. "Of course. She would be very

helpful; I've known her for a long time and she always has good ideas. I'll tell her about it."

After a little more conversation, I put Leeram back in the man purse and we all left. I had some planning, not to mention packing, to do. Lisa called me when I got home; she was excited. "I can't believe what you're doing! I just got off the phone with Suxie, and she wants me to go along! I can't wait to get out of that flower shop and go down to where they all came from."

Two weeks later, we were all in the line at Logan Airport, waiting to go through security. I did not dare to put Leeram in a suitcase, liable to be lost in transit—he would have to become carry-on baggage. I disguised him (after gaining his dubious and unprintable permission) by putting him inside a stuffed teddy bear that was in turn wrapped in gift paper. If asked, I would say it was going to be a present for a little girl. I hoped there was nothing in his physical presence that would show up on an x-ray, so I just put the bear in my carry-on gym bag, along with my toilet kit, a change of underwear, and copies of *Tales of Ordinary Madness* by Charles Bukowski and *The Boys from Brazil* by Ira Levin. (The Bukowski book reminded me of the strange, disjointed life I had been living recently.)

I was going to bring a rifle or shotgun in our checked luggage in case we wanted some game in the jungle—that turkey had liberated me from more than a few inhibitions. Pericles reminded me that if I did, we might run into problems boarding the plane, so I packed my trusty atlatl instead. We went through the checkline without a hitch. Suxie had bought us first-class tickets, so we boarded immediately, a privilege I had never had before. I opened the overhead locker and slid the bag inside, ready to settle down for a long flight. Just as I fastened the seat belt, the words "GET ME THE HELL OUT OF HERE" exploded in my mind. I jerked as though a sharp pin had jumped from the seat beneath me. Only the seat belt kept my head from banging into the baggage compartment. "Leeram, what's the matter?" I asked, audibly.

"I said get me out of here. I don't know what this thing is, but I don't like it."

It had never occurred to me that Leeram had never flown before. Some part of him was still a denizen of the rain forest. I unfastened my seat belt and Lisa, sitting next to me, asked what the matter was, had I forgotten anything. I knew that when it came to Leeram, Lisa still had some issues, which is why he usually only talked to me when she was around. This time, though, I could sense real fear in his voice. I stood up and took Leeram out of the gym bag. "Don't worry," I said. "This is a jetliner and we are heading to Brazil. It's perfectly safe."

"If you say so, boss, but don't put me back up there. It's bad enough inside this goddamned thing."

Boss? I wondered to myself. It was the first time Leeram had ever intimated that he wasn't calling all the shots. "I'll keep you here on my lap," I said, "but be nice to Lisa." Lisa glanced at the slightly gravid looking bear and up at me.

"Are you sure he doesn't have to pay for a seat?" she asked, only partly kidding. Just then the first-class flight attendant came by. She was better than pretty, almost a hologram of perfection out of a Lucasfilm movie, only solid.

"Would you like something to drink before we take off?" she asked, with a smile that would have charmed an inanimate object. Which it did.

"She can serve me anything she wants," Leeram muttered. "All of a sudden I like flying," he said. Lisa ordered a Fresca and I asked for a beer. I put a flight blanket over the bear, but it started to wiggle imperceptibly as soon as I did. The flight attendant looked at it sharply, but said nothing. Soon we were up and off, heading south, and the routine of folding into oneself in a cramped space on a long flight began. Pericles, Suxie, Lisa, and I all succumbed to the drowsiness that always follows the early morning scrum of waking, getting to the airport, going through the PSA line like prisoners in San Quentin, and finally strapping down into a tiny seat on the other end of it all. I was the last to doze off, wondering even then how absolutely improbable this whole thing was.

When I woke, Leeram was sitting next to me. Not just his head, but an entire human being, dressed in a loincloth and covered with tattoos. He was muscular and wiry and was actually quite handsome. The first-class seats were wide, and he was somehow between the sleeping Lisa and me. I was now alert, but somehow not surprised. "I wanted to see this big bird you put me in. Besides, I hate being in a stuffed animal, even if it's not real. It's not how I was brought up." I understood and apologized for his undignified container, but told him that there was just no other practical means of taking him around with me and not making life difficult for us both.

"I know," he said. "Doesn't mean I like it, but I know. I wanted to see this for myself, not just through your eyes. Especially that *bonita* who brought you the drinks." I wondered about what he said about seeing through my eyes.

"Is that what you do?" I asked. "What else do you do in my brain?" I was not surprised, just curious. "Do you live through me?"

He smiled. "I live through myself," he said. "You come in pretty handy sometimes, though." Just then, the gorgeous attendant passed by, oblivious to Leeram. He gazed at her behind as she walked down the aisle. "Not many like that in the rain forest," he said, grinning broadly now. I was, as usual, far too civilized to stare.

"What are we going to do, anyway?" I asked. "Once we get to Brazil," I added.

"Leave that up to me," he said. "I'm beginning to like this trip."

I wanted to ask him a few more questions but, being drowsy, forgot them, only to be awakened by the flight attendant asking if I wanted anything else to eat or drink. Lisa was stirring and Leeram was gone and the bear was by my side, quiet. Lisa and I were adjacent to Suxie and Pericles across the aisle; we were all awake by then and began to talk about our plans. The stewardess wrinkled her nose. "Do you smell anything?" she asked.

Later, I opened the Bukowski to pass the rest of the time aboard, immersing myself in his loopy dialogue somehow just this side of sophomoric. It seemed to help my peripheral vision.

The plane landed and we disembarked down a gangway into the refreshing Brazilian December air, a warm contrast to Boston's lowering winter. To our great relief, Customs was a breeze—we literally blew through it. Leeram could be very self-effacing if he felt like it. We climbed into a taxi that had just barely enough room for us all. Our luggage filled the trunk and the remainder, strapped to the roof, raised the vehicle's center of gravity to a dangerous height; we proceeded, it seemed, occasionally on two wheels as we rounded sharp corners. Leeram was silent but let us all know he was not at ease. Pericles had made reservations at a hotel designed for business trips and meetings close to the airport—nothing too fancy but very convenient. We decided to wait until we got there to organize the next leg westward up the river.

At the hotel, a generic Hilton, we shared two adjoining suites, with Suxie and Lisa in one, Pericles, Leeram, and me in the other. The door between them was unlocked at our request so we could more easily get together to make our plans. I took Leeram, who was just radiating irritation, from the bear and put him back in his man purse. I had begun to call it a satchel after Leeram complained that "man purse" was not a fit accessory for a real man. He said he felt like a miniature poodle in one. "You," I said to him, "are about as far from a miniature poodle as a bull moose with a tassel on its tail."

The next morning, Pericles called his contact in the Indigenous Affairs office in the Praca dos Tres Poderes and set up a meeting for the following day. We decided to spend the time in between just sightseeing and, after going over the attractions listed in the hotel's brochures, set out after breakfast, Leeram over my shoulder. Suxie had yielded him back to me with little resistance a while ago, but I caught her occasionally looking at his pouch in a wistful way. "I know," she said suddenly, "Let's get Leeram a proper home." A proper leather valise would do nicely, she suggested. Let Mambo Mama take care of it, she said in a way that ended any further discussion. There was no end of shopping opportunities for such a thing, and she found one in short order. The valise had a long strap that could support it on the carrier's back, yet looked businesslike. Good Brazilian leather, both soft to the touch, practically bulletproof, and with a pleasantly pungent smell. Leeram was quiet for a while after he got used to his new home, but finally, wordlessly, beamed satisfaction.

Brasilia is a big city only a little over half a century old and we were under no illusions we would be able to see most of it, or get a feel for the essence of Brazil, but we were there on business. We would have plenty of chances to immerse ourselves in Braziliana later. After another taxi ride, this time in traffic and therefore with far less nail-biting, we were at the city's tallest building, the Television Tower, and ascended to its top observation deck. From there, the view of this brand new metropolis spread out for miles and miles. "I don't know anything about this place," Leeram said, "but it sure ain't home."

When Leeram said something, I had no idea if I was the only one to hear him or if he was talking to us all. It was only when others responded that I had an inkling. This time he brought out the grammarian in Pericles. "Actually ain't isn't used now, but it was proper English a couple hundred years ago."

"Ain't that a shame," said Leeram.

"Let Leeram say 'ain't' if he wants to," Lisa said. "I like it when he does." It was the first time I had a hint that her attitude of reserved acceptance toward him had begun to soften into something like affectionate acceptance. We went back down and found seats in a fancy restaurant on the first floor. After lunch, we went on sightseeing and walked until our feet hurt, then went back to the hotel for a light supper and, jet-lagged, an early night's sleep. In bed, I thought about Lisa and wished that I wasn't sharing a room with the snoring Pericles. Eventually I drifted off, but not before giving a good night to Leeram. "Please don't wake me up," I said.

The next day we were in the office of the Assistant

District Commissioner of Indian Affairs, Northern Region. We had a short wait in a nicely appointed antechamber before his secretary ushered us into his chambers, decorated with modern versions of WPA-style paintings on the walls, showing broad-shouldered Brazilian workmen building grand structures designed by the great architect Oscar Niemeyer, who designed most of Brasilia. At least that is what the Assistant District Commissioner told us after we were seated on the other side of his desk. "Not many North Americans know much about our city," he said. "We are very proud of it. We have a great city and I am quite positive—*tenho certeza absoluta*—that within half a century we will surpass your country economically."

"Nice valise!" he said then, apropos of nothing.

We made some admiring comments about what we had seen so far, and then Pericles brought up the topic of Fordlandia. The Assistant Commissioner's expression shifted slightly; his eyebrows lifted. "Why are you so interested in that place?" he asked. "It is in the back of the way back. Even farther than that," he said, gesturing with his arms spread out. "Nothing but nothing up there. *Vazio*."

"Yes, but we want to help the indigenous people who live there, the *caboclos*," Pericles said. His Portuguese, hardly perfect, was better than ours, so he had become our spokesman.

The Assistant Commissioner's expression changed

again. He gave us a tired look. "That is government land," he said. "I'm afraid it's out of the question for you to go there." There was a moment of silence as we looked at each other. "And where is your NGO paperwork?" he added. We looked at each other. "You need a statute—three copies—also three copies of the Constituent Assembly minutes, a book of original proceedings, proof of payment of Civil Registry Office's fees…" His expression had become sadly formal, pouring out the same bureaucratic language that had dampened the ardor of so many other supplicants in so many other bureaus in every language everywhere in the world. He went on for a few more minutes, then paused for a response from us.

"Is that it, then?" Lisa asked.

"No, there is more," the Assistant Commissioner said.

"Is he the boss of all this rigamarole?" Leeram asked me.

"He is," I said. Suddenly I sensed a silent crackle and the smell of ozone filled the room.

Suxie sat up straight in her chair. General Schwarzkopf's personality came back for the first time since she had given Leeram back to me. She stood up and said, in a level voice, "We are going there. Make it happen." We stood up too. "I want a letter of authorization from you this afternoon; have it delivered to our hotel by courier before the end of the day." She spoke in English that seemed to be perfectly understandable to the Assistant District Commissioner, who was now sitting straight in his oaken chair.

Eyes wide open, he nodded speechlessly. "I will do so," he said in a shaken tone.

I heard Leeram say, "Good job, babe!" and we walked out.

Chapter 7

We had just returned to the hotel and were sitting at the bar when a uniformed messenger arrived, directed to us by the concierge. "Please accept the Commissioner's apologies for the delay," he said, handing us a large manila envelope embossed with the government's official seal. Inside it said: "The following individuals have exclusive permission from the Brazilian Department of Indigenous Affairs to travel to the area known as Fordlandia in the State of Para, and they are to have complete permission to act in the best interests of the native population there." Our names followed. "Visa extensions are to be automatically granted to these individuals for as long as they deem necessary." We looked at each other, and then gave ourselves high-fives.

"How about me?" said Leeram. "Who do you think made that little *merda* change his mind?" We did it again, looking a little strange to the other customers as we seemed to be high-fiving a leather valise, but we didn't care.

"Sorry, Leeram" I said.

Suxie also apologized. "I knew what was happening back in that office, that somehow you took me over as if I was a puppet. I couldn't resist, but the funny thing is that I didn't want to. You did it back home, too, when I first met you. You are the only person who I would ever let tell me what to do. You gave me back to myself then, Leeram, and I will always owe you for that.

The next morning, we bought tickets to Manaus on the Amazon River in the north, the capital of the State of Amazonia. Then, wondering why we hadn't thought of it earlier, I bought a satellite phone, guessing that where we were headed, cell phone towers might be few and far between. Manaus was the nearest big city we could find to Fordlandia and looked like the closest place to Fordlandia where we could find all the farm equipment we needed. We were back at the airport early the next morning, boarding a small twin-engine propeller plane and strapping ourselves in for another trip. Going overland, we quickly affirmed, over poorly maintained and widely detoured roads would have been too difficult, and it would have taken a flying boxcar to take all that equipment had we bought it in Brasilia. Leeram was almost cocky this time, as we climbed the boarding ladder. "Where's that stewardess?" he asked as we got settled in our seats. I had to explain that smaller aircraft like this one generally made do with the co-pilot, which in this case was a young man with lingering traces of acne, who looked barely in his twenties. "That kid?" Leeram asked. I had to reassure him that the kid most likely knew what he was doing. Leeram did not reply.

After we took off, leaving the incongruous city of Brasilia in the growing haze behind us, we spread our maps of the states of Para and Amazonia on our laps. The plane was half-empty and we could cluster around the aisle, speaking loudly over the dull but insistent sound of the props, weaving in and out of sync.

The little plane bumped and bounced its noisy way at low altitudes for hours and hours, boring over, under, and through low clouds that intermittently parted to expose the forest roof. Every now and then a little village would slide by underneath us, peeking up at us through the green carpet below. The settlements all featured circular, thatch-roofed enclosures with big, round open spaces in the middle. Thong-wearing natives and their little naked children would cluster around in the circle, staring at our noisy progress overhead. Leeram was unimpressed. "I never thought I would see this dump again." Dump? we said. "Yes, dump. Not much happening down there. Give those people half a chance to go north of the border and they'd jump at it."

"Look, Leeram," Lisa said, "we are down here to give them better lives right where they are."

"Sorry, I forgot I was traveling with a bunch of saints,"

he snarked back. It made me a little annoyed. I might have expected a little more out of the undersized but mouthy hairball that had egged me on to kill a wild turkey in the middle of Brookline's toniest neighborhoods.

"But it was you that made it possible for us to be here!" I said. "What is it with you, anyway?" When we finally touched down with a bounce and a lurch at the Eduardo Gomes International Airport in Manaus, those of us who had stomachs were a little off-kilter with motion sickness. The ground felt blissfully solid and soon we had forgotten any queasiness, heading for the baggage pickup area and getting ourselves organized again.

"Manaus is a big place, mostly quite modern," Pericles said. "All of those international mining, lumbering, and agricultural businesses have local offices there. It's a major Amazon River port." Once we had geared up, we would make arrangements to go downstream on the Amazon to the town of Santarem, then turn south to go upstream on the Rio Tapajos to Fordlandia. It was, we were told, mostly occupied by squatters and other indigents, way deep in the middle of nowhere. The words of the Assistant Commissioner were bright in our memory.

The taxi into town was driven at a speed resembling that of an oxcart rather than the velocity we had become used to in Brasilia. "Tell the *motorista* we don't have all day," Leeram said. "Step on it!" The cabbie looked around with a startled expression.

"What's your hurry, Leeram?" I said. The land around

us was different than that in southern Brazil, wilder and more humid. The air coming through the open windows carried exotic scents mixed with mud and a suggestion of decay. The cab driver began to give us his tourist lecture in passable English. He told us about the fortunes that were made here during the rubber boom in the late nineteenth century, pointing out some truly gorgeous mansions, most of which were in pretty good shape. Once in the city proper, he took us past the Opera House, the Teatro Amazona, a startlingly big, baroque old pile that looked like a cross between a Russian Orthodox Church and a Greek temple, surrounded by a vast plaza. We all said we would like to visit it on our return trip. The cabbie was in full tourista mode and we heard all about how the streets around it had been paved in rubber so that concertgoers would not be disturbed by passing carriages.

Leeram seemed nervous. Manaus was a cocktail of modernity and tradition in the middle of the jungle and it was making him very uncomfortable. "I don't recognize this place anymore," he said. "The sooner we're out of here, the better."

We decided on a hotel close to the Rio Negro, which flows into the Amazon nearby, and, after a surprisingly good dinner, during which Lisa hesitatingly, then enthusiastically ate the turtle soup, we set up a plan for the next day. Our first priority was to hire a boat big enough to carry us and our farming equipment. Right after breakfast the next day, we rented a car and drove to the waterfront, threading our way through a jumble of tin-sided shacks and small houses, the last few rows nearest the river on stilts. It was a kind of gradient of wealth, with the poorest citizens at the highest risk of flooding. Along the river's muddy banks were dozens of motor vessels, some quite grand and gaudy with two or three decks and room for hundreds of tourists. They left on a regular schedule, but they were crowded and noisy, usually with a bar on the upper deck that played loud *Corazao* music day and night. The locals called them *gaiolas* or birdcages, Pericles said. Passengers hung their own hammocks and brought their own food, although it could be had on board at a high price. With all our equipment, however, we needed a boat all our own, and after some time one, in particular, caught our eye. She was an old-fashioned stern-wheeler named *Dom Afonso*, about seventy-five feet long with a single lower cargo deck and shelter deck above it, capped by a wheelhouse and captain's cabin. Its paint was apparently fresh, which suggested that some maintenance had been carried out in a more or less timely way. We parked the car, gave a couple of *reals* to a kid standing nearby, and Pericles told him there would be more if the car was still there when we returned. We walked down the quay, and as we got closer, the *Dom Afonso's* captain came out of the wheelhouse as we approached. "*I pode adjuda-lo?*" he asked: "Can I help you?"

"We are looking for a boat to hire for a week or so," Pericles replied. "Is this ship available?"

The captain smiled and waved us aboard. "This is the finest vessel in Brazil," he said, praising her lavishly. "Almost a royal barge," he crowed. Despite the new paint, though, it showed the scars of many years of grinding up against muddy, jungle-fringed banks. She had, the captain said, been built during the rubber boom era back at the turn of the last century but had been maintained to A-1 standards! "Only 1,150 *reals* a day," he said. Pericles translated.

A silent but indignant snort emitted from Leeram's satchel. "He saw you coming," Leeram said. "Offer him two hundred fifty. In my time, that would have rented this lousy canoe for a whole year."

The captain's expression, when he heard Pericles's counteroffer, collapsed from ebullience to dolorous dismay. "I cannot possibly let this yacht leave the dock for such a tiny fee," he said.

At that, Suxie looked down at him with the full force of her Amazonian heritage. "We are leaving," she said and turned on her heel. We followed, leaving a slight whiff of ozone behind.

"*Esperar! Esperar!*" he shouted after us: "Wait! Wait!"

After catching up with us, he was all smiles again. "It will be a great honor to help you on your voyage. I will make a big exception to my normal fee and agree to charter her to you, along with myself and my crew, for just three hundred. It will be an honor to place myself and my ship at your service." He and his crew would take care of us on the trip in a style that no other riverboat could even dream of. "My name is Captain Primiero O. Segundo," he said, "and it is a great personal honor to do business with you." We shook hands and agreed to return in three days with everything.

Those three days were hectic, but with Pericles as our spokesman, backed up by Suxie's imperious aura of command (and her wallet), Lisa's femininity, and Leeram's photonic communications radiating from the satchel at my side, we arrived back at the *Dom Afonso* in a Jeep and a trailer loaded with tents, a generator, food, first-aid supplies, mosquito netting ("Not for me," Leeram said), machetes, fishing gear, an old Fordson tractor equipped with a plough and harrow, and much more to keep us going for at least a month. We had no idea what to expect. Not our least important purchase were large burlap bags of acai palm seeds and other native staples recommended by Dean Knotwell. Captain Segundo and his mate, a short, native Brazilian named Edson, helped us load the supplies and personal kits and showed us our sleeping quarters behind some canvas partitions where hammocks could be swung. We were finally ready, and at Captain Segundo's command, Edson cast off the dock lines right after the captain gave his whistle lanyard several good pulls that resulted in almost as many breathy toots from her horn. He eased the *Dom Afonso* away from the quay and edged her out into the river, clearing the two boats on either side by less than a foot. Full astern, the *Dom Afonso*'s paddle wheel started throwing spray, which blew all over us. We looked at each other. "No going back now," Pericles said.

"Don't be so sure about that," Leeram said. "Just don't forget and leave me somewhere."

Once in the channel, Captain Segundo called for full ahead and Edson threw *Dom Afonso*'s ancient oil engine into full forward, giving her headway, and our journey downriver officially began, just as the sun lowered into the jungle. The ship's cook, an ageless Chinese gentleman, had a large pot of stew that never left the galley stove, its permanent fire stoked now and then with fresh wood two or three times a day. The stew's ingredients were decanted for each meal and replenished periodically with whatever was available and the pot never washed, being constantly kept just below a simmer. It was now dark, and we all sat around a scarred wooden table on the main deck to eat, along with the Captain. Edson, who was at the wheel by then, the cook, and Captain Segundo would stand four-hour watches day and night until we arrived.

"What's in that stuff?" Lisa asked, pointing at the crusty pot. I had to admit, it smelled pretty good. When Pericles translated the cook's answer, she shuddered. "I brought some freeze dried ratatouille. Can you ask him to boil some water for me?" When he understood her request, he shrugged and put a pot full of river water on the stove.

"Let it boil for a while," Pericles said. "It'll be fine."

Lisa looked at it doubtfully, but finally nodded. "OK, I guess," she said. Later, after a ginger sip or two, she smiled.

"This stuff has never tasted so good! Interesting." I declined it with the excuse that we needed to make it last, and I would make the extreme sacrifice of eating the beefy soup. It was delicious. I was surprised to see Suxie eating it too and asked her.

"I have been wondering about something, Suxie," I said. "The first time I saw you was at that PETA demonstration. How come you're eating meat here?"

She smiled. "We Amazons have always eaten meat when it was available. What Lisa and I and a lot of other people object to is the casual way we treat animals in modern society. Sure, most of us are vegetarians, but just because you don't want to use animals for fur coats doesn't mean you can't use them for nutrition. You just can't be unnecessarily cruel to them."

Lisa looked at her, surprised. "I never heard you say that before," she said.

Probably to change the subject, Pericles asked the captain about the boat's name.

"Of course!" he said, obviously proud of his ship. "I would be delighted. *Dom Afonso* is named after a famous Brazilian sailing ship, a frigate that helped defeat the Argentineans during our battle with that country in 1851. It was called the Platine War."

"Ah yes," said Pericles. "We Americans think everything begins and ends in the northern part of this continent, yet this was an enormously important conflict—not as long or destructive as our civil war, but it came ten years earlier and some of its technology was the same. And it was essentially a conflict between Spain and Portugal, with the River Plata as its main theater." I thought I had a decent knowledge of history, but I had never heard of it. This little adventure of ours was opening many doors.

Wiping his mouth delicately, Captain Segundo rose from the table and left for the bridge to begin his evening watch at the wheel; shortly after we were joined by the now hungry Edson, who ate quickly and, despite Pericles's attempts at casual conversation with him, silently. When he was finished, we all rose and took our plates to the galley, washed them, and went to our hammocks. I was too tired to sleep and lay listening to the soft, rhythmical sounds of the ship's engine and the slide of her wake as we went into the night.

"Hey, Boss!"

I was suddenly awake in full.

"That guy Edson," he said, "keep an eye on him. He has a dark door in him. I can't go through it."

"What about the Captain?" I asked.

"The tip of his spear could use a new piece of flint, but he knows the river pretty well, and the cook's OK. He dreams of bird's nest soup and thinks that he is doing penance here for a past life."

"Don't ever think for a minute," I told Leeram, "that anyone is going to leave you behind."

I felt a sense of gratitude from him. "Do you ever sleep

yourself?" I asked, surprised that I had never thought of asking the question.

"Only when I get totally bored."

With that, I turned over in my hammock and let the river roll on.

Chapter 8

I woke to the sound of four bells: 6:00 a.m. When I pulled the canvas curtain back, I was in a silver ribbon world, the low mist on the water curling as it parted in our wake. The distinctive smell of tropical vegetation and river bottom was pervasive when we first started, but quickly faded into the background as the visual reality of the scenery took over in the morning. The forest, dark on each side, bordered our river universe, fringed with a line of mud and occasionally strewn along its edges with jungle flotsam that acted as a natural barrier, as though it was put there to keep trespassers away. The others were rising too. Edson showed us the bathing facility, a shower stall in the stern, open to the big paddlewheel that churned mightily just feet away, throwing more water on us than came out of the spigot. A short rail was the only barrier between it and us, making us huddle against the wall as far away as we could get. Canvas curtains on either side provided the possibility of privacy. The coffee-colored river water was the same, whether it came from the plumbing or more directly from over the stern. By the time we were done, feeling slightly cleaner, the cook had taken the large pot of coffee off the stove and was ladling it out into hefty navy style mugs, thick and chipped. It combined the flavors of coffee bean and manatee wake—not bad after you got used to it. Rows of freshly baked corn muffins slobbered with butter appeared from the old stove's oven, its doors were marked "Shipmate." We all dug in, even before the bacon and eggs reached the table; we had no idea if fresh food would be available when we reached Fordlandia, so we might as well enjoy this while we could. Lisa wrinkled her nose at the last two servings, but she loved the muffins. We had brought our own rations, but, "You'll get pretty sick of rice and beans and MRE's soon enough," Suxie said. We had purchased just enough to last two or three days; after that, everything we ate might need to be boiled in water or taken out of a can.

We were all beginning to blend into the surroundings; our clothes—easily washed cotton —were a motley collection that blurred gender. Except for Lisa's, which could not hide the fact that she was an attractive woman. Suxie was the tallest, but the only way to tell Pericles and me apart was that one of us was bearded. This was only a temporary distinction, though, I knew as I scratched my itchy chin.

Leeram had been quiet since the last evening. He was

stowed in my duffel bag, which seemed to have a dampening effect on him. "Are you still there?" I asked.

"Mmmph," he said.

"I can't take you out right now," I said, "I want to get where we're going. I can't let you scare this crew out of their wits."

"From what I can see, they don't have much to be scared out of."

"OK," I said, "but the Captain seems to know what he's doing. Don't rock the boat!"

The captain, cook, and mate were all up forward, so I took Leeram out of his valise, safely out of sight behind my curtain. There was something odd about him; his skin seemed less hard, less chalky. "Are you feeling OK?" I asked.

"I'm fine, goddammit! Just stop poking me!"

I put him back in the valise, but didn't bury him under all my gear this time.

"Just talk to us only from now on," I said. "Be cool."

By then, it felt as though the *Dom Afonso* had been slowly plowing down the river forever, her paddle wheel splashing rhythmically astern and her old engine thump-wheezing softly. The sense of present had almost completely taken over, driving out the past and the future; our universe was bounded by the jungle and river bends forward and astern. Occasionally a fish would jump and once we saw a large animal just below the surface, probably a crocodile. We would occasionally pass small settlements with dugouts pulled up on the riverbanks, the natives generally ignoring us, a common sight to them. There was very little river traffic at the moment, just an occasional tug and barge. Mostly we napped, read, or sat around the old table going over our plans. It was strange when we looked back on that time months later; we really did not have a working script of what to do the moment we arrived. We were almost as unprepared as the early English settlers in Jamestown, a reality that was just beginning to dawn on us.

"First we have to meet with the local authorities and convince them that what we have in mind is in their best interests," I said.

"Jeez, what a brilliant idea," Leeram interjected. "Why don't you just give them some money?"

Pericles looked at me. "He's got a point, Gilbert."

"I think we should just go right ahead and start planting," Suxie said. "They will join us on their terms. That way we can't be seen as interlopers." We had a couple of hundred pounds of seed—acai palm, guava, and aguaje. According to the Agricultural School, they should thrive along the Amazon and provide sustainable nutrition for a whole village. Now, on the river, Suxie changed almost by the hour. She was obviously in a place that suited her and it showed in her face; it might have been my imagination, but her eyes, originally grayish sky blue, now seemed to turn a darker, deeper blue. They gave her a kind of serenity, taking over from the severe expression she normally wore. At the table one evening, she looked at me for a while, then put her hand over mine. "Thank you, Gilbert," she said.

She was home, she said, home in the land of her ancestors. No more need for Mambo Mama, no more Gaia Galore. "I can't tell you how wonderful it is to be free, not to have to use those personalities to shelter me. I wasn't meant to live through New England winters, or those judgmental attitudes. It made me rigid and intolerant myself. Here, I can be what I naturally am—a proud Amazon woman." I remembered how uneasy I felt when I first met her in that bar, how I felt like simply running away. It was hard to imagine that now.

"We've both changed," I said. I told her she was absolutely right when she said I was full of it then. All I really wanted to do was get Leeram back, I said to her, and I concocted this whole thing just to do that. "I was thinking only about myself," I said. "It's hard to put my finger on exactly when this thing got out of hand and started to drag me along with it, but I know one thing for sure—I'm not the same man, the same Gilbert Greenbush that I was when you and I first met. I need to thank you, not the other way around."

We were silent for a while at the table, just looking at each other. When Lisa sat down next to Suxie, I felt almost annoyed, then had a flash of guilt for feeling it. "Hi guys!" she said cheerfully. "Captain Segundo says we will get there by the day after tomorrow." Too bad, I thought; I was almost hoping that the voyage would go on forever.

That afternoon, we reached the small city of Santarem at the tip of land between the Tapajos River and the Amazon and decided to push on. We could visit later. "Does anyone want to go ashore?" Captain Segundo asked. We declined, saying we would come back when we had time after we were settled in our destination. Segundo nodded and turned his helm to starboard. The *Dom Afonso's* bow responded and we passed through a vivid dividing line between the muddy Amazon and the far clearer Tapajos. We transited from downstream to upstream as we did so and the land on each side began to pass even more slowly. Other than the now much darker river water, the scenery was pretty much unchanged, and after we watched Santarem disappear astern, we went back to our usual routine of reading, dozing, and writing in our journals. Suddenly, there was a great splash alongside and we all rushed to the rail. A school of enormous pale pink creatures were playing in our wake, leaping out of the water and belly flopping back down. "River dolphins," Suxie said. They were some of the ugliest things I had ever seen in the water, with beaks that looked like yard-long clothespins. On top of their heads was a big round growth, the size of a medicine ball, and their coloration was that of a dead thing. "I love them," Suxie said. "They have the soul of the Amazon in them."

"The bump on their head is a sounding organ, like an

old Asdic depth sounder," Pericles added. "It's said that they can even stun their prey with it." We watched them for a few minutes until they disappeared and we went back to our books.

Soon it was time to get organized. I learned from the Captain that we would offload our supplies and equipment the next day from a ramp off the bow, as the dock, he said, although still there, was pretty dilapidated. He would secure the boat against the river current long enough to unload, he said, and then we would be on our own. When we needed him again, we could use our satellite phone. "But be sure to give me at least a week's notice," he said.

The next morning began early with a drift of low fog on the water, the riverboat slowly moving through it with just the pilothouse rising above into the clear. As I stood on the shelter deck, coffee mug in hand, the water seemed insubstantial, dreamlike. The wooded banks contained a ghost river. The day's warmth began to flood into us by the time we all gathered for breakfast, and the fog dissipated just in time for our arrival in Fordlandia. The first thing that appeared around the last bend was the improbable sight of a tall water tower on a hillside, that and a church. I looked at it through binoculars and thought I saw a faint, weather-beaten image of the Ford logo on its side, but it was just my imagination. A dirt road led down to a swaybacked dock, with a handful of local boats badly in need of paint, tied to it or just beached alongside. Captain

Segundo, not trusting the dock, chose a likely spot nearby and pushed the *Dom Afonso's* bow into it, then ran a gangway ashore. The business of securing the vessel with lines run ashore to nearby trees took long enough for us to finish our last meal afloat. We then pushed, carried, and dragged our equipment, including the tractor and jeep, ashore over the heavy gangway that Edson and the cook lowered. When it was all done, Suxie peeled off a number of Brazilian *reals*, large enough for Captain Segundo to smile and nod. "I'll be back when you need me," he said. "Just remember, a week's notice!"

After the gangway was lifted, the riverboat's mooring lines were hauled back aboard and she began to back hard off the shore, we had a moment to look around. By then, a crowd of people had gathered, at first thinking we were tourists when the boat first landed, but after about an hour when they saw how much gear we were unloading, they became confused and even alarmed, talking excitedly. Soon an older man joined us, and introduced himself as the Mayor of Fordlandia—or at least that was what we thought he said. Even Pericles did not understand the local dialect well enough to know. We had apparently caused a commotion that began to verge into anger as our inability to get across to them seemed to make things worse. Pericles had his hands full. Leeram, who had been silent the whole time, broke in. "Ask the Mayor to sit down with us inside that building near the dock. Bring a bottle of rum and don't forget me. You all have made a big collective jackass of yourselves barging in like this without doing any research and it looks like I'm going to have to pull your sorry butts out of trouble." He, of course, was exactly right. We had become invincible in our minds, with our secret satchel full of Brazilian magic.

"OK, Leeram, we've got it," I said, slightly embarrassed. "We need to communicate with these people pretty quickly. Can you at least somehow calm them down?" Leeram said he would try and he must have done something because Pericles got the old man to come inside. Lisa managed to find the case of Cachaca, a kind of sweet rum made from sugar cane, that we loaded before we left, and brought a bottle to the table, along with some plastic cups. I put the satchel on the floor next to me. Suxie had brought the valise with our documents and some plans we had written up. Once inside, Leeram told me he was ready. After we had poured a drink all around, I spread the paperwork out in front of us, speaking in English while Pericles translated to the best of his ability. As he spoke, his eyes widened and words began coming out of his mouth that he had never said before, in an accent that he had never used.

"This place used to be called Boa Vista," Pericles said to the Fordlandians, "because of the view. We have come here to make that view even more enjoyable to you, by bringing the means to make life more comfortable. Suxie, here, is a daughter of your land and is returning to it because it is where her heart is." He looked at me, his expression both amazed and amused. He paused, then in English he said to us, "It was like somebody else was talking...I knew what I was saying but Leeram was moving my mouth like I was a sock puppet."

"Just keep going," I said. "Go with it."

He proceeded to introduce us all by name, and we learned that the Mayor's name was Carlao Inocencio. "You can call me Carlao," he said, reaching out to shake our hands. Everyone here, we learned, had nicknames, informal and affectionate.

As the meeting went on and the rum bottle got lower, the Mayor began to smile and talked about how we might all get along for the common good. Pericles/Leeram reassured them that we were not there to take anyone's land, that we were not an advance party for some enormous agribusiness. Finally, after about an hour, he rose from the table and reached out to shake our hands. "You are welcome to stay here," he said. "We will do what we can to help." He went outside to talk with the crowd and when we came out in our turn, its mood had changed completely. There was a slight applause when we came into the sunlight, squinting a little after the shade inside.

"I don't know why I do this," Leeram said. "That was hard work. I'm going to have to rest for a while. If I hadn't done that, they would have thrown you back in the Tapajos. I'm beginning to wonder if I should even let you outside on your own."

We chose a vacant industrial building that seemed to

have a watertight roof and began to move our large pile of gear, food, and agricultural supplies into it. As we worked, more natives began to gather. They were shy at first. Pericles's Portuguese made little or no impression on them, so we tried sign language, also to no avail. "Tell them we will pay them to help us," Suxie said. When Pericles made the offer, holding up some money, their expressions went from apprehension to glee and they gathered around him speaking Tupi. They were from the Apiaca tribe, Pericles said, and mostly lived in a nearby village called Pau d'Agua and he knew a handful of their words. It was a beginning.

Lisa and Suxie showed them the seed bags and equipment we had and their leader, or at least the one who Pericles was able to talk to, began explaining our mission to the rest. They seemed to be excited and went off to get some others. One of them looked sharply at Suxie and immediately began talking to his friends. Suddenly, one of them spoke to her in passable Portuguese. Pericles translated. "He says you look very familiar. He says you look like one of them. He wants to know where you came from."

"Tell him who I am," Suxie said, drawing herself up to her full height. When Pericles translated her request, they all began speaking loudly, mostly to her.

"We are going to have to learn Tupi," I said.

"You sure as hell are," Leeram said. Later, he told me privately, "When I was alive here, I lived in this region for many years. These people talk pretty much the same as we did then." He sighed, and said, "It looks like I am going to have to give you enough Tupi to let them understand you."

When I passed that on, Suxie was ecstatic. "Even though I can't speak it, I have that language in my bones," she said. "I want to start now."

We arranged for a formal meeting with the Mayor and his assistants the next day. In the meantime, we had to set up camp for ourselves—not much of a problem with so many abandoned cottages nearby, a handful of which were already occupied by squatters. We took one of the larger houses reserved for the American management, situated farther up the hill. It had a great view of the river and also had the least amount of bat guano. We set up a Coleman camping stove in the kitchen to cook our supper. Later, when we were alone, I took Leeram out of his valise and put him on a table. It seemed polite. We ate freeze-dried food, boiled in Tapajos river water to save the bottled stuff we had brought with us. "When you are done with that," Leeram said impatiently to us all, "I'll start your education."

Actually he began sooner than that. By the time we were finished, we knew what the local words were for eating and drinking and what certain foods were called (there was nothing in their vocabulary for freeze-dried soup, but we didn't need to get that specific). Fire was *ata* and a house was *oka*. Tomorrow we would meet with the town (*taba*) chief (*morubixaba*) and so on. Anyone who peeked through a window and saw us would have been perplexed, perhaps weirdly so; we were all sitting around a table as if we were in a séance as he poured the information into us. When he gave us a word, we knew it immediately. No one had to ask questions out loud. After about a half hour, I began to feel a headache coming on, almost as if my cortex was being overloaded too quickly. I rubbed my temples and began to lose concentration. Leeram said, "OK, I know this doesn't come naturally for you, so I'll quit for now. Get some sleep tonight and we'll do some more in the morning." We all broke into conversation at once.

"Did you get a headache too?" I asked.

"My head is splitting," Lisa said.

"Mine too," Pericles said.

Suxie looked at us and smiled. "The words seemed to belong in my mind—they seemed to slide right into notches that were already there. They fit perfectly, and I feel great!"

I didn't sleep well that night. Not only was my cot, topped with an air mattress, as still as a stone after so long on the water, but the sounds of the Amazon basin were pervasive. Not especially loud, but all about me. I lay as quietly as I could, thinking about our situation. In the morning, we were going to have to convince these folks that we were actually going to try to help them, and, more importantly, that we were not going to take advantage of them. So many outsiders had victimized them since the early nineteenth century that their apprehension was as thick as a rubber tree's bark.

When I woke to the sound of my housemates moving about getting breakfast ready, I was surprised that I had actually gone to sleep. A big pot of water was boiling on the stove. "This stuff is a lot cleaner than the water in the Amazon River," Pericles said. "At least it doesn't have as many particulates suspended in it." We had gotten used to the brown Amazon water before turning up into the Tapajos, even though we had to let it sit for a while to let the heavier elements settle to the bottom of the bucket.

"It doesn't seem to bother the natives," I said.

"Well, they don't seem all that healthy," Lisa observed. "Maybe we can change that."

After coffee and some cereal, we settled down to wait for visitors. We didn't have to wait for long. A crowd of at least fifty appeared so quickly and silently that it seemed to have come when I turned my back for an instant. They were followed by smaller groups coming individually from different directions, until it seemed that the entire local population had joined the gathering. A small group that included some of the white-haired elders we saw the day before stepped forward to meet us. I went up to them with my right hand raised. I smiled. "Good morning," I said, only the words came out in Tupi-guarani, a language that crossed tribal borders. Even Leeram didn't know the local dialect perfectly. I started out at the beginning, a recap of what we said the day before.

"We have been given permission by the Brazilian government to start a farm here and when it is up and running, to give it to you." It was about as simple a way to put it as I could.

A voice in my head said, "You sound like Johnny Appleseed." Leeram couldn't help himself.

"You know nothing about Johnny Appleseed," I said back, silently.

At that moment, Suxie stepped forward and said, "I am one of you." They looked at her intently; she almost glowed, larger than life. "I am one of you," she repeated. "My grandfather is buried here; I would appreciate it if you can show me his grave." They huddled, talking among themselves, gesticulating.

The Mayor approached her; he was easily two feet shorter. "What was his name?" he asked, in a much softer tone than he had used before.

"Ubirajara," she replied. "My Amazon name is Araci—Mother of the Day. We all looked at her in surprise.

"You never told us that," I said.

The Mayor bowed. "You are truly one of us. We welcome you with all our hearts—our homes are your homes. My name is Carlao Innocencio."

"You never told me that, Suxie!" Pericles said. "Never as long as I have known you," he said in English.

The villagers offered to help us and promised to take Suxie to her grandfather's grave, but first they wanted to welcome us properly with a celebration. A homecoming party. They left to make preparations and we returned to our cottage. We had many questions of our own, the uppermost being about her name, Araci.

"I was given that name at birth," she said, "but in North America, it would have been confusing to people, especially to the kids I went to school with, so I became Suxie. My last name, Redbone, is an anglicization of the same word in Tupi."

I was dumbfounded. "Is that why you have so many names?"

"None of them were truly mine—they were just convenient for me at the time."

"What do you want us to call you now?" Lisa asked.

"Just Suxie, if you want," she replied, "We are good friends and good friends don't call each other 'mother of the day.' It sounds, um, a bit temporary, doesn't it?" We agreed. Suxie had become one of us and on a subconscious level we really didn't want to share her equally with the village tribes.

"What does your grandfather's name mean?" I asked.

"Ubirajara means either 'Lord of the Trees' or 'Lord of the Lance,' depending on whether he was at peace or in battle." We all didn't quite know how to grasp the subtle shift that had just occurred in our relationships. Leeram, however, did not have much trouble at all.

"I met your grandfather once," he said, with an overtone of respect. "Ubirajara was a man in full and now I can see him in you."

Chapter 9

The invitation came the next morning, presented by Mayor Innocencio and his wife, who came bearing a large basket of bananas and guava fruits, garnished with flowers. Bowing and smiling, they made us understand that the festivities would begin that afternoon. We were all invited; they would give us the best delicacies in the Amazon territory, they said. We didn't have to go very far—the festival grounds were about a half-mile downstream. Even the priest from the local Catholic Church would be there to bless the occasion, Mayor Inocencio said proudly. A soccer game would be played that afternoon and we would watch that too.

Then the Mayor took Suxie to her grandfather's grave in the local cemetery, first laid out by the Ford Motor Company. We followed them up the hill to see the gravesite, not far from the church. I had Leeram in the valise over my back. The burying ground was overgrown, obviously poorly kept, and the Mayor apologized. "We can't afford to hire someone to do it all the time," he said, "so when someone is buried here, his relatives will cut the grass around his grave. Sometimes they keep doing it, but time passes and then they forget." We finally found the little tombstone after pulling the weeds away. The letters UBIR were legible and after looking closely, we could make out the rest: AJARA. Suxie stood silently, and then knelt down to touch the stone. The year 1945 was engraved just below his name.

"He was a great man," she said. "I'll clean this up." We all told her we would help too, as did the Mayor.

We left, heading back down the hill with the Mayor behind us, trying to keep up. Suxie was in front, her long legs covering ground quickly. When I reached her and asked if there was anything wrong, she said in a low voice, "I just had a funny feeling. I'm still trying to figure it out. I don't want to talk about it right now."

We spent the rest of the day preparing for cultivation, organizing our equipment and, with the Mayor's guidance, mapping out the fields we would plant. There was more unused, open ground than we could ever hope to cultivate by ourselves. Late that afternoon, we joined a big crowd at the village soccer field, where the Mayor had invited us. A lot of Fordlandians were there already, drinking cachaca. "They also call it pinga. It's cheap and potent and it's their national booze," said Pericles. Others were imbibing a local concoction called alua, a low-alcohol kind of moonshine made of fermented fruits, which went down smoothly enough. "Not half bad," Pericles said, a mug in his hand. Before long, with the exception of Suxie, we had almost forgotten about her grandfather. The only one still brooding over the experience was Leeram.

"Later," was all he said when I asked him about it.

We watched the soccer contest, cheering both sides on, and were told later that, for once, the game ended peaceably without a drunken argument. They took their athletics pretty seriously here. "It is because you are with us," the Mayor said. "They like you." By the time we all were seated around one of many long wooden benches and the food was being passed around, it was almost like Thanksgiving. Several pigs had been roasted for the occasion and their fragrant meat, garnished with plantains, pineapples, bacaba, and strawberry guava, filled our plates—or most of them, anyway. Platters of fresh fish from the river were carried in, stewed in complex and delicious sauces. We looked at each other thinking of all the canned stew and freeze-dried foods we had so carefully provided ourselves with just a few days earlier.

"Well, we might need them someday," Pericles said.

"You know, Lisa," Suxie said as we were sitting down at the head table, "You should try this. It was prepared for us by people who normally can't afford such a feast every day. You will do them a great honor. Don't make them think you are not grateful."

Lisa picked up her fork and, with a quick wince, put a tiny piece of fish in her mouth. She looked up and said,

"This is excellent. OK, the vegetarian in me hates to admit it, but it's really, really good." We all raised our cups of alua to her. Later, I noticed that she went for a second helping almost guiltily, but not quite.

After everyone had eaten as much as they could, the Mayor rose to his feet and began ringing a triangle bell until the din of conversation finally died down. "You know why we are all here today," he said, in the manner of all dinner speakers everywhere in the world. "We are going into a new time here, a time of prosperity, thanks to these Americanos who have given themselves and their resources to us." The crowd, with the exception of a few here and there who just looked at their plates, rose to its feet and applauded us with gusto. I raised a cup of cachaca to acknowledge their praise. Before long, we were caught up in the celebration ourselves, feeling warm in their acceptance of us.

The party lasted into the night, long after we left for bed. We still had a lot to do in the morning, getting ready to break ground. After we climbed into our beds, we fell asleep quickly, even with all the shouting and singing in the distance. Despite good intentions, I didn't wake until much later the next morning than we had planned. I had a vague memory of a dream in which Leeram was calling for me, but I was too tired to help. When I did finally extract myself from a disturbed sleep, mouth dry and bladder aching, I had a funny feeling. At first it was just a sensation that something was missing; first, I attributed it to hangover guilt. Then it hit me suddenly: Leeram's valise was gone.

I was frantic. I overturned everything I had brought in to my room, then searched the rest of the house. I retraced my steps to the picnic grounds, stepping over empty bottles and trash. I even combed through the fire pits where the cooking had been done but there was no trace of Leeram's valise. I was dizzy and felt as though I had just emerged from the bottom of a scrimmage heap, hollow and sick. "What's the matter with you?" I heard Lisa say when I walked back into the cottage. The rest of them were just beginning to crawl out of bed.

"I've lost Leeram," I said. "Please don't ask me how, but he's not here." The shock in my voice woke everyone completely; they became instantly awake and all started to search with me. We looked everywhere—meticulously, inside the house and out. They, too, went back along the path we took to and from the picnic site and combed it, turning over trash, looking under tables and even in the latrine, which stank atrociously. Leeram was not to be found. Finally, after two hours, defeated, we sat around the table back in our house to make plans and assess our next move. For a little while, our heads in our hands, we said nothing.

Suxie broke the silence. "Listen. We came here on a mission. Let's just go ahead with it. If someone took Leeram, I'm pretty sure Leeram can take care of himself." Lisa got up and lit the stove. Pericles and I brought in a couple of gallons of water and we dejectedly set about making breakfast, though none of us was hungry. It was just something to take our minds off what had happened.

We decided to begin in the field that the Mayor had pointed out the day before as a good place to start. Pericles and I had gone over the mechanics of the tractor and plow back in Manaus when we first purchased the equipment with Suxie's money. We went down to the shed where we had stored it the day before and cranked it up after filling the gas tank. I drove it to the field's edge and lowered the plow blade, put the tractor in first gear, released the clutch, and aimed along a path that followed the contours of the gently sloping ground, according to the best practices guide I had read on the way from Brookline. Dean Knotwell had given me the book. The soil, silted over the years when the river flooded, was naturally rich. It curled off the blade like a massive brown peel, laying a clean furrow. When I reached the end of the field, I lifted the plow, made a wide turn, and lowered it again about a foot down from the first line. As the process went on and my aim improved, the furrows became straighter and closer together. It took concentration and gave me slight and momentary relief from the pain of my loss. Our loss.

Some of the villagers began walking up in twos and threes and by mid-afternoon, we had over a dozen volunteers. "We are farmers," they said. "Let us do this." Several of them, they said, worked for the local cattle ranchers but were excited about having the promise of something of their own. One of them, wiry and sun-toughened, offered to drive the tractor. "Mister, I have been doing that all my life, let me try." My hindquarters were feeling a bit sore by then, so I gladly climbed down and gave him the wheel. It took all day to plough, then harrow the field, and by evening we were exhausted. We decided to plant aguaje seeds the next day, when even more villagers told us they would show up to help. We had not forgotten Leeram, but the hard work had given us some small compensation. When we finally left, we were satisfied that we had made a good beginning. The first of many fields to come had been opened up.

We were subdued, walking back to our camp. Lisa was next to me and reached over to hold my hand. "I'm so terribly, terribly sorry," she said. It was all I needed. I began to weep, and she held me as I sobbed.

We had washed up and were beginning to prepare dinner when we heard a knock at the door. Lisa put down the bowl she had been stirring, wiped her hands on her apron, walked to the front door, and opened it to see nothing but quickly deepening twilight—no one was there. I was just in back of her and looked down. An envelope was lying on the doorstep. I tore it open and took out a note written in pencil in block letters: "If you want that thing back, one of you—and only one—bring twenty thousand BRLs to the cemetery tonight at exactly 10:00 p.m. Leave it at the Grave. If you are armed, the deal is off." BRLs, we decided, meant Brazilian *reals*.

Apparently Leeram had not gone unnoticed, and also, apparently, we had not been entirely among friends last night. At first I was so relieved that Leeram was still in existence, even though he was a hostage, I felt a spike of glee. It soon faded. "I don't have that much money with me," said Suxie. "Even if I gave them what I do have, we would have nothing left."

We talked angrily for a while, first Suxie, then Pericles, and then Lisa, each bringing up ideas, only to have them rebutted by the others. "The letter says 'leave it at the grave'; there can only be one grave he's referring to," I said. "That means that either the kidnapper was the Mayor or that the actual thief followed us." We all agreed that the Mayor would have been a very unlikely criminal; some people just ooze believability.

"I am sure whoever it was followed us," Suxie said. "I am a pretty good judge of character and if it was the Mayor, I'm a Girl Scout brownie."

She counted her remaining cash and it came to a little over fifteen thousand Brazilian *reals*. "This was supposed to support us for the next three or four months," she said. "Without it, we can't pay our help, and we can't get this whole thing off the ground. We can't even pay our fare back."

In the end, we agreed that we had no choice. I would go alone as the note demanded; the others insisted that they follow me far enough away so they would not be seen by the kidnapper but would try to stay close enough to help if they were needed. At 9:45 p.m., I set out up the hill. They waited for a few minutes then followed. We did not have a gun, but at the last moment I thought to put the atlatl and a couple of darts through my belt in back. It was dark by then and they wouldn't be visible from a distance. Exactly fifteen minutes later, I was standing at Suxie's grandfather's grave, now cleared of weeds for some thirty paces around. Suddenly a man approached. When he was close enough his face looked strangely familiar and when we were just a few feet apart, I saw who it was: Edson. "You!" I said.

"Yes, amigo, it is me." Edson looked around. "Are you alone?" he asked.

"I followed the instructions in your letter," I said. "We don't have twenty thousand *reals* with us, but we do have most of it. Where is Leeram?"

"You call it Leeram?" he asked mildly. "How did a curio like that get a name? Doesn't really matter. What I know is that you place a very high value on it."

Leeram had a right to be worried, I thought. "How did you get here? The last time I saw you, you were on the way back to Manaus." I felt both overwhelming joy at getting him back and an equally overwhelming fear of the moment.

"I got off the boat in Belterra when we pulled in for some cargo. I had the feeling that what you had here was worth a lot more than I could earn from Segundo. I hitched a ride back upriver and got in yesterday before that big party. You sure had a good time, didn't you? You didn't see me because I spent most of the time out on the fringes, but I learned about your big female friend's trip to this grave from one of the men who went up there with you when you first got here. You were so drunk last night that it was easy for me to pick up that valise. Couldn't believe what you had in it!" Edson swung the valise off his back and dangled it tantalizingly in front of me. "Give me what you have and I'll decide whether or not to give you this."

I took the money from my pocket and said, "Count it; there are 15,433 *reals* here."

Edson hesitated. "Give it to me," he said. I handed it over. It was dark but he had a flashlight, which he jammed under his chin while he flipped through the bankroll, his lips moving. Finally he switched the light off and looked up. "It'll do," he said, and tossed the valise to me, then turned and started to run toward the forest. I opened it up and saw a fist-sized stone inside.

"Where's Leeram," I shouted.

"I threw that goddamned thing in the river," he said, over his shoulder. Something snapped in me. I went into a red rage, beyond words, beyond even fear. I reached around my back for the atlatl, notched and hurled a dart with all my strength at the now almost invisible form, rapidly shrinking into the night. The form stumbled and said, "Huh!" then coughed, staggered a few more steps and collapsed in a heap. Suxie, Lisa, and Pericles were all close enough to see and hear what happened and they were next to me moments after I got to where Edson lay, one leg stretched out and the other curled beneath it.

"You motherfucker," I said, standing over him. "You motherfucking motherfucker." Edson lay there gurgling softly, the dart protruding from his chest.

"Fuck you," he said and then died. The part of my rational mind that still functioned mused that it just isn't fair that the dead get the last word.

For a few moments we were all silent. The fact that I had just killed a human being was just sinking in, but I didn't feel remorse. I felt like kicking the body. "We can't leave it here," Suxie said. I leaned down and tugged out the dart, grabbing it with both hands and bracing a foot on Edson's torso. It was as though he didn't want to give it up, but finally it slid out. Then I cleaned it with a couple of swipes on his shirt.

"I might need this again," I said.

"I'll go get something to wrap the body in," Pericles said. "Let's just throw it into the river." It seemed like a good idea; a grave would be easily discovered and the banks of the Tapajos were sparsely populated for many miles. The fish would take care of it before long. Pericles went to get the Jeep, and when he returned, we rolled the corpse into a blanket and hoisted it aboard. I thought of the turkey in Brookline, a place that seemed so distant now, almost as though it had never existed. We were in the only real world right now. There were no witnesses to see us drive the half mile or so to the riverbank or to hear the soft splash as we launched Edson to join Leeram.

At least, we agreed, there was one good thing. Suxie got her money back.

Chapter 10

During the next few days, the group of natives who wanted to join the farm grew until we had nearly a hundred. It looked as though we were assembling an Amazonian kibbutz. Some of them even moved into the empty cottages, giving the place less of the feel of a ghost town.

We knew we had a finite amount of money, enough to carry the project for about four months. After that it would have to support itself. It was a deadline that we had anticipated, even to the extent of keeping a sufficient sum aside to get home. The native Apiacans, including descendants of the Munduruku tribe, were enthusiastic by now and we followed many of their suggestions. We began rising with the sun and working until late morning, when it became too hot. Like them, we began taking a siesta in the shade, eating a light lunch, and then working until dusk. I had read that Henry Ford hated this relaxed regimen and, from the distance of his headquarters in

River Rouge, imposed a standard, continuous eight-hour workday on them, feeding them a large, hot midday meal in a sweltering dining hall. That, and many other impositions, eventually led to a violent, destructive uprising. Suxie's father survived it and caught the eye of his employers when he tried to get the rioters under control, telling them that they were hurting themselves more than their bosses.

The routine, once we fell into it, was comforting. We hadn't forgotten Leeram, but could at least put him in the back of our mind for most of the day. His memory was constantly with us, but we only spoke of him in the evening, when we would talk about him during supper. Many times, I would catch myself thinking that he was still "alive," but then would wake up, knowing we were on our own now and were entirely capable of carrying on. That knowledge was sad but comforting. My old life seemed as though it existed behind a veil—everything that I did before meeting Leeram and going to the Amazon was hazy in my memory, everything after, sharp and clear as the sky after a cold front had passed through. Every breath I took now somehow spiked new energy into me.

***

"*Voce esta preso!*" (You're under arrest!)

The words were bellowed at the break of day one morning when our front door was violently broken open and the room suddenly filled with armed and uniformed men. We jumped out of bed and looked, blearily, at them, uncomprehending.

"Get dressed. You are coming with us."

We were dazed. "What's this all about?" Pericles asked in Portuguese. We were given enough time to pull on our clothes and get the papers we were given by the Indian Affairs office, then were told our questions would be answered at the police station in Aveiros. We were handcuffed, then hustled into a waiting (windowless) police van with two long, facing benches. Lisa was sitting next to me, our hands gripping each other despite the tethers on our wrists. We looked at each other wildly as the van bounced and jostled along for an endless time. Finally, the driver jammed on the brakes and we all accordioned into each other, pressed against the partition that separated us from the two *officials de policia* in front. They got out, came around to the back, and unlocked the rear door, motioning us toward them. We climbed out and were escorted into a cinderblock police station, where we were told to sit on some chairs along a wall. We waited for a long time.

"Why did you arrest us?" Lisa asked the sergeant sitting behind a steel desk, chipped and rusty.

He just looked at her, and at us, and said, "*Calar-se!*"

"That means shut up," Pericles said to us.

"*Caramba! Calar-se!*" the sergeant said angrily to Pericles.

After what seemed like hours, a man in a suit came in,

nodded to the sergeant, then turned to us. "You are here illegally," he said. "You are henceforth under orders of deportation from the government of the State of Para."

"Just a minute," I said. "We have legal permission from the Office of Indian Affairs—look, it says here," I said, holding out the official documents we had received in Brasilia.

The man gave the papers a brief glance, handed them back, and said offhandedly, "All well and good, but this is the State of Para. Those people in the south have no idea what goes on up here, or in Amazonia. You have a choice: post a bail of fifteen thousand BRLs and return to Fordlandia until we send you away, or just stay here."

Some choice. What a coincidence that our bail almost equaled the cash we had on hand, we said to each other. Suxie had grabbed the money before we were taken away, only to have it confiscated almost immediately. "I want a written receipt," she demanded. He ordered the sergeant to type up the receipt, signed it, and handed it back to Suxie. "What are the odds we'll ever seen that again?" she asked dryly.

We were driven back to Fordlandia at a slower but still bumpy pace and arrived back at our house in the early afternoon, starving and thirsty. None of the locals were to be seen. The fields were empty, even the squatters had left the handful of cottages they had been living in. What happened that morning had spooked them badly; the authorities apparently had a reputation for sudden, unbidden violence.

After eating our first meal of the day, now in the early afternoon, we sat around the table going over our options. We had enough money to get us through the next week. I thought, suddenly, of the satellite phone we bought at the beginning of our trip. We had more or less forgotten about it, not thinking it would be of any use until it came time to leave, and that time had come a lot earlier than we had planned. It was in the bottom of my duffel bag, which I had not even completely unpacked. I took it out, put in fresh batteries, and dialed the Department of Indigenous Affairs, then gave the phone to Pericles. After giving our names, he asked for the Assistant District Commissioner.

"I'm sorry, senor," the replay came, "but the Assistant District Commissioner is at a meeting." When would he be available, Pericles asked. "The meeting is all day," came the reply. Tomorrow? Pericles asked. "He will be at meetings all day then also," came the reply again.

We looked at each other. It was pretty clear that someone was washing his hands of us. We were on our own. "Well, I don't know about the rest of you, but I'm here and I'm not going back. I don't even have to go native; I am native," Suxie said. "You folks should probably go. You have lives to live elsewhere. I'll buy your tickets."

I turned to Lisa. "I'm so sorry I got you into this mess." She put her arms around me.

"Gilbert, don't blame yourself for this. Don't forget I

was the one who insisted that you go through with it, back in Massachusetts." She gave me a kiss and I felt my backbone take form again.

Lisa, Pericles, and I reluctantly agreed. We had to go. I found the number that Captain Segundo had given me and called him. The *Dom Afonso* was in Belim, down on the Atlantic coast. She had just loaded a cargo of fertilizer for Belterra's big new industrial soybean farms and was about to head west with a few passengers. "I'll pick you up when I get there," he said. "If you want me to go all the way to Fordlandia, it will be extra." By then, we were so discouraged that it didn't really make much difference. Hell, we said, we could go down the river in a goddamned raft if we had to, I said.

We spent the rest of that day deciding what to do with our farm equipment and fruitlessly looking for any official who could help us. The Mayor threw his hands up and looked genuinely distressed. "I would do anything to help you," he said, "But these people are very powerful." We had become pariahs. We would, we agreed, assess things in the morning and take some kind of action. Our brains just weren't up to insightful conclusions that night. As I lay in bed sleeplessly, I began to wonder what Henry Ford would do in our position. I began to try to visualize the Father of Mass Production way up in his River Rouge plant in Dearborn. I had read that he never once came down to Brazil to personally inspect his rubber plantation. What a contradictory character, I thought—half-shrewd, half-provincial. Bad dad, great father to the automobile.

I was certain it was probably just wishful thinking when a slight hint of ozone seemed to suffuse the air in my bedroom, just before I fell asleep. But then, even before I knew I was asleep, I began to have a vivid dream—a dream so real that I could almost breathe its air. At first I thought it was just a waking dream, since I knew, or thought I knew, that I was awake. After all, I had been lying there for hours wondering what we were going to do the next day. I was on my back in the forest; I was warm and dry. The light was clear and slightly tinged with green as it filtered down through the forest's thick top hamper and flittered slightly as jungle birds and monkeys passed through its rays. I felt quite comfortable and not overly concerned with the oddness around me. I turned my head and an Indian was sitting patiently, his back against a tree and his arms around his knees. He looked at me as I saw him. He was very familiar.

"Well, that took a while," he said, smiling. Then he got up and walked over to me and squatted down again.

"Leeram?" I said.

"Leeram," he said.

"Last time I saw you in person, you were on that plane," I said, happy for the first time since he was taken away. I had almost forgotten what not being utterly depressed felt like. It was actually Leeram!

"I'm not as good-looking as that 'stewardess,'" he said, "but, yes, it's me."

"How did you..." I began to ask.

"Better start by asking how you got here," he interrupted. "In a way, you are in my valise now. I got you through a wormhole — not your body, just you. Don't worry, you can't stay very long because you'll go away, but I can hold on for a while."

"But you are gone in the river," I said.

"Yes, in your universe for now. I don't mind. It was a pretty cramped way to get around anyway. I want to thank you, by the way, for killing that Edson cocksucker."

"It was my pleasure," I said politely. "I'd do it again, anytime."

"It was doing that, you know, that made it possible for me to reach you," Leeram said. "The act of taking his life to revenge me gave me the opening into this existence to pull you through. I can't explain it in any more detail, but it worked."

"Do you know what's happening to us now?" I asked.

"Nothing very good, I'm sure," Leeram said. "Without me, you all are pretty helpless. I should know better, but when things were aligned just right, I took the chance to pull you across to here because I might be able to do something."

"Is there any way I can pull you back?" I asked.

"Not without my head," he said. "It's the only thing that can anchor me in your world."

"Look," I said, "the police took all our money and have ordered us to leave. Even the natives are avoiding us. We need your help, Leeram! Don't you have anything else of yours we could use?"

He shrugged and picked up a coconut. "OK," he said, "This is now my coconut," and tossed it onto my lap. "Worth a try," he said. The coconut sat there like a heavy, hairy ball. I felt it land.

"It doesn't much look like you," I said. He thought for a minute, then took out a knife, carved a little smiley face on it and put it back on my lap.

"Primitive art is never representational," he said. "I don't know if it will work, but it's better than nothing." He sounded very un-Leeram-like. Primitive Art? Unrepresentational? I said that to him. "Someday I'll tell you a few things," he replied cryptically.

"Before you send me back," I said, "what about Suxie's grandfather?" The thought came subliminally. If Leeram lived here, why couldn't he?

"Ubirajara?" he said. "Wait here." He rose and then he was gone. I tried to sit up but couldn't move; it was not an unpleasant paralysis, I was just curious. I could look around, or at least was aware of my surroundings, but other than that, I was in a kind of stasis. Just as I had absorbed everything that I could see around me without much emotion, Leeram reappeared, this time with another tribesman a good head taller. I wasn't surprised by that either. It was as though I had taken a bucket of Valium.

"You know my granddaughter," the man said to me. It was not a question.

"She resembles you," I said.

"Your friend took a long time to find me," Ubirajara said. "I was very far away." Time and distance must work differently around here, I thought.

"You are on Araci's mind always," I said. "She used the money you left in the form of stock certificates to get a first-class education; you made her a wealthy woman in every sense, and now she is in Fordlandia to help your people."

"My own children never really understood the world outside of the Amazon," Ubirajara said. "They could have used that money themselves, but at least they didn't throw the certificates away. They chose to stay close to home after I died, but gave their daughter freedom to follow her own path, even encouraged her. For that, I love them as much as I love the one I never met—Araci."

I decided to ask him about the grave. "When you were buried," I asked, "did they leave you with anything of great value?"

"They did, but nothing anyone would recognize," he said.

"It was..." I started to say.

"My badge. That badge was the most precious thing that I owned, other than the portfolio of shares in General Motors."

I didn't understand why, and said so.

"It looked just like all the thousands of other badges, but it wasn't. I was a simple rubber tapper when I first started with the Ford Company as a translator, and when they gave it to me, I took it as a talisman, not just a sign to identify me. I took it to our medicine man, who in turn knew another medicine man with certain powers and gave it to him." Suddenly Leeram looked up sharply at Ubirajara.

"I remember it," Leeram said. "It was special, but I had no idea it was yours. I sacrificed one of our slaves to ennoble it with good fortune."

"I was planning to give it to my children but I had no warning before I died and never got the chance. They buried it with me," he said. "When you return, I want you to give it to Araci."

"You have to go now," Leeram said. "Or you may be stuck here like a statue in the middle of this forest forever." But I didn't want to go just yet; the longer I was awake in this strange place, the more questions began boiling in my mind. "Leeram, let me stay for a minute or two. I have to know how I'm here and why you can't come back."

"This universe and yours were never meant to interact, but nothing in all creation is perfect. The transit between them is supposed to be one-way only, and it is, for the most part, but there are a few exceptions. Don't forget, I was a medicine man when I was on your end and we knew a few things your modern scientists overlooked. You don't have time for me to tell you everything, but I'll work on the connection. Now, you really have to go."

"Can I talk to you again?" I asked.

"You bet," he said.

And then it was dawn in my bedroom. Lisa was standing in the doorway. I could smell the coffee. I looked down at my midriff and saw a prominent rise in the sheet. Lisa said, "Sorry," and quickly shut the door. I pulled the sheet away and there was a coconut with a smiley face, grinning away at me to beat the band.

Chapter 11

We all met in the kitchen for breakfast. Pericles and Lisa had been up for hours and Suxie joined us—like me, another late sleeper that day.

"I had a strange dream last night," Suxie said. "I don't exactly remember what it was, but I think I liked it." I didn't want to say anything about my own nocturnal adventure right away; I was still trying to make sense of it myself. Before I left my bedroom, I put the coconut into Leeram's valise, where it took up a little more space than its previous inhabitant but still fit comfortably. I wasn't in a mood just yet to show it to anybody. In the meantime, we had to get ready to vacate Fordlandia.

When we finished eating, we began gathering our belongings, not saying much to each other except for the occasional, "Where the hell did I put that seed reference book?" or something. After we had packed for about an hour, amazed that we had carried so much with us, we heard a knock at the door. It was Mayor Innocencio.

"I came here to apologize," he said in Tupi.

"Why?" I said. "You didn't arrest us."

"I know," said the Mayor. "They come when they want something. We can't stand up to them. They think you are dangerous to them, that you don't belong here."

"Until they arrested us," Suxie said, "we weren't dangerous to them." We all looked at her. She was back in full Amazon mode now, radiating quiet anger. "I'm beginning to think that we shouldn't run away so quickly."

"But they have the guns," Lisa said. "They can force us to leave, and don't forget, they have your money."

"Did you ever really think we'd get that money back?" Suxie said. I had to admit that we hadn't either.

"So what do we do?" asked Pericles. The Mayor was standing in the doorway, looking at us, his hat in his hand.

"I beg your forgiveness for what I said yesterday," he said, looking at Suxie. "I apologize for my fear; it was why I said what I did. I was not thinking. You are one of us—that we know—and it would help us make amends for not being with you when all this happened, if we could help you now. You have done so much for us since you came." We were silent for a moment, not sure how to respond.

"Come in," Pericles said, breaking our startled silence. He offered the Mayor a chair in the living room.

"What do you have in mind?" Suxie asked the Mayor in a level voice.

"You can pretend to leave," the Mayor said. "We can

hide you and when they go away, you can come back out and we can go on the way we were."

"Without any money we can't pay for your work on the farm," I said.

"Your money was of more help to us than you can imagine," the Mayor replied. "It is we who owe you. We will give you our labor."

"But what about the *Dom Afonso?*" I asked. "Captain Segundo is going to show up pretty soon to take us aboard."

"Let him," Suxie said. "We can board the boat, leave with him, get off a few miles downstream and come back. We will leave some of the farm equipment here with the Mayor, so it will be here when we return."

"But how are we going to pay Segundo?" I asked.

"We'll give him our Jeep. If that's not enough, we'll give him some more."

I was still confused. "Ok," I said, "but how about when we really have to get back?"

"Don't you have any confidence in yourself, Gilbert?" Suxie said. I was a bit miffed, though I knew back home she would have called me Greenbush. I must have come up in her esteem. If Leeram had given me anything, it was confidence in myself. Was it overrated? We agreed on the plan and started going over the details. We would make a big show of embarking in full view of anyone who might be reporting back to the authorities, then meet some loyal natives at an arranged location several miles away. They would guide us back to Fordlandia.

"But what if Segundo or his crew talk to the authorities when they get to Manaus?" Lisa asked.

"Leave that to me," Suxie said. For some reason that seemed sufficient.

"You can also leave that to me." It was the unmistakable voice of Leeram!

"Is that really you?" I said out loud.

"Who do you think it is," Suxie said, with a hint of impatience.

"Sorry," I said, "I thought I heard something."

"One other thing," Suxie said to the Mayor, "I would do this myself, but we don't have time. Can you get some people up to the cemetery and put my grandfather's grave to rights?" The Mayor bowed and said he would take care of it immediately, then shook our hands and left.

I was stunned. Could it possibly have been Leeram? I excused myself and went outside. When I was alone, I said, "Leeram, can you hear me?" His voice was muffled and distorted, but I could just make it out.

"These goddamned wormholes are hard to talk through," he said. "Can you understand me?"

"Thank God, you're back!" I said. "The coconut isn't as good as your own head, but it is one hell of a lot better than nothing!"

"Well, it was a long shot and I didn't honestly think it

would work, but I thought, what the hell. That coconut is mine, after all, even though I only had it for a moment."

"Could Suxie have the same link with her grandfather's badge?" I asked.

"I think she could, but I'm going to have to talk with the old man, show him how to use it. By the way, thanks for connecting me to him. I think we can work together." Leeram was back! I had my personal wise guy back!

"Talking with you through a wormhole to a coconut is like talking through tin cans connected by a string," he said. "It just wrings all the horseshit out of conversation." That made sense, I thought. "I can get through to you, but not the others like I could when you had my head," he said. "Also, right now I can't see you anymore or get into your head like I used to, and I can't talk to anyone else either."

I went back inside, not sure of how to tell them. Or should I tell them at all? They were still glumly shoving their essential belongings into duffel bags. The *Dom Afonso* was due the next morning and we had to give the appearance of taking everything with us, yet leaving enough behind enough so that lugging everything back overland wouldn't be too hard, even with the villagers helping us. Later, the Mayor reappeared in our doorway. "Tonight we are going to give you a feast," he said, "A feast for your departure. This will convince the authorities that you are actually going to leave. We will make it as loud as we can with many speeches and toasts." We thanked him, and he gave us an exaggerated wink as he turned to leave.

We all looked at each other. "Well, OK," Suxie said dubiously.

"I suppose it can't hurt," I said. "Might as well set out with a full belly." I turned to her later when we were alone. "I need to tell you something. Let's go up to your grandfather's grave." Just before we left, I picked up a couple of shovels.

"Hope you're not planning to dig him up again," she said.

"Well, actually, yes." I told her everything about my dream, her grandfather, and the badge. "It may do the same thing for you that Leeram's head did for me, and it might be the only way we can find a way to stay here."

At first, Suxie was incredulous and not a little angry, then curious. "This is going to be very, very weird," she said.

It was hard work, but finally we reached the wooden coffin, which by now had little more consistency than the dirt around it. With a few final scrapes, the remains were visible—bones, bits of the clothes he was buried in and, right in the middle, attached to a leather thong, was the badge. Brushing the dirt away with the tip of my shovel and ignoring the very faint odor that began to fill the bottom of the pit, I could see it more clearly. The initials "C.F.I.B." in raised lettering were stamped under a busy rendition of a factory, complete with smokestacks and below, two small ships. A badge number was on the top and the famous Ford logo in the middle. "He must have worn that badge every day he worked there," she said. With Suxie holding my ankles, I reached in with my hand and picked it up, then struggled back out and handed it to her. "I don't know if it's just me," she said, "but this badge is warm." I hadn't felt that myself, but it belonged to her grandfather, not mine. We rested for a few minutes, and then filled the grave back in.

About an hour before dusk, after washing up, we walked down the hill to the picnic ground, already filled with the now familiar and appetizing smell of roasting pork. We filled our cups with alua, avoiding the more powerful rum, and mingled with the villagers. They were tearful and many embraced us; they were convinced we were leaving for good. Our knowledge of Tupi had improved enough to let us talk with them almost without effort, given the head start Leeram had implanted in us. Now we were able to understand nuance, to read faces, much more easily than when we first arrived.

The Mayor led us to a central table where his wife and family were already sitting. Others crowded around in nearby tables; only a few villagers hung back, sitting at the fringes, talking among themselves. We knew that distance alone was not enough to indicate disloyalty but we observed them carefully anyway. "Look at that one," Leeram said. "The one with the hat." I turned my head and saw a short native, wearing a stained, brown fedora. He was gesticulating as he spoke, and the people around him were paying full attention. "That son-of-a-bitch is a spy," Leeram said. I walked over to Suxie and pointed him out.

"Funny," she said, "I got the same feeling." It was hardly enough to convict him in our minds, but it did give us a sense that we might be able to go further. I decided that I would have to open up to her about my experiences last night and with Leeram today. I took her by the elbow and we moved to a private place, behind some trees.

When we were completely out of sight of the others, I opened the valise and showed her its contents. "Say hello to Leeram," I said. "He's back. He says the guy is a spy." She looked down at the valise and then up at me with the most Redbonian disdain.

"That is a coconut with a smiley face, you idiot!"

"Well, you're not wrong about that," I said, "but it is Leeram anyway." I then told her everything, every detail of my dream and waking up this morning with a pup tent in my sheets and her grandfather and the badge. She took the badge off her belt and looked at it intently.

"How do I do it? Can I talk to Ubirajara with it like you do with Leeram?" she asked.

"I really don't know," I said, "but I think that Leeram does. Let's wait until he shows us how." That didn't satisfy her.

I thought for a moment, and then said to Leeram, "Can you ask Ubirajara something about Suxie that only he knows?"

Leeram was silent for a moment, then said, "Her mother had a pet donkey called 'Bebe.'" I passed that on.

"Leeram!" she shouted. "Let me talk to my grandfather!" I said I didn't think he could communicate with her directly without his actual head. I told her about the string theory, and she looked dejected. "Maybe I just have to try myself," she said, softly this time.

"You can't force these things," I said. "It is really up to them to get the ball rolling." We walked back and rejoined the crowd.

A short while later, maybe ten minutes, Suxie said excitedly, "There's another one!" She pointed discreetly at a short, mustachioed gent sitting by himself, one hand on a glass of cachaca. "I'm not sure of how I know, but the badge is warm in my hand. Feel it." I did, and it was indeed warm, not too hot to touch but definitely hotter than the air around it. I got the sensation that I had when Leeram was with me, almost a tangible presence but not exactly physical. It's hard to describe.

"I think that communicating between their existence and ours must take practice," I said. "Leeram has had many years because his head was in our living world so long, but your grandfather was six feet under ever since he died. I'm not surprised that he can't talk directly to you, but I did meet him and I know he is there. I also know how he feels about you. Give him some time."

We sat down as the Mayor made a farewell speech, wishing us a safe trip home and thanking us for all we had done, regretting that we could not continue. We stood and thanked him in turn and wished the villagers the best of luck in bringing the cooperative farm into being. We left early, saying that the next day was coming all too soon. Back at our house, we exchanged notes.

"There were definitely two spies," I said, and Suxie agreed.

"I wasn't aware of any more, but those two are bad to the bone," she said. We sat around the living room and went over our options.

"We can't do anything about them until after we leave," said Pericles. "They will have to inform their bosses that we actually have left, but we are going to have to neutralize them before they can report that we're back." It was a delicate problem.

"And we are going to have to make sure that our guides for the trip back, once we get off the boat, keep their mouths shut, too."

"Not to mention Captain Segundo and his crew," added Lisa.

"Not to mention everyone else in the entire village," I said. We all looked at each other silently. It was, I decided at that moment, the time to introduce everyone to the new Leeram. "Suxie already knows this," I said, "and I was going to tell you this at the right time. Well, now is the right time. We have Leeram back! He looks a little different now, but don't worry, he is with us." I opened the valise and took the coconut out. Consternation replaced happiness all around, except for Suxie, who looked amused. "At this point, he can only communicate with me," I said. As I spoke, I realized that Pericles and Lisa were going to have to put great faith into what I was saying; after all, I was standing in front of them holding a ridiculous object.

"I know," I tried to reassure them. "It's just a coconut, but it is Leeram's coconut, and since it belongs to him, he can link to us—not as easily as he could to his own head, but he can still link!" Suxie stepped in.

"It is Leeram," she said. "I can't talk to him myself, either, but Gilbert, through Leeram, has given me information that only Leeram could get. Believe me, he's real."

Everyone started to clap, laughing and whooping. Lisa's and Pericles's eyes welled up. "I don't know how," he said, "but for the first time since we were arrested, I feel sure that we'll survive this thing."

"Better than survive," I said. "We will win."

At dawn the next morning, in the distance, we heard the hoarse, breathy sound of *Dom Afonso's* whistle, beginning with a hiss, building to a shrieking crescendo, then dying back to an exhausted finish. The show was now on the road. By the time we finished a hasty breakfast, a dozen or so villagers were at the door to help us carry our baggage and load it aboard. Captain Segundo was waiting at the top of the gangway to greet us elaborately, a big smile on his face. Even the old cook was grinning heathenishly.

"I have a surprise for you," Segundo said, turning and beckoning behind him. Suddenly, from the wheelhouse door, a woman appeared. It was Dean Elizabeth Knotwell, dressed in khaki shorts and wearing a pith helmet. With her were two young men, blue-jeaned and jungle-shirted.

She stepped down the gangplank and gave us all a big hug. "I have to apologize for arriving unannounced this way, but I had no way to get in touch with you." I suddenly realized that we had not used our satellite phone to call her, once Suxie decided to finance this expedition by herself. What with Leeram and Suxie, we had almost forgotten completely about the grant request we had made. "We got the funding much earlier than I ever thought we would, but I had no way of calling you," she said, "and I took a leave of absence, a sabbatical if you will, to come down in person. I arrived in Manaus and was told that Mr. Segundo here was about to leave for Fordlandia, so I hopped aboard and here I am!" She turned to the two young men. "Meet Ben and Seth; they are graduate students of mine and will be helping us while they work on their dissertations."

We all shook hands and introduced ourselves to the students, then I told everyone to put down their bags and wait for a while. "This changes everything," I said. "We have to talk."

When we were all back inside, we filled her in on our dilemma. She looked at us for a long time, then said, "Let's have some coffee. Can you put this whole scheme of yours on hold for a while?"

"That would be very difficult," I said. "Maybe for a while, but the *Dom Afonso* is due back downriver and can't stay here very long."

"Before you make up your mind to leave," she said, "I must tell you that I have two things: authorization from the US State Department and cash money from the Agriculture Department to fund the Fordlandia Project. That's what it is officially called," she said. "We are going to stay here, to work with you, to get this off the ground." We told her about the events of the past few days; she was silent for a moment, then said, "We're aware of the situation in Northern Brazil where some of the local authorities occasionally take matters into their own hands. I am not without resources to deal with this," she said.

I was both stunned and relieved. The ludicrously haphazard plan that we had pieced together had already started to come apart. It was just too complicated—it would have been like trying to plug a dike with a dozen holes and only ten fingers to close them. For one thing, we would have had to permanently silence several people, a job that I doubted we could handle ourselves. If we were to believe Dean Knotwell, the local authorities might be overruled, yet they were here, not in Brasilia. And they had guns. We debated what to do in great concentric circles—leave, stay, or just delay. Suxie suddenly took her grandfather's badge in her hand and closed her eyes.

"I am going to stay," she said. "It is the right decision."

I knew what was happening. It was time to tell the others what I had seen the other night—her grandfather and the provenance of the badge. As I spoke, Suxie nodded confirmation. "So as you can see, we are not alone here," I said. Dean Knotwell was listening intently.

"I would have thought the bunch of you were certifiable candidates for a secure mental facility," she said, "if you hadn't shown Leeram to me back in Massachusetts."

"Well, he's not all that presentable right now," I said, "but he is still with us, or with me, anyway." I showed her the coconut. She peered at it, then up at me.

"If any other person from academia or government was standing here in my shoes, that person would climb right back on that leaky old steamboat and head home. Even though I question my own sanity, I will stay and help you with everything I've got. I'm in, believe me, I'm in." We all laughed and embraced each other. "Let's get to work," she said.

First we had to tell the Mayor and Captain Segundo of our change of plans. I went down the hill and gave the news first to the Captain. "Here's some money to compensate you for the trip," I said, giving him the last of Suxie's bankroll. He counted it, then looked up and smiled.

"Please remember me when you do actually need me," he said, and ordered his crew to hoist the gangplank. "Lost one of these guys. Hard to hang onto them these days," he said, then waved. "Adeus!"

"Adeus," we said.

"*Boa viagem,*" Pericles shouted at the retreating boat. "Have a good voyage."

The Mayor's reaction was more emotional. "The authorities will put you in jail, or maybe worse!" he said. "I want to protect you because you have done so much for us, but I don't know how I can if you defy them." I introduced him to Dean Knotwell.

"She is here as a representative of the US government," I said. "If any official or unofficial restraints are placed on us, it becomes an international affair. I think that the authorities should be informed of this as soon as possible. We are staying." The Mayor still looked worried.

"If you are certain..." he said, uncertainly.

"Don't be afraid," Dean Knotwell said, putting her hand on his shoulder. "We have resources and we're well able to use them." The Mayor, smiling weakly, turned away to tell his people about the abrupt change in plans and the five of us went back inside. We had a lot to discuss.

Chapter 12

"Tell me how to work this thing," Dean Knotwell said as we came up to our tractor. I had been showing her around, describing the farm equipment we had brought with us.

"It's pretty simple," I said. "You hold the clutch down, set the throttle where you want it, put it in low gear, and release the clutch slowly. Just steer where you want to go, and remember, when you are making a tight turn, there are two brake pedals. Push the one on the inside of the turn, both if you are going straight ahead." We climbed aboard and she sat in the cupped driver's seat. It was an old Fordson, one of the many pre-war Ford-built machines still around and still running, just like all the old 1950's era cars in Cuba. When we bought it in Manaus it looked almost new. I showed her where the various pedals and handles were, then she started out with a jerk, releasing the clutch too quickly but she soon learned. Ten minutes later, after a drive to the field and back, she returned, grinning like a kid.

"That was really fun," she said. "I'm ready to go!"

Ploughing and planting began again, and the villagers came back to help in greater numbers than before. Everyone felt defiant. Anger and solidarity replaced the resigned submission that had filled the air just a day ago. We joined ranks against the people who had jailed us. The two spies were not to be seen anywhere. At first, nothing happened. A few weeks passed uneventfully and we were beginning to think that nothing would happen. Then one morning, a black SUV arrived, followed by two canvas-covered trucks. They came to a sudden halt, the dust they had been trailing bunched up around them. Tailgates opened and soldiers dressed in camouflage poured out. They lined up, weapons in front, held at the ready. The doors of the SUV opened and two officers emerged, followed by the man in the white linen suit who had taken Suxie's money. The two spies from the going-away party were in their ranks.

Suxie and I walked up to him. "I want you to halt this operation immediately," he said, in clear English. "If you do not, I will order my men to start shooting." Suxie looked down at him. Dean Knotwell joined us.

"I suggest we go inside," Suxie said, in a tone that countered his. She said it without raising her voice, but in a way that made it apparent that there was no alternative. He nodded and we went into our house. Lisa, Pericles, and the two agricultural students were still out in the field, working with the villagers. When we were sitting in the living room, Suxie said, "You may not be aware of this, but if you or your men lift a finger to disrupt our activities here, you will experience the full force of the United States Government. I would like to introduce Dean Elizabeth Knotwell, representing the US Department of Food and Agriculture." The white-suited one looked at her, then his eyes lost the glitter of command and became uncertain.

"I am going to talk to the *Comandante*," he said, and rose to leave.

"One more thing," Suxie said quietly, "If I don't have my money back by tomorrow at this hour, my government will do what it has to do." As the white-suited one walked through the doorway, accompanied by his two officers, he turned and spat on the ground. Within five minutes the entire platoon was gone, the two spies looking confused. We all turned to each other with a big communal embrace, laughing.

"That was way too easy," I said. "What happened?" Wordlessly, Suxie handed me the badge. It was warm to the touch. "Your grandfather? How?"

"I'm not sure myself," she said, "But I felt he was somehow next to me. It gave me a sense of invincibility."

Lisa and Pericles, having seen the invasion from a distance, had just arrived, followed by several villagers. Ben and Seth were there too. We told them what had just happened. "Do you think you will actually get that money back?" Pericles asked.

"If I don't, that little prick will be missing a couple of body parts," she said.

I took a moment to walk outside and have a quick word with my coconut. "Leeram, what next? What do you think we should do now?" At first there was no response, then:

"I was out when you called," he said. "What do you want me to do, hold your hand? You people seem to be doing fine just by yourselves. I think you guys have someone else looking out for you. Not just me anymore." I relayed what he had just said to the others.

Suxie smiled. "We do," she said.

We were back in business. I began to think about my own investment in this project. It had begun as a means to an end, then became an end in itself, but Leeram was right. I knew that I wasn't going to spend the rest of my life here, but on the other hand, it was the most interesting, challenging thing I had ever done. My old, feckless life must have been lived by someone else. I didn't recognize that person anymore.

"I envy you; I wish I could talk with my grandfather," said Suxie, watching me with my coconut. She turned away. "I'll see you later," she said over her shoulder and started up the hill. I ran across her about a half hour later in the cemetery. The grave had been put to rights, fresh turf placed over the filled hole. She was sitting cross-legged next to the gravestone. She had the badge in her hand. "Don't worry about me," she said. "I'll be back down by suppertime."

Around the table that night, a table that had grown considerably in recent days, we had much to talk about. Our three new companions had acclimatized quickly. Dean Knotwell's attire became indistinguishable from ours. Our days started early and ended with the fall of night and our hands and backs had hardened from the work. Right after they arrived, we hired a local couple to do the cooking and help us out in other ways. When there were just four of us, we could handle all that by ourselves, but we decided that we needed to concentrate on the project and just didn't have time for much else. Slowly, the houses and outbuildings around us were being revitalized, a lot of the work being done by villagers. The really big ones, the sawmill, hospital, and water plant remained untouched. Their ghostly broken windows and leaky roofs were too much for us to deal with, but we had plans to patch them up eventually and use them for storage. The water tower was too dangerous to use, but the purification equipment that was built to process the Tapajos river water was repairable. Seth, who had great mechanical skills, set about to fix it. Within a week, using cobbled-together parts, he had it producing first a trickle, then gallons of potable water. "If we had a better source of electricity than this little generator, we could make a lot more," he said. We all indulged in luxurious showers and the atmosphere around us became much sweeter, losing a funkiness that Pericles and I had actually gotten used to. The women did not miss it.

Our routine began to take over now that the threat of eviction had passed. I realized that I was speaking to Leeram less often, and it bothered me. Was I ignoring a friend? I picked up the nut and called him. "What's up?" I said.

"What do you mean, what's up?" he replied. "What's up is that you are still in the most boring part of the world."

"But they need me here," I said.

"You may be overestimating yourself," Leeram replied. "Why not just put Redbone in charge?"

"She doesn't have the kind of help I get from you. Without that, she may get into trouble," I said.

"OK," he said. "Are you saying that I am the only thing that's keeping you here?" I replied that I hadn't thought about it exactly that way. "Let me see what I can do," he said. "I'll talk to her grandfather."

Meanwhile, the work continued. We had, by that time, around a hundred villagers helping us, most in the fields but the ones with carpentry and mechanical skills fixing up the infrastructure. A big gang was working on the dock, pulling up old pilings and replacing them with new ones. At first we felt a little guilty about that since all the good local hardwood trees had been cut down years ago and we wanted to avoid aggravating the deforestation problem, even in the slightest. One day, Suxie said, "Why don't we look over there," pointing to a section of riverbank. "I have a feeling that we might find something." She was holding the badge. "Dig there," she said. When we did, we found a stash of logs that had been stored underwater nearby at the river's edge. They were intact, perfectly preserved for almost three-quarters of a century; in fact, they were better than new, having seasoned for so long. "I just knew," she said. "Don't ask."

We formed a group called the "batshit team" that went from house to house cleaning guano and washing them down with bleach. Minor repairs and fresh paint were all that most of them needed, and with the water plant operating, they were inhabitable for the first time since 1945, the year that the last Ford employee left. The money that Dean Knotwell's grant provided was being wisely used—not wasted at all. Our neighborhood once again began to resemble old Henry's vision of a perfect little Midwestern city in the middle of the Amazon. Well, not quite, but a reasonable facsimile anyway.

I almost forgot. Suxie didn't get her money back the next day, but about a week later, a government boat pulled up and several state officials came ashore. "You have done an admirable job here," their spokesman said. "The State of Para has been in contact with the Department of Indigenous Affairs in Brasilia and it is our opinion that you are doing a great service to this community. We apologize for the regrettable error that occurred right after you arrived and will compensate you in full for any damages our local officials might have made." He handed me a bulky envelope full of BRLs, saying, "I believe this is your bail." I counted it and handed it to Suxie, who had just joined us.

"Thank you," I said, diplomatically. "I am sure it was a misapprehension and we look forward to working with you closely in the future."

Somebody sniggered, but only I could hear it. "Come on, Leeram," I said silently, "We have to say things like that; after all, we got the money back."

"In my day we didn't have diplomats. Life was a lot simpler."

The delegation from Para left, their river launch burbling away into the distance downstream. We had a little celebration that night. Dean Knotwell and the two graduate students shared the house next door and we gathered in our dining room. We opened a bottle of rum, while Lisa and the Dean sipped agua, laced with a little cachaca. "Success to the Railroad," I said.

"Railroad?" Seth asked.

"It used to be a toast to celebrate anything that went well," I explained, feeling a little old. We ate and drank more than usual that night and retired late. I had a long, dreamless sleep, which had not been the case with Suxie. The next morning she joined us at the table with a strange, almost unreadable expression.

"I met my grandfather," she said simply, after sitting at the table for a long while. "My Grandfather!" she repeated. "It was not a dream—he was in my room. It was as though I had known him all my life." We were silent, not wanting to think she was raving or had somehow come loose from reality, but half-believing her. After all, we had Leeram, so nothing was impossible.

"He told me never to lose his badge, as long as I had it, he would be with me," she said. "He said I had come home and would be with him in full if I stayed here." That sounded a little ominous, and I said so.

"No," she replied, "don't worry. I am more alive than I have ever been and intend to stay that way for as long as possible. I will never leave this place."

"But eventually we will," I said.

"I'm not leaving until this project is complete," said Dean Knotwell, to everyone's general agreement.

"I met your grandfather also," I said. "Leeram introduced me to him. He's an impressive man."

"I know. We had a long talk," Suxie said. "He is very angry about what is happening to the rain forest. He talked a lot about working for Ford for so many years, not realizing that it opened the door to all of the modern business world that is clear-cutting the trees and ruining his homeland."

"Maybe it was just time for everyone else to come in," I said. "I don't know if Henry himself was responsible." For some reason I was moved to defend the old guy who had suffered from a lot of historical revisionism in recent years—some of it entirely justified.

"Since World War II ended," Dean Knotwell said, "this place became fair game for big Brazilian companies and also a lot of foreign companies too. There is just too much valuable timber standing in topsoil, good for five or ten years of harvesting before it wears out, but it's easily replaced by cutting more trees."

Pericles stepped in. "And nobody gave a flying you-know-what about the natives who lived there in the first place. Your grandfather was one of those natives. I'd really like to know how he felt about the changes in his world."

"Does he know why we're here?" I asked.

"I told him," Suxie said. "He is with us. He is very angry, not just at the foreigners but with himself for having been so distracted by the magic of new technology, blind to what was actually going on."

"He should be very proud of you," I said, "but also of himself for buying those stock certificates. He was a man far ahead of his time, his people, and his situation. You wouldn't be here now if it hadn't been for what he did."

"Can we talk to him, too?" asked Lisa.

"It's not like with Leeram," Suxie said. "And now, Leeram can only talk to Gilbert. I have no idea what goes on between his world and ours. By the way, where is Leeram?" I hadn't heard from him for a while myself, I thought. I picked up the coconut.

"Leeram?" I said. No reply. I shook it a little and asked again, looking directly at the smiley face. Still no reply. "Come in, please," I said, as though I was speaking to a mike. I could almost hear an echo, as though my voice was caroming off distant cliffs somewhere.

I had almost put the coconut back in my satchel when I heard, "Why are you calling me at this hour of the morning?" His voice sounded as though he was hungover.

"I'm sorry, but I have no idea of what your time is. I can call back later."

"No, don't bother, I'm awake now."

"Listen, Leeram, we need your advice on a few things," I said. "Suxie has just had a long meeting with her grandfather and he says he will help us. Can you communicate with him now?"

"If it's all that important to you, yes, I can." I had no idea of whether he was rubbing the sleep out of his eyes, but it seemed that he was. I remembered what he said about sleep on his end when we were on the *Dom Afonso*.

"Have you been bored lately?" I asked.

"Gotta admit that this place can get a little slow now and then," he said. "Not much goes on. When you had my head I was with you all the time. Now, sometimes it seems I just exist in a big soup of neutrinos that resembles a rain forest."

A strange thought just struck me. "Are you dark matter?"

"Well, I'm not as fair-skinned as you are."

I sensed that the conversation was not going in a productive direction. Leeram's funny bone obviously no longer existed, so I changed the subject. "We've got to find a way to get you back, a man in full, so to speak." I relayed the parts of the conversation that I could to everyone around the table. We had not told Ben and Seth yet about our link with Leeram's universe, although Dean Knotwell had mentioned that we had a secret during their travel down here. They were full of questions and not a little dubious about our sanity. Unless anyone had met him in person, as the rest had done back in Massachusetts, it might take a leap of faith equivalent to Evil Knievel's when he jumped over the Grand Canyon on a motorcycle, to accept what we were saying at face value. "Look," I said to them, "I know what you are thinking, but there are no loony bins in the middle of the Amazon rain forest. Things happen here that are outside of human experience." They nodded uneasily, and then looked at each other. I realized that to them it must sound as if I was telling tales around a campfire.

"OK," Seth said, "Then what's for breakfast?"

***

That morning, after everyone had gone back to work, Leeram's coconut and I walked uphill to the foot of the old water tower. I took it out of the satchel and turned to gaze at the view back toward the river. The Tapajos shone silver in the sun, not quite at its zenith. My shadow, short at my feet, pointed toward the river, as did Leeram's, looking like a bowling ball with a cone head. "Are you there?" I asked. He said yes. "Listen," I said, "I have a question: If you need to have something physical of yours in this world in order to contact us, does it work with others on your side? Others, I mean other than Suxie's grandfather?"

"Yes, it does sometimes, but whoever it is on my side has to want to make contact with your world—our own former world, that is."

"So it's kind of like a séance?" I said.

"Yeah, we get those vibes a lot, or used to anyway. They dried up about fifty of your years ago. Problem with séances is that most of us have no intention of ever setting foot on earth again. We treat those séances the way you treat robocalls at dinnertime."

"I wonder if Henry Ford would like to come back for a while," I mused. "Is there any way you could contact him, like you contacted Suxie's grandfather?"

"What do you have of his?" Leeram asked. "Without a physical object that belonged to him, you can't even get to square one. Besides, he never went to Fordlandia in his life!"

My next thought came completely out of the blue: "This entire place belonged to him," I said. "If you could hold a coconut for a second and give it to me, and have that be enough of an anchor on this end, why can't this entire plantation be enough of a draw for him?"

"Dunno," he said. "I ain't the answer man."

"Leeram," I said, "Please. I know it's a lot to ask, but I have to know. You found Suxie's grandfather. Is everyone in your universe still there? Do people even die there?"

"No, and they don't even fade away. I think we have had

this conversation before. You have no idea how hard it is to find anyone here; the world just gets bigger as people cross over. I only found Ubirajara because I once met him when I was 'alive' and with all my body parts. We had a connection. It would be like finding a single grain of sand on a beach for me to find your Ford character." I thought about that.

"What is going on," I said. "Is this some kind of a Mormon thing? How about getting him to come to you?"

"No, it's not a Mormon thing, you idiot. And please don't ask me to find this guy; you have no idea how hard that would be."

I have a stubborn streak and I wasn't going to give up that easily. For some reason, I really wanted to talk to Henry Ford. "Leeram, you owe me a big favor. I have the feeling that the sooner we can find Henry Ford, the sooner we can get out of here and back to civilization." Total silence. "Maybe you can get him to come to you?" I thought out loud.

"I owe you a favor?" I had never heard Leeram speak in anger—annoyance, yes, even pique, but never anger. I was puzzled and a little set aback.

"Look, I'm sorry if I annoyed you, I really never intended to have it come out that way. Please, Leeram, it's not that important to me and I'm sorry if I pissed you off."

"Just don't keep talking about Henry Ford," he said, sounding a little mollified. "I'm sorry that I lost my cool, also. If I had a back, I know you'd have it."

So that's that, I thought, and went back to work.

***

Lisa seemed more beautiful than she had been back in Brookline. The tropics seemed to have agreed with her, giving her a glow that was somehow accented by her working clothes. She had opted for cool cotton dresses rather than blue jeans and was like an open jar of honey to Ben and Seth. I was jealous whenever they monopolized the conversation with her at our table and elsewhere. When one of them mentioned that they needed some equipment that we did not have in Fordlandia, I had an idea.

"I'm going to take the ferry to Santarem," I said, "and try to find what you're looking for."

"We'll go with you," they both said.

"No. You are needed here. Lisa will come with me," I said. "Is that OK?" I asked her. I was hugely pleased, more than I could have imagined, when she smiled and nodded her head vigorously.

"I really need to get away for a little while," she said. "I love it in Fordlandia, but we never got a chance to see Santarem on the way here." Pericles looked a little miffed, but I explained that he would get a chance later, but right now, he was needed on the farm. He and Suxie were a great team, I said, and between them they could handle anything that could come up. The two students reluctantly gave me a shopping list and I added several things that we needed ourselves. We were also going to establish a bank account in Santarem and the whole trip would take several days. We bought passage on a ferry the next day—the first one that stopped in Fordlandia—and boarded with backpacks, cash, and a couple of hammocks. I had wanted to get away for a little while, and to have Lisa along was perfect. Ever since we left Brookline, our relationship had been, well, delicate. We were very different people; she was much younger than me, as were her friends. She wasn't much older than Ben and Seth, for that matter. I had never found the right words to completely cross the barrier and our dealings with each other had been friendly but celibate. It had a lot to do with Leeram, I knew. Before we left, I decided to forget to pack the coconut.

Once aboard the ferry—nondescript and crowded compared to the *Dom Afonso*—we found a space for our hammocks as far from the bar as possible, where a loudspeaker was blasting samba music all day long. We had brought our own food for the trip. Aboard, we were surrounded by chickens, families with large broods of children, mostly crying, and men who never moved from the bar except to pee over the side. Here I was, alone with Lisa at last, and lacking the tiniest sliver of privacy, but somehow, our hammocks side by side and almost touching, we managed to create a kind of intimacy during the trip, especially after nightfall. We spoke in low voices to each other and more or less willed an invisible wall around us. Once, when the din was replaced by the muted rumble of snoring, diluted and softened by the ferry's engine, I reached across and took her hand. She squeezed mine and said, "I'm so glad we are by ourselves, finally." My heart jumped.

Early the next day, we woke to the jostle of passengers pulling their belongings together and rolling their hammocks; Santarem was coming up with the dawn and before long our riverboat was wedged in between dozens of other river ferries, so close that they literally touched. Much scraped paint on all the boats attested to the tight quarters. We disembarked behind a couple of men on each end of a pole on their shoulders from which five or six chicken cages were hung. Dogs and children were underfoot, making the gangway a perilous road to shore, but we made it without a muddy mishap, a feat that not everyone managed. We took a cab to a decent hotel that was recommended by the ferryboat captain, and in fifteen minutes found ourselves in a modern, air-conditioned lobby. We were in a world a thousand light-years away from the one we had left the day before.

"We would like two rooms, please," I said to the clerk and was about to pull out my wallet when Lisa interrupted.

"Just one," she said. "We need to be careful with money." I looked at her and she smiled.

"One room," I stammered, and the clerk gave me a key. I felt myself blushing and extraordinarily happy. We had very little baggage other than the knapsacks we carried. I took hers and slung it over my shoulder with my own and we went into the elevator. When we were inside, by ourselves, she kissed me and suddenly we were all over each other, the knapsacks on the floor. When the door opened, far too soon, an older couple standing outside watched us with amusement as we picked everything up and went down the hall. We found our room and as soon as we were inside, we pulled and tugged each other's clothes off and were on the nearest bed while I was still kicking my pants away from my ankles.

The shower came much later.

Chapter 13

It was fortunate that Brazilians normally ate late, since Lisa and I didn't get down to the hotel's dining room until around 11:00 p.m. that evening, and when we did, we were famished. After we were seated, I immediately ordered a bottle of Vieuve Cliquot that I saw on the wine list, to my surprise: "We're in heaven," I said, when the waiter drew its cork with a satisfying pop, and we touched our flutes together. That champagne tasted like no other wine has tasted before or since.

I hadn't felt such a buzz since I was a teenager and it was all I could do to keep the worst clichés in check but not successfully enough, I knew, as I went on and she came back with equally affectionate banality. Thank God, I said to myself, Leeram isn't here to tell me I sound like a high school freshman with his first girlfriend. I hadn't been exactly celibate before, but I had never been a collector of women either. When the menu arrived, we combed it silently for a while. "I don't see any vegetarian food," she said. I had almost forgotten about her eating habits and my sense of absolute joy deflated slightly.

"Would it be all right," I asked, "for you to try the fish?" The menu listed some fresh-caught local items, straight from the Amazon River. She had certainly enjoyed it at the feast when we first arrived in Fordlandia.

"Right now, with you, I'll crumple up my scruples like an old newspaper and toss them out." I didn't say a thing and we gave the hovering waiter our orders. After a long, long study, she asked for a fish stew well stocked with carrots and other veggies, and I chose a savory Brazilian pork rib dish—not to rub it in, but the carnivore in me just took over. We had this slight difference between us but the gap was narrowing. When the food arrived, we ate like the starving people we were, silently at first, then when our stomachs began to fill, talking again like crazy. "This is delicious," she said and smiled wickedly. After a glass of sauterne and a tasty flan (pudim de laite) for her and ice cream for me, we left to go back to our room with at least one of our appetites sated.

Late the next morning, we came downstairs to do what we had come for, and spent the rest of the day trying to look serious. We went to the city's financial district, full of architecture from the early twentieth century when the first wave of big business from outside washed through. It was also the last big heyday of the rubber boom and there was plenty of pre-depression money to be spent. We set up an account in the Banko da Amazonia with a check written out for that purpose. The bank officer was a good source of advice, recommending several agricultural wholesale dealers for us to choose from. After visiting them all, we decided to present our findings to the full group in Fordlandia and inform the dealers of our decision in a week or two. In the middle of the serious business part of our trip, it was hard to keep from holding hands at moments when we thought nobody was looking. Afterward, we went sightseeing, during the times when we had clothes on, and reluctantly boarded a boat for the return trip a couple of days later. We staggered aboard under boxes and sacks loaded with purchases and supplies when we knew we couldn't postpone it for another moment. We stowed everything here and there, and finally, when we had a little private space, began to talk.

"Gilly," she said, "I have never been as happy in my life as I am now with you." She reached out with both her hands and took mine. "At first I thought you were much too old for me, then our ages stopped making such a difference. You really are as young as me, or maybe I'm as old as you. I don't know, but it just seems right." I was silent for a moment because I couldn't speak. We were sitting cross-legged on the deck, sheltered by bales and crates from the rest of the passengers.

"I love you, Lisa," I said, overwhelmed. I squelched an impulse to shout the words out to the crowd, then said it again to her, softly, almost falling headfirst into her gaze. "I love you, Lisa."

The trip back upriver was like the one down, except a little longer. The boat, garishly painted and decorated, was overcrowded and like the one on the way down, without a shred of privacy. It didn't really matter that much; we spent the time in each other's company talking inside an invisible shield that blocked out everything else except the passing shore. Screaming babies, barking dogs, clucking chickens, and squabbling families might as well have been in another boat. We sat for hours with our backs against bags of flour or grain or potatoes and our feet resting on the low rail, only aware of each other. Once we passed a fisherman hauling a net bursting with a sizeable catch. I thought of our dinner the first night in Santarem. And porpoises were all around, following in our wake.

"What was it like for you, eating that fish stew?" The thought crossed my mind as we watched some natives hauling in a net.

"I was so hungry that I had eaten half of it before I remembered that I was a vegan," she laughed. "Sex made me into a carnivore, or at least whatever you are when you eat seafood!" I laughed and said that by the time we came back from the Amazon, even the horses would have to look out when she was around.

Chapter 14

Our arrival back in Fordlandia was a little more subdued than our departure. Everyone treated us with polite circumspection; we answered their questions about Santarem, describing the city and the river voyage. The obvious change in our relationship was politely ignored all the while. Pericles was especially discreet, and Seth and Ben seemed resigned. Suxie was delighted, taking Lisa aside at the first opportunity to chat privately. While they were at it, I went back to my room and took Leeram out of his valise. Once we had a connection, I told him about the trip. To say the least, I was nervous—I thought I would have some "splainin" to do. He was quiet for a moment, then said: "Well, good for you, my friend. I was beginning to worry about you. Not enough sex can give a man the willies."

"Well," I said, "it's not just the sex; I really think I'm in love." This set Leeram back a little.

"Let me give you some advice," Leeram said, after a

pause. "That's all well and good, but you are going to need some clear thinking soon, my son, and you have got to get your priorities straight. I can't see forward in time. Nobody can, even here, but I do know you are a long way from being safe." I promised him that I would be careful and I reassured him that he and I were still best buddies, no matter what.

"Do me a favor," he said. "Do not ever leave that goddamned coconut behind when you go out again." I promised.

Shortly after we came back, Lisa and I moved into our own little cottage. We had plenty of choices and we picked one that needed a minimum of work to make livable and was not too far from our main house.

By now we had settled into a routine: clearing, plowing, tilling, and planting enough acreage for all of the seeds we had brought with us. With the Mayor's permission, we used pastureland to plant in that had been grazed by cattle; there was enough of it for all of us—plenty more for the cows. The number of natives that joined us had grown every day until the Mayor could not find work for them all. There was less and less for us to do, so we put all our energy into rebuilding Fordlandia itself. We planned to use the time until harvest to make the town livable for a long time to come. The two agriculture students were now used to our references to Leeram, even to Suxie's talk about her grandfather, and had more or less accepted it as gospel, though in the way gospel is accepted in our secular world as parable, not revealed truth. Despite that, they blended in well with us, coming up with good ideas that surprised even Dean Knotwell. "I thought I would mentor you," she said to the two young men one night over dinner, "but I'm beginning to learn from you." They even renovated an old tennis court nearby, originally built for the American families. We reached an agreement with the Mayor; he would take full charge of the farm workers. He would be the one to settle disputes, hire people, and assign tasks, while we would give the project overall direction. Actually, I was beginning to distance myself, bit by bit, from the whole thing. I had begun to think more and more of my old life up north. I had no intention of backsliding into the sleepwalk I had left, though, and there was still a lot more to do here. When Leeram and I (and Lisa) finally did return to the United States, I wanted to make a clean break. Adventures are great, I mused, but then they need to be replaced with new ones when they get old.

For some reason, I couldn't stop thinking about old man Henry Ford. Henry came to my mind every time I looked around Fordlandia, at those huge buildings with their acres of broken glass panes and pieces of industrial equipment just too big to carry away for scrap metal. The Ford logo was everywhere in fading paint, sometimes almost obliterated by the weather. The water tower, for some unlikely reason, was still there, hundreds of feet in the air, but none of us dared to climb its rusty ladder. It would surely come crashing down any day. The hospital still contained a few examination tables and a dentist's chair, covered with bat guano like everything else. If he were here, would he pick up a broom and start sweeping?

To our surprise, and contrary to what we had been told, when we first arrived, Fordlandia had not been entirely abandoned. A fairly large population of squatters had been living there for years. It's a very large place, big enough to absorb many things in its vast, decrepit sprawl. One new building housed an operating sawmill and was actually doing a thriving business with shredded pulp used to make pressboard. We invited the mill's owner to dinner one night, just to introduce ourselves, a practice we started with all the other local notables, including the priest from the big, relatively new church near the water tower. The last thing we wanted to do was come off as ugly Americans.

Dean Knotwell had really taken to farm life. She loved the tractor and I could often see her on it, wearing bib overalls labeled Oshgosh and a big grin, off to do some chore like pulling a manure spreader to fertilize and replenish the fields. The Mayor, graciously, let her do a few jobs like that, even though there were plenty of his people available. Thanks to the local cattle farmers, there was a lot of manure. We had taken over a small outbuilding that had originally been part of the old power plant—a really big structure, one of the first projects in Fordlandia. Back then, in the beginning, Ford knew it would take about five years for the newly planted rubber trees to mature enough to start producing and, in the meantime, the company planned to cut and sell timber, mostly valuable hardwood, to make money. We patched the leaky roof and made it into a relatively dry, habitable place for storage. It was now almost entirely full of our gear and even more equipment that we had bought after we arrived, and we were already thinking about rehabbing another building.

Now that the preliminary work was done, I had much more time on my hands and set out each day on short trips just to explore and look around. Back in Manaus, we had bought an aluminum skiff with an outboard engine for use on the river and I was on it frequently, going up and downstream a little farther each time. The Tapajos connects many small settlements; one of them across the river, Urucubituba, was close enough to be visible from Fordlandia and I had long been curious about it. One day when I had nothing else to do, and everyone else, including Lisa, was busy, I took the coconut and climbed into the skiff to explore. Leeram's coconut was with me during every waking hour during the day now, so attached that if I ever found myself without it, it was as though I had forgotten to put my pants on. Needless to say, that morning, Leeram was not happy when we were on the Tapajos. "Is this necessary?" he asked. "I tried to tell you before we got here that I hate this goddamned place."

"Sorry, Leeram," I said, "You're better off with me than lying under my bed where some armadillo might eat you."

He didn't have much of a response to that. "Or maybe a two hundred pound capybara," I added, just to see if I could get a rise out of him.

"You, my friend," he said, with enough ice in his voice to make sure I understood the word 'friend' was maybe not applicable at this particular moment, "had better watch where you put your feet around here. I am only with you because I want to be; it's my choice."

I was, I admit, chastened. "Leeram," I said, "if I offended you, I am truly, truly sorry. It's the very last thing I would do willingly." He accepted my apology and I promised we would be back on terra firma soon.

We pulled ashore at a public landing. A lot of Urucubitubans had crossed from there into Fordlandia in recent weeks to work with the local population; they were part of the larger native community that had always lived and traded together on both sides of the Tapajos. Many were related. During the rubber plantation days, this little settlement had many bars and sporting houses for workers who got tired of Henry's puritanical rules for daily life on his side. The village had become known in those days as "the Island of Innocence" just outside of company reach, where workers who got tired of the Midwestern morality imposed on them could go for relief. Ford had forbidden his employees such temptations on his plantation, which, obviously to anyone but him, made their availability just a short boat ride away even more enticing.

"Look, Greenbush," said Leeram, as we walked down a

once-paved road with little square houses here and there, goats and chickens underfoot, and children running around everywhere. "Look around you. Why, in the name of all that is good in your world and mine, do you want to come here?" Actually, it didn't seem all that bad to me and I said so. No response.

The shore was so low-lying that it was remarkable to think that anything could be built on it, much less a camp of carnal pleasures. A few fishermen's shacks and other structures necessary to the town dock were there. Most of the streets ended at the river's edge. As the land rose and became less exposed to flooding, the place became more defined with houses and the streets improved. In the distance, slightly higher up, I saw a corrugated tin-sided bar with a Brazilian beer sign, cerveja, next to the door. A big wooden sign read Casa Lugar Perfieto and, on impulse I went in, transitioning instantly from hot tropical sunlight to a dim world smelling a little like jungle juice and Lysol. It was cooler and that was a relief. The place was almost empty, except for a couple of men asleep at a table, heads resting on arms. One of them got up when he heard me. "Em que posso ajudá-lo?" he asked, or at least I thought it was a question. Leeram said, "He wants to know what he can get you."

I pointed at the tap handle with a Brahma Chopp logo, the beer I had tasted in Santarem; the man nodded, went behind the bar, and filled a large pilsner glass. I sat down, put a couple of reals down, and took a long swallow. To my surprise, it was cold and pretty good. I nodded and gave the bartender a thumbs-up. I silently remarked to Leeram that there must have been many places like it in the old rubber plantation days.

"Yeah, it was livelier then," he said, "but it's a lot safer now. You had a pretty good chance of leaving with a knife in your belly in those days. I know, I stuck a few in myself." Every now and then I got a hint of Leeram's business end, so to speak. The bartender, under a stained, straw fedora with a hole in the fold at the top, was like bartenders everywhere. His companion, still lying on the table, was obviously not in a conversational mood, and I was available, so he wanted to talk. Leeram was my silent translator and facilitator at the same time, handing me the right Tupi/Portuguese words when I needed them.

"You're one of them American farmers in Fordlandia?" he asked. I had the feeling that "farmers" was not the precise word he used, but sometimes Leeram could be a little diplomatic if he didn't want to see a fight break out. I replied that I was, and that the people who lived there were happy we were there. "A lot of our people go over there—they come back here after work and they got money in their pockets. That's good! Welcome to my Casa." I asked him about the name. "Lugar Perfieto means Heaven," he said. "Don't you feel like you're there?" he asked, with a grin. He went over to his dozing buddy and swatted him with his hat. The man raised his head, blinking. "This gentleman is one of those people building up the farm in Fordlandia," he said. "Maybe he can give you a job and you can pay off your tab." I told him to show up tomorrow, sober, and report to the Mayor. If the Mayor approved, he could go to work.

"Almost like the old days," Leeram said. "More booze around this place than anywhere south of Belterra."

I finished the beer and went back out into the sun, blinking a little. If in Europe, all roads lead to Rome, here most of them just petered out in the Tapajos. After about an hour of sightseeing, I was ready to go back to our boat, when Leeram said, "That house over there, do you see it?" I looked. The buildings high enough for protection from floodwaters were generally older and some were actually attractive. One of them, larger than most and well painted, had two stories and double-deck verandas on three sides. It stood out clearly. "That's the house that was owned by a family who used to own all the land that Fordlandia is on," Leeram said. When we got closer, I could see some laundry hanging inside the shelter of the porch. It was obviously occupied, though I couldn't see anyone around. I'll be back, I thought.

"You know this place pretty well," I said.

"I do," he said. "I used to get away from the forest to this island now and then when I wanted something a little stronger than coconut milk."

"And now?" I asked.

"Coconut milk is about all I have on this end," he said,

sounding resigned. I climbed back into the skiff, pulled the starter cord, and headed back across the river.

The next day I decided to spend some time with Suxie. Ever since we stepped off the riverboat, the change in her that started on the Dom Afonso had deepened. Physically big and indefinably attractive back home, she always exuded a sense of almost military authority. Now that aura had softened into one of peace. Her smile, which rarely showed itself before, was now more frequent and welcoming. Before, she would flash annoyance when someone did or said something that showed ignorance; sometimes it would be more than just a flash, but now she seemed to have acquired patience. She was more accepting, less demanding. We had all slowly lost the sensation of walking on eggshells around her. She was calm now, not disengaged, but serene. Now that our project was more or less firmly on track, I felt I could have a non-threatening conversation with her. She was by far the most interesting person I had ever known, other than Lisa and Leeram, of course.

After breakfast, I walked down the hill with her toward our "office," the building that held our equipment, and began. "You said you felt your grandfather's presence a while ago. Do you still sense it?"

"More than you can imagine," she said. "I would have thought I was crazy if I hadn't meet Leeram. Now I know a lot more." She then said that she and her grandfather continue to have long conversations. "You are one of the few people I feel OK talking with about this," she said, "but sometimes, I am not even asleep when we talk. He's right there in the room with me. I would never want to leave this place if I didn't think I could take him with me. That's fine, because I'm home now and I have no desire to be anywhere else."

Leeram had been silent until this moment. "I can't talk to Suxie directly," he said silently to me, "at least not through that nut you carry around, but tell her that I have been seeing a lot of her grandfather on this end lately. He's all right, that one, and he has never been happier since he found his granddaughter. Makes him feel alive again," he said. I relayed this to Suxie.

"It doesn't surprise me," she said. "Ubirajara also tells me a lot about Leeram too, although that isn't his real name." That stopped me cold. He had been nothing but Leeram for so long that somehow I never thought about the fact that he must have had a name that a mother or father gave him. I opened up the satchel and took the smiley-faced coconut out; it seemed a more formal thing to do under the circumstances.

"Leeram," I said. "I know this is quite late in our relationship, and I should have asked this question a long time ago, please forgive me, but, um, what is your Amazon name?"

"Names are given by our mothers," he said. "We only have one. My mother named me Araribóia, after a famous man in our ancient history, but everyone just called me

Jose. If you want to know, I kind of like the name Leeram. Keep on using it." I felt relieved at that. It was far too late to start calling him anything but Leeram. I told all this to Suxie and she smiled.

"I'm glad he likes the name you gave him," she said. "I do too." As we walked on, she continued about her grandfather. "Ubirajara would rather be called Ubirajara. He says the name has resonance in his world and he is very proud of it. I didn't know very much about him at first, but he has told me a great deal—what it was like to live here and work with the Ford Company. He is very patient and very, very intelligent; when I am with him, our minds connect on every level. The Americans recognized his intelligence very early, especially after he learned enough English in the first year or so to act as an interpreter. When the riots broke out at the beginning, when the natives rebelled at having to pay for their meals and sign in with time clocks and everything else that was foreign shoved down their throats, he took the management's side, thinking that his people were destroying their own future. He thinks differently about that now. After those disturbances, he was given the job of head of native personnel and given a very high salary. They valued him greatly and he never stopped learning from them. Right now he is delighted to be here, with me, and he wants to get involved."

"Ask him, when you think it's right, if he has ever met

Henry Ford," I said. "Leeram keeps putting me off when I talk about him."

By then we had arrived at our storage building; the others were already there and we started planning the day's work. The villagers arrived soon after and the Mayor huddled with them to discuss plans. I appointed myself to be the scout for our project, to spend more time exploring what might be going on around us. I never thought we could get this far so quickly; sure, we had help from the other side—the universe Leeram and Ubirajara lived in—but even with that, our progress had been so fast that a part of me had its guard up. Good attitude for a scout, I said to myself.

The next day Lisa and I took the skiff back across the river. "I've been wanting to explore the other side ever since we got here," she said. "I would have gone with you the first time if I hadn't been so busy." It might provide a prospective on Fordlandia, she said, put it at a distance that might reveal things that were too close to see on our side of the river. We walked up to the Casa Lugar Perfieto. This time there were a few more drinkers gathered at the bar, including two men in clean clothes who were discussing a map laid out on the flat surface in front of them. We eased into a space next to them and I ordered a Brahma. There was no wine, so Lisa ordered a glass of alua. The bartender recognized me immediately, of course.

"Hey Americano!" he said, "Welcome back, my friend!" The two map-readers turned to look at me. One of them folded the map and put it in his pocket. "This guy is with that new farm in Fordlandia," he bellowed. "He's going to make us all rich."

Chapter 15

Make us all rich! The bartender's voice was of the booming kind and everyone in the place turned to look at us. I had their undivided attention, whether I wanted it or not. My mind went blank. "Insha'Allah," was all I could think of to say. The words from Arabia flew right over their heads. They looked at each other, then back at us.

Leeram interrupted, coming to my rescue through the coconut. "I hope he's right," I heard myself saying. Leeram fed me the words. "But it will take a lot of work. You can help too in time. If our project is going to be successful, we'll need your support. We're not here to take from you, but to give you an opportunity to help yourselves." The crowd buzzed like a beery beehive. The two men with the map left almost immediately. "Leeram," I whispered, "why did you make me say that? I sounded like a cut-rate politician."

"Buddy, in this place and time, you are," he said. "Trust me."

I spent the next half hour talking about the Fordlandia project; most of them were familiar with it and had a lot of questions, mostly about how to get work there. I told them all to talk with the Mayor. Later, we left to explore a little more of the village and headed back toward the old house I had seen earlier, the one with the verandas. When we got there, an elderly couple was sitting on a swinging porch chair, protected from the sun but right where the breeze could work its cooling bliss. Impulsively, I walked up to them, while asking Leeram to help if I needed it. "At least this time, make me sound like a human being." They rose and we shook hands. "Good afternoon," I said in my best (or Leeram's best) dialect. I introduced Lisa.

"You have a lovely view of the river from here," she said.

"It's too hot to be walking all over the place," the old man said. "Have a seat." He rose and pulled one back for Lisa.

We thanked them, sat down, and looked out toward Fordlandia. The river, now a kind of muddy blue under the high sun and cloudless sky, underlined and accented the distant buildings in Fordlandia and the hillside they occupied. The water tower and church were still dominant, even at this distance. The woman, whose face still had great beauty despite the mark of years, offered us some lemonade. I realized that it would make an excellent change of pace. I thanked her gratefully and in a moment she was back with an icy jar and some glasses. The lemonade had been sweetened with sugar cane, giving it an oddly satisfying taste. The woman told us that she had inherited the house from one of her paternal grandparents who had lived here long before the Ford company had come. "Actually, he sold much of that land to Ford," she said. His name was Franco. Alberto Jose da Silva Franco."

"We have been watching your progress for some time now," the old man said. "You and your friends are doing good work here and my wife and I would like you to know that we appreciate it very much. I must tell you that we both lived in Fordlandia many years ago before it closed; we moved over here when the place was abandoned. It was safer here. Now, we rarely ever go back." Their names, they told us, were Gustavio and Gabriela Carvahlo.

They told us what life was like back then, when the plantation was in full, if futile, operation. All the natives, or at least most of them, hated the lifestyle superimposed on them by the men from Michigan. They were used to foreigners coming in either to change the world or escape from it, but they resented being thought of as primitive or stupid. They did appreciate the good pay and the medical care that they got. "A lot of children were born there who would have died without that hospital," said the wife. After 1945, when the whole place was handed back to the government, discipline and order fell apart and they moved here, they said, where their life became simpler, if duller. I asked them if they had ever heard of a man named Ubirajara.

"Oh yes" they both said together. Gabriela went on.

"He was well-known. Some people thought he was a traitor, but the ones who knew him best thought very highly of him." I told them that his granddaughter was in our group, and that her name was Araci, though we used the name she had in the States. As I spoke, I realized that the words were mine, not Leeram's. He had managed to silently, unobtrusively retreat, leaving me on my own. I was swimming, but I wasn't afraid.

"Would you like to come inside?" she asked.

"We would like to very much," I replied, and they got up to lead us in; it was surprisingly cool with high ceilings and windows on all sides open to the breeze. When my eyes adjusted, I saw a living room furnished in a Victorian style, dark wallpaper and high-backed upholstered chairs. Photographs and prints in elaborate frames were everywhere on side tables and hung from the walls. Most were landscapes and pictures of what must have been relatives. Alone, on a shelf in the center of the room, was a framed picture that intrigued me from a distance; when I came up to it, I realized that it was none other than Henry Ford, and when I looked at it more closely, I could see that he had signed it.

"A few of us were given that picture by the managers as a reward for good work," he said. "We have kept it over the years just for sentimental reasons. He looks pretty stern, doesn't he?" I had to agree. His sharp nose and long, thin face framed unsmiling eyes. The portrait was obviously posed to radiate authority, almost like a Russian icon of

Saint Nicholas. I wondered how many mantelpieces it once sat on across the river.

After a little while, we thanked the old couple for their generosity in giving us a little respite from the heat and left for the dock. Aboard the skiff, heading home, I had an idea. "Leeram," I said, "That photograph of Ford, I was thinking, does that count as something of his? I mean, he did sign it, just as you carved the face onto the coconut. It did belong to him originally and he personally put his signature on it." Leeram didn't respond right away, and when he did, it was noncommittal.

"Maybe, maybe not."

I wondered if there was more than one way to skin this cat, but wasn't ready to take it any further right now. It was still early in the day, and after we landed back in Fordlandia, Lisa went to find Suxie to help on a project of theirs. I walked up the hill to where the two agriculture students, Ben and Seth, were working in a wing of the old hospital, a corner that still had a tight roof and most of the glass in its windows, giving plenty of light but big enough to circulate air. They had set up a lab of sorts with rows of small pots scavenged from the area. The pots held seedlings of various local plants and they were experimenting with ways to combine them. They had brought some equipment with them aboard the Dom Afonso, including a microscope and some lab glassware. They were able to get an Internet connection via the satellite phone and had logged onto various sites that gave them access to their specialties. They made us, the original "settlers," look like trogylites. We thought that a simple telephone connection would be sufficient!

They were trying to develop, they said, ways to crossbreed native species of fruit to increase their production and protect them better from disease. They had been able to give their full attention to the project once the Fordlandian natives had taken over the farm work. When I came in, they looked up and greeted me with deference; I was the root cause, they would joke, of the whole Fordlandia project. They had been attracted to it, they told me, largely because the Amazon rain forest is a hugely fecund and variegated place. When it comes to plant life, "it's the biggest salad bowl on earth," as Dean Knotwell called it once. It was the perfect place for their post-doc work.

"We are kind of stumped," Seth said when I came in.

"It's a little bizarre," Ben added. "We've been going over this with our colleagues online and we're really not too sure what's happening." They had been experimenting with various grasses and other plants that they found growing naturally at the edge of the forest and found that the instruments, which measured photosynthesis, were giving unpredicted readings. It was as though the plants were producing electricity all by themselves.

"You see, plants absorb photons from the sun, beginning a chain of photosynthesis that splits water atoms into hydrogen and oxygen," Ben explained.

"Electrons are produced by this—an equal number of electrons to the number of photons that come from the sun, it turns out," Seth added. "Normally, those electrons go through a system of thylakoids, which converts the electrons into the sugars that directly feed the plant. We don't know exactly what's happening here, but there seems to be an excess of electrons in these plants. We don't know why or where they are going, but I can tell you I've never seen anything like it before."

I acted suitably impressed. Thylakoids? "That's amazing," I said, completely in the dark as to what it all meant. "So, then, where do you think all this is going?" They didn't know themselves at the moment, but told me they might know a lot more in time to come. In the meantime, they wanted to order much more equipment, which would mean another trip down the Tapajos River, at least as far as Santarem if we could locate it there. If not, it meant going all the way to Manaus.

Meanwhile, as I learned when I finally got back down to the riverside, a yacht had just tied up at the dock and a group of men, obviously not tourists, disembarked. They were poking around, taking photographs, and asking questions of the men and women working in the fields. Suxie, Lisa, and Pericles were not around so I walked up to one of the strangers. "Are you in charge here?" he asked.

"I'm one of them," I said.

"We would like to talk to you," he said. I replied that any serious conversation would have to involve all of us.

I told them to wait at the dock while I gathered everyone and in the meantime, I said that I would appreciate it if they stopped interrupting our work. I found everyone, but decided to leave Ben and Seth in their lab, way up the hill. They were too deeply involved in their own experiments to be interrupted. When we were all finally sitting in the yacht's main cabin, lined with the soft elegance of oiled cherry wood and mahogany, and served tea by the steward, the leader of the group introduced himself and the others with him, as representatives of one of the largest agricultural businesses in South America, Chefe Agro, S.A.

"This land is owned by Brazil," he said. "We have determined that its best use is in the production of soybeans, a staple crop already growing, as you must know, in Belterra. Even though we have title here, we recognize your efforts here on behalf of the native population, and are fully authorized to make you a substantial offer of cash to reimburse you for anything you have spent," he said. It was so unexpected that I couldn't think of a thing to say. I looked around at our group and saw that they were as dumbfounded as I was.

Dean Knotwell was the first to respond. "I really don't think you understand, but this is a non-profit project partly funded by a grant from the US Department of Agriculture. It is not ours to sell to anyone." It was the visitors' turn to look at each other.

"Apparently, there has been some misunderstanding,"

the spokesman said. "Our company works very closely with the USDA on many levels. Who is your liaison officer in Washington?" he asked. Dean Knotwell gave him the name. "Thank you," he said. "We will be on our way. You seem to have done a reasonably good job here. I will mention that when I see him in Washington." It was obviously the end of the conversation. We did not need to be told that it was time to go back ashore and no sooner had we set foot on the dock (which had been substantially repaired by now), when the crew began to cast off her lines, and the yacht swung gracefully back into the river. We had found our voices by then and started talking all at once. Suxie's face was set in an expression I hadn't seen since we were back up north.

"Those bastards with their fancy boat and their fancy shoes are going to get a boot where the sun don't shine," she said levelly, her voice speaking the truth. At least I hoped it was the truth. After a lot of astonished and angry words, we all slowly separated and went back to our tasks for the day. At least they did. I had no task, other than toting a coconut around.

"Did you hear anything?" I asked Leeram. Silence. It was not like the old days when I had his actual head. Now it seemed that I could only talk to Leeram when he was in the vicinity, in earshot, so to speak. Sometimes it was as though he had just wandered off for a while, and there was no voicemail on his end of the string, either. We were on our own until I could contact him. I decided to talk to Suxie and went up the hill to the old hospital building where she had set up her office. It wasn't far to her grandfather's cemetery, where she had taken to spending time. "Don't worry," she said to me once, "It's not morbid, but it's as though I can talk to him when I'm there, especially when I have the badge."

She was sitting at a desk when I found her, looking at a pile of papers. "I really don't think they can do this," she said. "It says here that we have the necessary Brazilian permissions to live here and carry on. And the grant itself means that we have a green light from the United States. My life is right here," she said. "Here and nowhere else." She put her hand down flat on the desk with a thump. "I am not leaving," she said, with some of her old Schwartskophian emphasis. "I am not leaving Ubirajara."

The conversation at dinner that night was not hard to predict. Seth and Ben were shocked. "There is no effing way we are leaving here," Seth said. "This place is like paradise to us. I could spend two or three lifetimes just doing pure research here."

Ben chimed in: "We may be on to something right now that I don't think we could replicate anywhere else on earth." The case of the curious electron, I thought to myself.

Lisa, who had been nearly silent at first, said flatly, "I agree with Suxie. We need to stay here to finish what we started. Gilly, what does Leeram have to say?" I told her I'd find out.

Later, back in my room, which thanks to a couple of screened windows open on two facing walls, was comfortably cool, I tried to reach Leeram again. Lying on my back, I put the smiley-faced nut on my stomach and spoke to him, my head propped up on a pillow. "Leeram, if you hear me, please copy."

"Not so loud, goddammit!" he shouted and I jumped. "I'm not deaf!" I apologized and told him that I had been trying to reach him ever since I got back. He apologized to me, saying that he had been away from our wormhole for a while, hunting, and was tired. "It sounds like you need Ubirajara," he said.

"We need the cavalry," I said. "Suxie thinks we will stay, but I'm not sure myself. There's too much money involved and it makes me nervous."

"Sounds like the old samo-samo," Leeram said. "Those bastards have been trying to get rich off us since before I was born. I'll bet I knew their great-grandfathers."

"You said we need the grandfather, speaking of grandfathers," I said.
"He knows this place better than I do, and they just might be able to work together."
"But can he do it from your end?" I asked.
"Maybe," Leeram said. "It's up to him."

Chapter 16

The next morning, after breakfast and our usual meeting to plan the day's activities, I decided to go back across the river. I wanted to visit the Carvahlos again, to bring them some books I had run across and to add to the journal I had been keeping since our arrival in Fordlandia. I had many questions. Leeram's objections to being on water had quieted a little, probably because there were more coconuts where this one had come from. I was extremely careful with it anyway since I had no real guarantee that another one would work, or work as well, but at least it would float, I told him. We (the coconut and I) set out again in the skiff and headed across the river while it was still relatively cool, the morning sun shining off the surface and through a rapidly melting cover of mist. By the time we reached the landing, the air was tropically hot again. As we passed the Lugar Perfieto, I paused. I realized that I had never seen it without feeling a twinge, a tic, the sensation of something odd. Even though the ozone smell that I had gotten so used to when Leeram was around was not apparent, something in my brain told me that it should be. I shook the feeling off and walked toward the Carvahlos' house. I was sweating. No one was on the porch, so I climbed the stairs and knocked on the screen door. Gabriela appeared behind it and smiled as she recognized me and motioned me into the relatively cool air inside. "It is a pleasure to see you again," she said in Portuguese. Thanks to Pericles, Leeram, and simple immersion in the last few months, I could understand her, even if I was far from fluent. "Gustavio will be down very shortly. In the meantime, would you like some coffee?" I thanked her, saying that I would. By now I had learned that a hot cup of coffee or tea was the perfect thing in a tropical climate, tricking the mind into thinking that it was actually cooler than it really was. Arabs have known this for centuries. Gabriela and her husband appeared together soon after, bearing full cups, and we sat down on the porch. I gave them the books, one an atlas of the Amazon region and the other an illustrated historical account of a group of former Confederate soldiers who had resettled in the Amazon after the Civil War. The books were in English, but Gabriela said she could read them well enough. They were delighted and over my not-too-strenuous objections, offered me lunch. We sat at the table for a few minutes making small talk, and then Gabriela said, "You have no idea how far the news of your communal farm has spread." After the visitation we had gone through on our side of the river recently, I was not surprised and told them so.

"In the last few days, there have been scouts for at least four or five big companies in town," Gustavio said. "They are everywhere. They've set up camps here in our village." I thought of the two men in the bar with their map.

"When we came down here, it was just to help the caboclos," I said. "Looking back on it, I realize how naïve we were."

"Before you arrived," he said, "this whole region had been totally forgotten about, other than a few tour boat operators out of Santarem. The place was treated almost like a temple in the deep forest built by distant ancestors that people only knew a little about—nothing except for some local farming and fishing was going on here. Nobody knew or cared what went on out here. Now, I can't remember seeing so many strangers in my life, and the only thing people talk about is Fordlandia." I replied that I had seen some yachts and other boats at the town landing, boats that were obviously not used for fishing or tourists.

"They've just started to show up; their people only go ashore to look around and then spend the night back aboard," Gabriela said.

We chatted for a little while longer, then I left after thanking them gratefully. They had become instant friends and I told them so. On the way back, I decided to check out the Lugar Perfieto again just to see if any of our "scouting" friends were inside. It was midafternoon by then, and it took a moment for my eyes to adjust to the much darker interior. The casa was crowded, probably because it was the only watering hole in town. The bartender recognized me and I knew I had made a mistake. He boomed, "Hey, General, welcome back!" I turned back toward the door when a large figure appeared in front of me, blocking my way. It held out a massive hand.

"My name is Franklin Bouchard Calhoon," it said. "If I am not mistaken, you are Gilbert Greenbush, the gentleman who runs the new plantation across the river."

I looked more closely and saw a tall man in a big Stetson. He was dressed in ironed jeans topped with a massive silver belt buckle inlaid with gold initials spelling FBC, and a fitted cotton shirt with snaps in the pockets.

"I am," I said. His hand was still out and I shook it. It was like gripping a drilling clamp.

"You've caught a lot of people's attention," he said, his voice straight from the tar sands of southern Texas. I replied that it certainly appeared that way. "Let me buy you a drink," he said. I started to say I was sorry but I really had to go, when he put his arm over my shoulder and literally turned me back around toward the bar. We sat down and I ordered a beer. "You're famous, son," he said. "We need to talk."

"I don't know exactly why," I said. "All we've done is organize a collective farm in Fordlandia to help the locals make a sustainable living."

"Yes, yes, I know," he said, with an exaggerated wink

and then chuckled. "Best bullshit I've ever heard. Listen, my people and I want to talk to you in private. Want to come down to my boat?" At first I wanted to make excuses and just leave, but a little Leeramish voice was curious about what he had in mind.

"OK," I said. We finished our drinks, he tossed some money on the bar, and we left under everyone's gaze. His "boat" was a big, steel commercial vessel festooned with satellite navigation and communication antennae and a corporate logo on each side, reading IMEX. Her name was Gold Digger and under the name was her hailing port, Galveston, TX. I looked at Calhoon questioningly.

"International Mineral and Energy Extraction Services," he explained. "We're worldwide, operate out of Dallas. Come on aboard." A steward welcomed us at the gangplank and we went into the main cabin, which resembled a boardroom, nicely paneled. "Would you like another drink?" I declined, saying that I had to get back pretty soon. "Suit yourself," he said and the steward brought him a glass of whisky, straight up.

"I've got a proposition for you. I know you know that there are very valuable deposits of manganese and other minerals all along the property you are leasing from the Brazilian government. Our geologists also tell us that there is a good chance that oil shale is down there too. Gotta tell you that my hat's off to you for thinking about telling 'em it's all about farming. What I can do for you is give you our help and equipment to extract the stuff and you take a good chunk of the profit. You couldn't get a fraction of that ore out that we can, so we both win this way."

It was probably the very last thing that could have entered my mind, and I was speechless. Manganese? "Let me think about it," I said. "I really do have to leave now." Mr. Calhoon rose with me.

"Of course, I understand," he said. "I know others have spoken to you about this, and I know you undoubtedly have plans of your own, but I can tell you we are the biggest, the best, and have the most solid government connections on both sides of the border than anyone else here. I can tell you we have always gotten what we go for. I'm a gambling man and I'm willing to bet a lot of money that I'm right about this, but don't worry, we can make you very, very rich."

Back in the little skiff, heading on a course to Fordlandia, I asked Leeram what he thought of it all. "Buddy, you're going to need me. This guy can crush you," he said. That, I thought, was pretty obvious. All he needed to do was grab me with one hand.

"We need some Amazonian help," I said. "Is there any such stuff around?" By the time I got close enough, I could see a couple of unfamiliar boats at our dock, obviously not in the tourist or fishing trades. It was close to our dinner hour so I went up to our communal house.

While we were all at the table, I described my experiences in the village, both with the Carvahlos and Mr. Calhoon. "Nobody's approached us," Pericles said, "but I've seen a lot of strangers around here. They're not tourists, for certain. By the way, anyone seen Suxie?" She had been missing during a lot of our evening meals lately, only showing up in the mornings looking tired. She was not there the next morning, and not in her room, either. Everyone scattered to look for her.

"The graveyard?" I asked Lisa. She nodded and we went up the hill. Nothing there. The others opted for the docks and the big machinery buildings and the town itself, after we all agreed to meet at noon back at our headquarters. We combed Fordlandia, asking everyone we saw. It was fruitless. Lisa and I were the first back and opened the door to our meeting room, to find Suxie sitting at the table. She was sitting next to a tall, muscular native who was, if anything, taller than she was; they had an overwhelming familial resemblance. The old familiar smell of ozone was in the air.

"I'd like to introduce you to my grandfather," she said. Ubirajara stood slowly, unfolding into a statuesque man in the prime of life, dressed in a loincloth. His badge was on the table in front of him.

"Ubirajara!" I said, bowing. I recognized him immediately from the dream. "We are honored beyond my ability to express it." The others, who followed right behind us, stood silently, dumbfounded. We looked at Suxie.

"I was down at the riverside with the badge on my belt and I felt it vibrate," she said. "It scared the hell out of me.

I thought something had bitten me. When I looked out on the water, I saw someone swimming toward the shore. He had a steady overhand stroke, the kind really experienced swimmers have, and I felt very, very strange, but I wasn't afraid. When he reached the shore and climbed up the riverbank, I knew who he was. I felt calm and I wondered why because I should have been frightened out of my wits. He held out his hand and smiled. 'Hello, my granddaughter,' he said. For a little while, I didn't know if I was asleep or awake and I think I lost consciousness, because the next thing I knew he was kneeling next to me. He said, 'It is me. This is my real body, you are not dreaming. I have come back.' And now he is here with us."

We all started talking at once and Ubirajara held up his hand.

"I am here," he said in a deep voice, "because my granddaughter Araci needs my help. Since I will help her, I will help all of you." His voice hinted of the lowest notes from a stately old church organ, pulsations from its largest pipes more felt than heard. "My granddaughter has explained to me your motivations and your situation."

"You look a lot better than the last time we saw you," said Pericles. "How did you manage that?" The tall man looked at him steadily for a long time. "I'm terribly sorry," Pericles said, "I realize that sounded impertinent and I didn't mean it that way. Please accept my apologies."

"I understand your question," Ubirajara said, finally. "I am here because the risk of coming back was worth more than staying where I was. Even the smallest chance of coming through that passage alive was worth an eternity on the other side. I don't know how long I will live here, but every minute that passes here is worth a thousand years back there."

"Did you come through a wormhole?" I asked.

"That is what your friend, Araribóia, I mean Leeram, calls it. It is not exactly a hole, more like the inside of a whirlpool that twists and turns and sometimes closes off completely. It goes between two worlds with different measurements of time and distance, so it is almost infinitely long and infinitely short at the same time. To come from the other end to here is like swimming up a waterfall or crossing a bottomless canyon on a tightrope. When this one is open, it comes out in the forest in back of a bar in Urucubituba. There are a lot more around this world, of course, but it's the nearest one to us."

"But Pericles was asking about your physical body right now," I said. "How did you get it?"

"The process of returning is so excoriating that everything must be put back together in the end. Why not do it, right?" Ubirajara seemed to tire of the conversation. He turned to us all and said: "My granddaughter has explained your situation and we have work to do." He sat down, and we all crowded around. "I want you to continue as you have been doing for now. Don't approach the strangers; act as though they are not there. I will study and react when the time comes. In the meantime, since I now exist in your world, I need to eat and sleep as you do. Prepare a room for me." He rose; we rose.

As he was about to walk away, a thought occurred to me and I had to ask him. "If things are so bad over there, why don't more people come back like you did?"

"I think I told you," he said, turning back. "It is very dangerous. Most people would rather live in peace and safety, even if they miss the old days. And don't forget, most of the ones who try do not get through, or if they do, are very, very different when they come out than when they went in."

"You can stay here in this house," Suxie said. "There's a bedroom we are just using for storage. I'll move into it and you can live in mine." She led her grandfather away. Pericles, Lisa, Ben, and Seth emptied the spare room of everything we had tossed into it over the past few months, carting it all to an adjacent cottage. Suxie would have to make do with a cot and an air mattress until we could find an honest bed.

"Leeram," I said after they left, "can you tell me just what in the holy hell is going on?"

"He's known about your situation ever since I gave you the coconut. I can tell you one damn thing for sure—he must have wanted to cross over to your side a lot more than I thought. There's no guarantee he can get back. You couldn't pay me enough to do it myself."

"Is he doing it for his granddaughter or his people? Or both, maybe?"

"Beats me, but he's taken one helluva chance."

"Just as long as you're with me through this thing," I said, hand on the smiley face.

"My friend, I will always be with you," he said. "You and your young lady." I did not expect him to say that and I was touched. I told him so. "Don't get all wobbly," he replied. That evening, Lisa and I went for a long walk after dinner. We headed down to the river, where the dock was empty after dusk. We sat on a crate near the shore.

"I keep thinking about what I was like when I first met you," I said. "I was like that thing out there." I pointed at a piece of driftwood just visible in the moonlight, slowly passing in the current. We gazed at it for a while as it approached and then passed, going downstream. "I don't think I gave my life any more examination than it does," I said.

"I like you a lot better now," she said. "You've changed in so many ways. You've gotten younger."

"Or you older?"

"No, we've both done that, I guess, but we are so much closer now. I've left a lot of my old self back in Massachusetts and you have too," she said. I thought about that. The piece of flotsam was out of sight by now and the river smelled of the rich jungle. If I had somehow gone through a loop in time and met my old self, would I even recognize him?

"You even look different," she said. "You're thinner, your face is sharper. You're even a little buff," she said, half-jokingly. I laughed. "What am I, Johnny Weissmuller?" I said.

"Who's Johnny Weissmuller?" she asked, and I remembered our age difference all over again.

"He was Tarzan," I said. "Don't you remember?"

"Vaguely. Before we left, I read that Alexander Skarsgard is going to be playing Tarzan in a remake."

"Who is Alexander Skarsgard? Never heard of him."

"Didn't you ever watch *True Blood?*" I had heard something about it, I said, but, no, I had never seen it. We laughed and embraced. The hug turned into more than a hug and soon we were making love on top of the crate, Tarzan and his Jane.

***

Our world had changed dramatically in one way, but in all the others it remained the same. It was finally time to harvest the first field we had planted all those months ago. The aguaje plants, looking a little like miniature palm trees, had not reached their full height, but their fruit was already appearing, buriti, as it was called by the Brazilians. They were a chestnut color with a yellow pulp inside. Dean Knotwell was ecstatic. "They are delicious," she said, biting into one about the size of a peach. "These things are so rich in vitamins! You can even make wine from them," she said. I tasted one and felt my saliva glands explode. It tasted almost like ice cream with a hint of pumpkin pie, caramel, and lemon.

"Wow," I said. "I had no idea."

"Wait until you taste it frozen," she said. "They make them into popsicles."

Pericles chimed in. "These grow in the wild," he said, "but that's a problem because the naturally grown trees are so tall that the most practical way to harvest them is to cut them down. The Amazon has lost more than half of them that way. Our farm here will help show the way to end that kind of thing."

By then we had chosen a wholesaler from the list we had acquired earlier in Santarem and after a week of picking, a full boatload was headed downriver aboard the Dom Afonso, accompanied by our supercargo, Pericles, who would handle the details. Two days later, he returned with a check—the first money to come in rather than go out from our farm. It wasn't much after paying the freight bill, but it was definitely worth a celebration that evening with the Fordlandians, attended by the Mayor, a big crowd of local farm workers and, of course, ourselves. Even Ubirajara put on some new clothes we had made for his extra-large frame; he was accessorized with his old Fordlandia badge hanging from a string around his neck. "I had forgotten how good this tastes," he said, after a long drink of rum. "I think I'll stay for a while," he said with a straight face.

Chapter 17

Strangely, it was Dean Knotwell who had the strongest reaction to Ubirajara's sudden appearance in the flesh. Ben and Seth took it pretty much in stride, as did everyone else, even Lisa. By now the strange, green embrace of the Amazon basin was so pervasive that we took the mysterious as just another surprise—something to be remarked upon but in the end, not totally unbelievable. Nothing, that is, that would make us doubt our sanity. We had been through so much that a simple reanimation of a dead man seemed, if not exactly ordinary, at least perfectly feasible. It didn't take long for Ubi to fit right in like a distant uncle home from a long sabbatical on Mars. Yet Dean Knotwell still jumped whenever he entered the room. "I never know what to say around him," she said to me privately. "I know he means well, but I'm just tongue-tied when he talks to me." She couldn't keep her eyes off him, with his loincloth just barely covering what it needed to. "Why can't he dress like he did when he worked here before?" she asked, arms akimbo.

In the first few days and weeks after his appearance in Fordlandia, Ubirajara spent most of his time just walking around the place exploring, sometimes with Suxie and other times by himself. "Getting reacquainted," he said. His vocabulary was sophisticated and illuminating for someone who had never had a formal education. He had done an enormous amount of reading in the years before he died; his mind was supple and inquisitive. "Actually, I was getting pretty bored on the other side," he told me, when I worked up enough courage to ask him what it was like. "I missed my old books. Your friend, the one you call Leeram, was one of the few who engaged me over there." Having one's head in circulation here in this universe was a blessing in disguise, Leeram once told him, he said. Leeram could live a dual existence, which helped a lot. He could safely skip over to this universe whenever he wanted, Ubi said, without actually having to go through a wormhole. I asked him what dead people did when they became, how should I say, terminally bored. "Some of them try to act out their religions," he said. "But they get frustrated when nothing turns out the way they expected. A lot become nihilistic; others just want to travel infinitely, thinking that their salvation is around the next bend. The Mormons are just very confused since their families are so scattered that they rarely make contact with other Mormons. It doesn't stop them from trying to convert us, though," Ubirajara said. I described a book called Riverworld, written by Philip Jose Farmer, which depicted a planet with a nearly endless river bounded by unclimbable cliffs that looped back-and-forth endlessly. Everyone who died on earth woke up there. I asked if his world was anything like that. "No," he said. "Not at all. It has something to do with the different dimensions there. Here you have height, width, and depth, just three of them. The fourth one takes up the overflow."

"Well, OK," I said. "But in Riverworld there was a godlike race of beings that set it all up for reasons of their own. Is that the case where you came from?"

"If it is, they exist on a dimensional plane that we didn't have access to," he said.

Ubirajara insisted that we call him Ubi, despite the fact that his imposing presence made the diminutive name a little awkward for us to say. Even though he had done nothing more at first than transform Suxie with his presence, he began to give us all a feeling of invincibility, of calm strength. He and Suxie spent a lot of time walking around Fordlandia and even well into the jungle as they talked about many things. The change in her that had begun aboard the Dom Afonso on the trip up, the indefinable blurring of her hard edges, had accelerated. She now radiated a softly regal beauty, a mysterious sense of the land itself.

They met with the Mayor, although they were careful not to mention who Ubirajara was. She introduced him as an uncle who had heard about her arrival and came many miles downstream from a distant village. Their strong family resemblance made the story believable.

It was a lull, we realized much later. A necessary lull that allowed us to consolidate our base. Even Leeram, who complained constantly about wanting to get back to civilization, stopped carping sarcastically and began making helpful suggestions. "I have no idea why he jumped over," he said, "but Ubirajara is one good man, on your end or mine. You're very lucky he did it." I wondered, when he said that, if he could talk to Ubi, if there was a bridge between them. "I'll do my best, buddy," he said, noncommittally.

Ubi was especially interested in the graduate students Ben and Seth. He spent hours with them, listening to their theories and observing their experiments. "I might be able to help," he told them one day. "I learned a great deal on the other side. You speak of something you mysteriously call dark energy, but I know what it is, and I can sense its presence here. In the end, it's not all that mysterious, but it is not as apparent to you as it is to me."

The two young men didn't know quite how to respond. They had been vigorously trained in the scientific method and here they were casually talking to a resurrected human being about dark energy. To say their minds were in turmoil would be an understatement. He offered to work with them. "I might be able to help," he said, and they accepted his assistance mostly, they told me later, because he just exuded self-assurance. They couldn't think of a way to turn him down.

At the time, none of us were aware of this collaboration, which went on for weeks. Ben and Seth were in their lab for ten or twelve hours a day, with Ubi making frequent visits when he wasn't with Suxie and the rest of us. Their project was never mentioned in depth at our nightly dinner table, where we normally brought each other up-to-date on things, a tradition that had grown over time. Those meals didn't just have an educational function; they were a way for us to simply blend into the family that we had become. Ubirajara sat at one end and Suxie usually sat at the other with the rest of us scattered along the sides. We would have a glass of alua or perhaps a beer and talk about the day's events, then have dinner and generally go to bed not long after. Like farmers everywhere, we rose at dawn and worked all day.

By now we had begun to assume that the Fordlandia Project would go on long after some of us had left, with Suxie and Ubi in charge. Pericles began to talk about returning to academia; Lisa occasionally mentioned how nice it would be to see Boston again, and I agreed with her. Dean Knotwell and her two doctoral students wanted to stay longer because, "There is no place like this on earth," she said. Ben and Seth were completely absorbed in their research, which had become incomprehensible to me by now.

One evening, Ubirajara said to me that he was going to

take a trip upriver and asked if I would like to go with him. I jumped at it. "Of course," I said. My work in Fordlandia was taking less and less of my time, and I was more than happy to go exploring with him.

A couple of days later, Ubirajara and I began loading the skiff with extra cans of gasoline, food, and camping gear. It didn't take long before we both realized that there would be more gear than the little boat could safely carry. "We need a dugout," he said. "A real dugout."

"Doesn't that mean we need an enormous log?" I asked, thinking about deforestation and keeping the old major trees intact. "Also, doesn't it take a lot of time to make a dugout?" He replied yes, and "normally" yes.

"But we have help. Don't forget, we have your modern tools. It won't take as long as you think." I was a little skeptical, and said so. "As far as the logs go, we don't have to cut down any trees; they were harvested many years ago; I know where they are," he said. "They're buried in mud right inside that little inlet to preserve them." He pointed to an indentation on the riverbank not far from the sawmill. "When the Ford Company first came here, it clear-cut hundreds of acres of old hardwood, planning to sell it later. It was so tough that their mill equipment kept burning out and they finally gave up. The wood was forgotten about once their other problems got bigger. I helped put those leftover logs in the mud myself; they should be as good now as the day we put them there." When we got there, I realized that it was the exact spot I had found wood earlier when we were rebuilding. I must have just seen the logs closest to the surface, not realizing they were just the tip of the iceberg.

We found them after digging with a borrowed backhoe for about a half hour; there were hundreds of them, still covered with bark, lying side by side, looking like a corrugated substrate under the mud. I remembered reading in the papers about a similar find in Boston Harbor where they found "live" oak logs set aside by the navy one hundred fifty years ago and forgotten. When they dug them up they were still good as new, perfectly preserved by the mud. Ubi chose one, hauled it out with the tractor, and, afterward, used the tractor to cover the rest with mud once more. The logs were all old-growth mahogany that once towered everywhere on land now used for cattle farming. Once we hosed off our log, it looked as though it had just been cut down the day before. We collected about a dozen men who knew what they were doing, according to Ubi, who really did know what he was doing, and supervised their work as they dug into the log with a chain saw. Amid the smell of gasoline and the sound of the motor, the sight and odor of fresh wood jumped out almost immediately. Once the external shape of the dugout had been roughed out, they used sharp axes to finish it. Then they took acetylene torches and quickly burned the inside, then scraped the charred material out. In a couple of days, we had our native craft, altered slightly to take the outboard motor, but twice as big and burdensome as the old skiff. After we loaded everything aboard, including fishing gear and a couple of shotguns, Ubirajara and I finally shoved off, heading south up the Tapajos. Just before leaving, Ubi also loaded a dozen buckets and two shovels. When I asked what they were for, Ubi shrugged and said, "We'll need them." Once we were underway, the canoe seemed to shrug off the occasional wake from passing boats, and I began to relax. It swam in the river imperviously like a big wooden alligator, unbothered by waves. On several occasions we passed other craft, almost identical to ours, and I began to understand how well these dugouts were suited to the Amazon.

We motored on until dusk, then pitched camp in a clearing by the river's edge. Ubi had a miraculous touch with the fishing rod, knowing exactly what to use for bait, and before long we had a big pirarucu, more than enough for supper, roasting over a fire. Pirarucu is an air-breather, I read in a guidebook, an ancient species of catfish that dates back to prehistoric times. As we cooked some big chunks over a fire, he said he and his tribe used to hunt them with spears, but he couldn't resist all the fancy modern fishing equipment. "It's like a toy," he said, laughing, waving the rod in the air. We ate until we couldn't eat any more, but there was more than enough left for the next day. Finally, after cleaning up and putting out the fire, we climbed into our sleeping bags under mosquito netting. I slept a dreamless, refreshing sleep and literally woke with a bang at dawn. Unzipping the tent flap, I saw Ubi, a big grin on his face, walking back from the woods, open shotgun crooked over one arm, and a large bird hanging by its feet from his other hand. He was clearly enjoying every minute of his new life on earth. "I shot it, you clean it," he said, tossing the bird to me. It was one thing I really knew how to do.

By the time we were underway again, midmorning, we were indistinguishable from any native craft on the river. I had not known Ubi to be a voluble talker before, but now his words seemed to flow, as if the river and the surrounding jungle had woken a long dormant stream within him. "Do you know what we are really after?" he said. I replied that I assumed that he wanted to look around, now that he was back, and that I was eager to explore as well. "That, of course," he said, "but your young friends need some help and I think I know where to find what they are looking for."

I replied that I knew their research had something to do with electricity. "It does," he said thoughtfully. "It does. Have you ever heard of the word 'chemurgical?'" It seems I was being taught English by a denizen of the rain forest.

"No," I said. "Can't say that I have."

"Well, chemurgical means making new products from plants. In the old days, I was always reading about Ford's chemurgical experiments in company papers. For example, his labs made a kind of artificial leather from wood chips, but I don't think he ever managed to pull something like that off here. Well, your young friends are right on the edge of a chemurgical discovery here and we are going to help them." Then he looked at me and his expression suddenly became playful.

"Like the plants and insects, there are about twice as many species of fish here than anywhere else in the world, including one that will swim right up inside you, and there are animals you haven't even discovered yet," he said, after a pause. "Right now there is a school of electric eels on the bottom, just under this boat." I looked nervously over the side, but I couldn't see anything. He smiled and said, "The only way you could see them is to jump overboard and go for a swim," and he started rocking the boat. I grabbed the gunwales, my knuckles white. I was suddenly more aware than ever of how close we were to the water, a distance that seemed to shrink by the second.

"Be careful, for crissakes," I shouted. He laughed. I was dealing with a reanimated corpse who was just a kid at heart!

Ubi turned back to the river and steered silently for a while, looking carefully along each bank. Suddenly, after we came around a bend, he spotted the mouth of a small tributary, almost invisible from the middle of the river. We headed for it. "That's where it is," he said. "I remember now. We have to go up that stream for a while, but it's there."

"What's there?" I asked.

"What I'm looking for," he said, unhelpfully. The

riverbanks, now only a dozen feet away on each side, were overarched by tall trees and vines. At times, the sun was completely blocked by the foliage, and I realized that everything around me looked like the place in that dream. The outboard motor had become jarringly noisy and before long Ubi shut it off and picked up a paddle, motioning for me to do the same. We paddled for two hours against the languid current. Sweat began to drip through my cotton headband and my hands had started to blister annoyingly when suddenly he stopped. I did too, gratefully. Momentum carried us forward until our speed just matched the current and the land stopped moving. Ubirajara sat still, sniffing the air. "We're almost there," he said and dug in with his paddle with even more energy than before; I started again, not wanting to show weakness. When we came around the very next bend, a big, grassy clearing came into view, filled with sunlight. We paddled up to it and climbed out onto dry land, tying the dugout to a tree at the clearing's edge. "Take off your shoes," Ubi said. I did, and when my bare feet met the ground I felt—wonderful! I walked in circles, rejoicing in the curious but very pleasurable texture of the grass and the soil it was on. I had a slight tingly sensation each time I put my foot down.

"This is it," he said. We picked up the buckets and the shovels and he started walking on the grass as he looked for the right spot. "Don't dig in the middle," he said. We went to the edge, near the tree line. As we got closer, the tingling sensation intensified. "Here," he said, and pushed his shovel into the dirt, bringing up a sizeable chunk of the grass and its roots. I followed his example and before long, all the buckets were full.

On the way back, Ubi caught a couple more fish, which we ate at the next campsite. He carefully watered the plants, which took up all of the available space aboard the dugout. From a distance, we must have looked like a floating island. Since we were going with the current this time, the trip back to Fordlandia was a lot faster. We were at our dock by the following afternoon. When we unloaded, almost all of the canned and freeze-dried food we had come with was still there, packed and untouched.

Ben and Seth were at the dock within minutes. They went right for the buckets and were hugely excited. I couldn't understand much of what they were saying, but then Ben looked up at us and said: "Ubi, we can't thank you enough!" We all carried the buckets up to their lab, where they transplanted the grasses into long beds. Some were placed in soil, others in a hydroponic substrate. That evening, we all met at the dinner table and celebrated Ubirajara's find. "They look really healthy," Seth said. "We'll give them a week to stabilize, get used to their new home, and then start with our experiments."

By now, life in Fordlandia had almost, I hate to use the word, turned more or less humdrum. Our fields were now entirely planted, and the natives in surrounding villages like Boa Vista and even across the river in Urucubituba had accepted us almost as though we had been there since time began—quite a change in their attitude since we first arrived. Every now and then, a riverboat full of tourists and other strangers would tie up at our pier, spend a few hours ashore, then leave. Before long, we had settled back into our routine and just let the Amazon rain forest and all its tributaries flow all around us. Our role as farmers of traditional crops had decreased, and our new role had yet to become apparent. In the meantime, we began to concentrate on the physical infrastructure of Fordlandia itself. We weren't equipped financially to do too much ourselves, but local Brazilians began to step up. There were some big cattle farmers in the region before our own arrival, and even a working sawmill. Slowly, local folks who had pretty much accepted the status quo before we arrived began to invest in the place and by now, Fordlandia was in the middle of a real transformation. We became construction coordinators. Homes were repaired and painted at an accelerating rate. The electrical and plumbing infrastructure was refurbished, and even the old water tower was reinforced and repaired to the point at which we could safely climb up to it and gaze at the vast rain forest around us, neatly bifurcated by the winding Tapajos River, which ran through its lush green blanket like a mysterious silver snake.

Chapter 18

For a short while, things proceeded on an even keel, if I can be permitted to use a nautical term, and then one morning, everything changed. When we came down to the dock after breakfast, a large, familiar steel vessel was tied up to it. I recognized the IMEX logo immediately and had a bad feeling. Mr. Calhoon was surely here, high, wide, and handsome. Nobody was on deck, but after we had been back to our office for a short time, we heard a knock at the door. A stranger, underneath a big Stetson and wearing an open-collared gingham shirt already spotting with sweat, was standing there when we opened it. "I represent Mr. Calhoon, the president of International Mineral and Energy Extraction Services, Inc.," he said. "Mr. Calhoon would like to meet with you aboard our vessel at your convenience. May I tell him when that might be?" Something about that invitation implied that a negative response, or one that set the meeting too far in the future, would not exactly fly.

"Of course," I said. Suxie looked at me sharply. I turned to her and the others. "We're going to have to deal with this; it might as well be sooner than later." Turning back to the emissary, I said "Tell Mr. Calhoon that we will meet with him at 1:00 p.m. right here in this house, this afternoon."

"Our ship is air-conditioned," he said, "and we have much more suitable conditions for a meeting," he said, a little plaintively.

"We will meet you here." The words came from Ubi, who appeared in the back of the room suddenly, like a big, dark jungle cat coming from behind a tree. "Here. Not on your boat." The man in the hat jumped.

"I will tell Mr. Calhoon," he said, and with a short nod of his head, turned and went back downhill. We all sat down immediately and everyone started talking at once.

"Who is this man Calhoon?" asked Ubirajara in his low voice. It seemed to rumble from everywhere in the room. I told him of my meeting with Calhoon in Urucubituba. "He thinks we want to dig for gold?" Ubirajara asked in an astonished tone. "He thinks we are going to cheat our own people?" I nodded.

"He doesn't understand us here," I said. "Where he comes from, there is one man on the top and everyone else beneath him. He thinks we are like him." I then tried to describe the world he lived in—everything from the worship of sheer size, to barbeque. The outside world existed to people like him as a two-dimensional abstract,

I explained. He was here in person, surely, but on some level it wasn't as tangible as his favorite seat in a Dallas restaurant with a cold bottle of Lone Star beer waiting for him there. They love a game called poker.

"What is poker?" Ubi asked.

"Well, it is a card game. They must have played cards in Fordlandia," I answered. "You're dealt cards and bet that you have the highest hand. The thing about poker, the way he plays it, is that there are no limits on what you can bet. You can win with a weak hand if you just bet so much that everyone thinks your hand is better than theirs and then they fold or drop out, leaving their bets on the table for you to take. People do a lot of bluffing, or pretending their hand is better than it actually is, but it's risky, because if you are bluffing and someone else actually has a better hand and calls your bluff, you lose big time." Ubi was silent for a while, taking that in.

"I look forward to meeting this Mr. Calhoon," he said, finally. Then, after a pause, he said to me, "I would like to talk to Leeram." I handed the satchel to him.

"I'm pretty sure he can only contact me," I said, "but give it a try." He held the coconut for a while, looking at it intently. After a while he handed it back. "Try it yourself," he said. "When I came over, I crossed a rope bridge over an infinitely deep canyon. I think it broke when I reached the other side."

"Leeram," I said out loud. "Leeram, come in please." The coconut's face seemed to have lost a bit of its smile as its function was now reduced to a hand-held, two-way radio, temperamental at that. There was no response. "Leeram!" I almost shouted this time. Silence. I was about to put the coconut back in its satchel when I heard a faint sound.

"Greenbush." At first I couldn't understand the word. "Greenbush." Then I heard it.

"Leeram, I'm here. I'm with Ubirajara and Suxie and everybody. Ubi wants to talk with you; can you hear him?"

"I can hear you," he said, a bit louder, "but that's all. Tell Ubirajara I think he's nuts to have crossed back over to your side but I admire his balls."

"I suppose he has them back," I said, "but as far as I know, he's happy he did what he did. He wants to talk with you."

"You need something better than my coconut if that's going to happen. Or he does." I thought for a minute.

"Ubi, did you leave anything of yours on the other side...anything that Leeram might be able to find?"

Ubi scratched his head, then said, "Before I came over, I laid aside everything that contained metal. Metal is dangerous to take with you. Tell Leeram that he might be able to find my old knife." I relayed the message.

"I'll get back to you," Leeram said. Which he did almost immediately. "I spent the last two days looking for his damn knife and I found it sticking out of a tree right in back of where I was when you asked me to look for it." His universe and ours obviously were on different time scales.

"Is he still there?" I said he was. I handed the coconut to Ubi, who folded it into his arms. He closed his eyes, then suddenly they opened wide.

"I need to see what's going on down there," Leeram said to Ubi, and this time I could hear him also. Ubirajara and I could hear him together!

"Put that badge next to the coconut. Make them touch," Leeram said. Ubirajara gave it to me and I leaned it against the smiley face.

"This is more than just a little silly," I said, "but what the hell." A minute or two passed and we all sat around holding our breath. Then, suddenly there was an audible snap and the room filled with that old, familiar ozone smell. Somehow, the badge and coconut on our side and the knife on the other had made a Rube Goldbergian, patched-up wormhole, an improbable bell, book, and candle link through which visible light on our end was translated into whatever equivalent it had on Leeram's universe.

"Well, cut off my head and call me a cantaloupe," said Leeram. "I can see you now. Not as good as I could before, but it'll do." We all high-fived each other, even Ubi, who was a quick study.

"Can you see cards?" I asked. "You know, playing cards?"

"If you point me in the right direction, sure I can," Leeram said. I put the coconut on a shelf, facing our dining room table.

"Can you see cards on the table from this shelf?"

"Clear as day," Leeram replied.

I turned to our group and said, "I have an idea. Please go along with me." Everyone agreed. Reluctantly. "Look," I said, "you have to trust me here. I know these Texans. They have a particular sense of honor when it comes to cards. It's a Southern thing and it's especially true in Texas. We're going to literally bet the farm." They all looked at me as if I had turned into Ronald McDonald.

"Greenbush, I have gone along with you on everything you have done here," Suxie said, "but I can't do it now. I have never heard of such a lunatic idea. I will not allow you to lose this whole project in a damned game of cards." The others nodded, agreeing with her. I felt my plan slipping away.

Then Ubirajara spoke, the windows rattling slightly. "Granddaughter, this man knows what he is doing. Leeram and I may have more to do with the outcome than you might think."

"I would never do this without your permission," I told everyone. "Please believe me and Ubi. Do you think I would do this just depending on sheer luck? All those in favor, please raise your hands." Nobody moved a muscle for a long time and I began to think I had lost the argument. Then Dean Knotwell's hand slowly began to climb, then Pericles, Lisa, Ben, and Seth raised theirs. Suxie was stock-still then reluctantly raised her hand to shoulder height.

"I hope you know what you're doing," she said, with an edge of menace that I had not heard since I first met her. "If you lose, I will kill you."

A half hour later, the front door opened and in walked Franklin Bouchard Calhoon, trailing his posse. "Can't understand why you wanted to meet here," he boomed. "My boat is a hell of a lot more comfortable than this shack."

"We will meet here or we will not meet at all," said Ubi.

"Who in jumping hell are you?" said Calhoon.

"My name is Ubirajara and I was born here. This is my granddaughter and these are my friends. I advise you to walk carefully among us on this land."

Calhoon looked at me and said, "Look, let's cut out this bullshit. Let's get serious. You've got a good thing going here, but you don't have the resources or the connections to make the best use of your position. I'm prepared to make you an offer that will be big enough so that you never have to think about money again and you can use the rest of it to fund your favorite tree-hugging charities. Goddamn it, time is money and I don't want to waste it here."

We were silent for a moment. I knew what was going on under Calhoon's big hat, but this was the first time the others got a look. Ubirajara's pipe organ voice was the first to break the silence. "Time is not money. Time is time. Only a very foolish person would say what you just did." Calhoon's face got red. He sputtered.

"I'll show you what time is," he finally shouted. "Let's get out of here," he said to his men and they all started for the door.

"Wait a minute," I said. "Why don't we sit back down. Let's settle this a different way. You told me you were a gambling man. How about playing a little poker, winner takes all. If you win, we will pack up and leave and the place is yours. If we win, you have to agree to leave us alone."

Calhoon hesitated, then turned and sat back down. "That's a very interesting idea," he said, with a hint of oiliness. "I like a sporting proposition, I really do."

"Since the stakes are so high," I said, "we have to have cards we can trust, so why don't we get a new deck from a neutral source. You can inspect them and we can too. We can look for some cards here in Fordlandia or order some from Santarem."

"Santarem," he said. "I'll get my copter to fly a couple of new decks here this afternoon."

"Fair enough," I said, and shook his hand.

He got up and for the second time walked toward the door, his people with him. Just before he left, he turned and said to me: "Lookin' forward to this, son. I didn't tell you that I used to play cards professionally. Have a good night."

As soon as they were gone, everyone started talking at once. "What in the hell are you doing?" Suxie said. "This guy is going to eat us for breakfast!" I let the din go on for a minute, then held up my hands, flat over vertical, forming the letter T.

"Remember, you voted for it, so trust me," I said.

"A couple of things," I said. "First, I know how you feel, Ubi, but please don't piss this guy off unnecessarily. He's going to be mad enough as it is. The second is that, as they say, you have to make your own luck. Have you been listening, Leeram?" I said.

"You kidding? I haven't had this much fun since you got here."

"Do you know poker?"

"Does a bear befoul the woods?"

"Well, bears doing their business where nobody can see them and the finer aspects of card games don't have much of a link, but I take that to mean you know poker."

"Look, son, don't forget my head was on top of a pile of chips once. Believe me, I know poker."

With everyone's assistance, I wrote up an agreement that put our wager on paper to be signed by both sides. Essentially, it stipulated that if Calhoon won, we would agree to hand over any and all rights to our Fordlandia project, leave Brazil, and agree never to return. If we won, Calhoon and his business would agree to leave, relinquishing any claim on us and promising to forgo any future claims on us, and to leave the Amazonian rain forest in a pristine condition, whatever else they did. At Suxie's request, I also stipulated that if we won, the IMEX research vessel would be given to us. That was a stretch,

I knew, but something told me that these Texans were so sure they would win that it wouldn't matter.

The coconut was smiling away on a shelf overlooking the table when Calhoon and three of his men came in a few hours later with new decks of cards. He tossed a half-dozen on the table, all wrapped in cellophane, and a brand-new box of poker chips. "Choose any deck you like," he said. "Feel free to open one or two or all of them and check them out as much as you want." We did so, passing them around. I had a magnet and an ultraviolet light from our lab, passing them over each card to make sure that the face cards weren't implanted with anything that I couldn't see. I gave him the wager we had just finished putting on paper. When Calhoon reached the part about his boat, he stopped and looked up. "That boat's worth a lot of money," he said.

"Your company can afford it," I said. "This project is all we have. I thought you guys like to take a chance."

"OK, OK," he said, "It's in the pot, too."

"The cards look fine to me," I said. "How about you guys?" Pericles, Lisa, and the rest nodded and said that they looked clean as far as they could tell. "Do you want to play a couple of hands first for cash before we get serious with the unlimited pot—the really big one?" I said. "They're only two of us, so I guess it will be a short game. Also, does it matter what the chips are worth, considering that we both know what's at stake in the end? Any particular rules we need to talk about?"

"With just two of us, what kind of game do you want?" Calhoon said. "We can do Hold 'em if you want, but maybe just a game of five-card draw works best here." I agreed. Hold 'em was really designed for a crowd. "Another thing," he said. "All of you on your side of the table and all of us on the other." Most of us were already seated facing the wall, so we nodded. After a quick look around the room for hidden cameras, stopping at the shelf to pick up the coconut for a closer examination and putting it back in its place on top of Ubi's badge, Calhoon and his crew sat down in front of us. "Hell of a decoration," he said, chuckling. "What is that? A good luck charm? You'll need it."

"Might as well loosen up a little," Calhoon said. "How about the whites are worth one hundred and the colors go up by fifty each." His men began to laugh at such peanuts. "And in Brazilian reals! Hoo boy." Ignoring them, I cut the deck and Calhoon spread the cards in a fan, face down, and looked at me. We each took one; his was a ten of clubs, mine was a seven of hearts. "I'm the button," Calhoon said. "I'll deal."

"Ready, Leeram?" I asked silently, concentrating my gaze on the table. We bought in with a couple of white chips each, then Calhoon dealt five cards to himself and me. I picked up my hand and thrilled to see an ace, but then realized that the rest was pretty much garbage, not even a chance for a flush. "I'll take four," I said, and he grinned as I tossed everything but the ace away. He dealt me a ten, a five, another five, and a seven.

"Dealer takes two," he said, with a glint in his eye. "I'm in for a thousand, he said, pushing ten white chips into the pot.

"He's got you there," Leeram said. "He's holding two pairs—sixes and eights." I folded.

"My turn," I said, and shuffled the cards.

"You ain't going to last long at this rate," Calhoon chortled.

Four more chips in the pot and I dealt. This time I was luckier with a pair of aces. After Calhoon's request for two, I took three, a deuce, a nine, and another two. "Two pairs!" I said silently to Leeram.

"He's still got you, buddy," Leeram said. "Three tens." I was a little worried. We didn't have all that much cash. I folded again.

"The hell with this," I said. "Let's just go for the big one." Calhoon was amused.

"Anything you want, son," he said. He picked up the deck, shuffled, and offered it to me to cut. I split it three ways.

He dealt the cards, back and forth, one to him and one to me. When he picked up his hand his expression never shifted from the bland, somewhat bored looking mask that he had assumed from the start.

"Not bad," Leeram said. "A pair of fives and a couple aces." I was holding three of a kind, eights. "Dealer takes one," he said and couldn't keep a note of triumph out of his voice.

"Didn't help him at all," Leeram said.

"Hit me for two," I said. Calhoon dealt them, and it took every atom of my willpower to keep my face a mask. They were a pair of threes, giving me a full house. "Did you do this?" I silently asked Leeram.

"Maybe," he replied.

"How about throwing in that helicopter?" I asked.

"What have you got to match it?" Calhoon snorted, then he laughed. "Seeing as you're going to lose anyway, sure I will."

The moment came and we put our cards down on the table. Calhoon's eyes, hooded until that moment, flew open and he slammed his hat on the floor, standing up so suddenly that he knocked his chair over. It took him a few moments before he could get enough control over himself to speak. "You are very lucky," he said in a strained voice. "You are lucky twice. You not only won this game, but you are also lucky that I am a man of my word."

All I could think of to say was, "I'm sorry, but you dealt that hand."

For our part, we were stunned. We didn't even begin to talk until they left, but when they did, we were all over each other. Pericles went into the pantry and came out with a bottle of rum, pulling the cork as he returned.

Chapter 19

The next day, as Calhoon had promised she would be, the Gold Digger was tied to the Fordlandia dock, devoid of paperwork and equipment that belonged to IMEX. I marveled again at the strength of Calhoon's chivalric code. We climbed aboard and paced off the distance from bow to stern to get a rough measurement of her length: around ninety-five feet. We climbed to the bridge and found a signed bill of sale on the chart table, along with her Federal certificate of documentation papers naming the ship and her official registration number with the US Coast Guard. The stated sales price was one dollar and considerations. Alongside were similar papers for the helicopter—everything we needed to officially transfer ownership.

"Until I saw this," Pericles said, "I couldn't believe we actually pulled this off. I kept thinking there's got to be a hook somewhere."

"Calhoon's a man of his word," I said. "He may be many things we don't like, but you've got to give him that."

We were still in disbelief as we explored the little ship. Gold Digger had three decks, with the bridge on the top, sleeping cabins, a galley, a big cabin used as a meeting room on the middle deck, and what looked like a machine shop and lab on the main deck. Her engine room was below that, and when we descended into it, the low headroom indicated that she had a fairly shallow draft, perfect for river use. It was spotless, a sign of expert maintenance. Two big diesel engines and a separate, smaller genset to produce electricity took up most of the space, all surrounded by a maze of color-coded pipes and wiring. On its upper deck was the helicopter. Calhoon and his crew were nowhere to be seen. They must have taken one of the vessel's small craft back. Its absence was almost like a parting insult from a poor loser. A really poor loser wouldn't have given us the Gold Digger at all though, I had to admit.

"How are we going to operate this?" Pericles said, his arms waving it all in. It was an obviously practical question and one that hadn't come to us the night before in the midst of our almost delirious celebration. "We need a crew for the boat and a pilot for the helicopter."

"Why don't we trade the helicopter for the skipper?" Lisa asked. Everyone looked at her.

"Brilliant!" said Pericles.

"Who wants to go over and ask them?" I said. I was

beginning to feel that what we had just pulled off was so improbable that there had to be a catch somewhere. I wondered if the helicopter might have been one step over the line.

"I'll go," said Suxie. "I'll go with Ubirajara."

"I'll go too," I said.

With that, the three of us—and a coconut—climbed into our dugout and headed back across the Tapajos to Urucubituba. We arrived at the dock just in time to see a large yacht, her engines running, getting ready to cast off. Crewmembers were standing by the dock lines, ready to retrieve them when they were let go by men ashore. I hadn't seen this boat before, but she was bigger than the Gold Digger and a lot fancier. She must have arrived yesterday. Her name, we saw when we were close enough, was Gold Rush out of Galveston. We waved and Calhoon stepped out onto the bridge deck. "We need to talk!" I shouted. Calhoon disappeared back into the bridge and in a moment the dock lines were tightened again.

He reappeared. "What? Do you want to rub it in?" he asked.

"No," I replied, "but we had an idea that might be mutually beneficial."

He asked us reluctantly to come aboard. We tied the skiff to the boarding ladder and climbed to the vessel's teak deck.

"We want to make you an offer," Suxie said, standing next to Ubirajara.

Ubi looked directly into Calhoon's eyes and said in his best echoing voice, "I misjudged you when we first met. I know now you are a man of your word. Judging by your success in life, I also know that you are respected for that as much as you are for your success in business." He now had Calhoon's full attention. "I know that you regret so casually throwing that flying machine into the poker pot yesterday, and we have come to a decision that might help. We will give the machine back to you, if you release to us the boat captain and a month's salary for him."

Calhoon was silent for a moment, then he picked up a mike and said, "O'Malley, come up to the bridge." He turned to us and said, "I learned something. Never underestimate the strangest bunch of people I ever met." It was an odd moment; we couldn't find the words to answer him. A grammarian he was not, but somehow a kind of mutual thaw appeared between us.

"You, sir, are a gentleman," I said. "Maybe someday you'll be glad you did this."

He laughed, "That'll be a hell of a while!" Just then a middle-aged man in a golf shirt and khaki cargo shorts appeared. "Meet your new employers," Calhoon said. "Captain O'Malley, this is Mr. Greenbush, and this is...ahh..."

"Suxie Redbone and Ubirajara," I filled in.

"Yes," he said. "You don't need to take that little boat back to Fordlandia. I'll give you a lift." Towing our dugout astern, the Gold Rush was back at our dock in less than twenty minutes. The helicopter was transferred to a similar flight deck on the yacht, we handed back its bill of sale, and shook hands once again. Once it all had been accomplished and after a slightly awkward round of handshakes, the yacht turned downriver and disappeared around a bend.

"Looks like you're on our team now," Suxie said to the captain. Nonplussed is a word that is rarely used precisely, but in this case it fit Captain O'Malley to a T. He looked as though he had just stepped into a funny farm. But in the end, it seems, he was a man who could apparently land on his feet. Calhoon had obviously neglected to tell him anything about the sudden change in events, so we did. As we filled him in, his expression shifted from perplexity to amazement to out-and-out amusement.

"You won me in a poker game?"

"You're not the only one around here that that's happened to," I said.

"Let me get this straight," he said, in a Gulf Coast drawl. "I understand that I now work for you. Calhoon is a pretty impulsive guy, I think you know that by now. There's always something new around the corner, but this one beats all hell. What do you want from me?" Had we known ourselves what was going to happen, we explained, we would have hired a captain ourselves, maybe Primo Segundo, but here we were, and here he was. "OK, I get it," he said when we finished. I asked him if he could show us around our new possession, which he said he would be glad to do. Our previous, and only, tour was hasty and raised more questions than it answered.

"Do you realize that you also own about twenty thousand gallons of diesel fuel?" asked Captain O'Malley. "I don't even know if Calhoon realized that I topped off our fuel tanks before we left Manaus to come here. We paid about $4.50 a gallon in US dollars. I was going to give him a regular monthly inventory next week, but this, ah, transfer came up first. He never even asked me. That'll last for six months at the rate we were using it."

He took us on a tour from stem to stern, aloft and below, pointing out the vessel's systems and equipment. The galley was much better equipped than our own kitchen ashore, and for that matter, the living quarters were nicer, too. His cabin was spacious and right behind the bridge and the whole ship was air-conditioned, powered by the discreet generator that ran day and night, emitting a low thrumming sound that seemed to give the ship life. If we did nothing but stay at the dock with the genset running, the fuel we had on board would last a decade, he told us.

The little ship had been built to supply offshore oil rigs in the Gulf of Mexico before IMEX bought her, so she was somewhat ugly as ships go, but very functional, with a broad, flat, open deck aft and a big hydraulic crane for lifting heavy objects on and off. Some of the cargo space had been made into the living quarters we had so admired, but there was plenty left. We decided to use her at first to bring us supplies and deliver our produce to market. But I'm getting ahead of myself.

"I really hate the name," Lisa said; she rarely mentioned anything that we all agreed on so thoroughly. Even Captain O'Malley remarked that it had always bothered him too. The very first thing on our agenda was to change it, but to what? Everyone chimed in: the "Amazonian?" No. "Brown Water Queen?" Nah. That one might have been a sick joke.

"How about Soul of the Jungle?" Dean Knotwell suggested. She had been mostly silent as we explored the ship.

"Lord Jim?" Pericles offered.

That one was tempting and we almost went for it, until Suxie said, "Don't underestimate the people who live here. Once they realize we are referring to the heart of darkness, they might not be so amused." Her point was well taken. Naming boats can be a delicate thing. We didn't want something heavy-handed or vague enough to be meaningless. It couldn't be frivolous like the names of a lot of pleasure craft, yet it had to resonate. Suddenly it came to me.

"How about Araci," I said. "It's your name, Suxie, and it has a deep meaning in Tupi." We all agreed, including O'Malley when we explained it to him.

"Very appropriate," he said. "Araci it is, then. Easy to say on the radio, easily spotted at a distance. These are important considerations in a ship's name. Well, the paint's in the paint locker. Let's do it." We rigged a scaffold over her transom and within an hour, Araci announced herself to the world. The big IMEX logo was painted out. We would come up with a new one, we agreed. When we were done, Suxie went forward and, leaning over the bow, poured a bottle of cachaca into the water, sprinkling the last few drops onto the deck.

"I name you Araci," she said. "If we had champagne, I would have used it, but cachaca is of this place and it does her honor." Everyone applauded and we got to work cleaning up.

Almost from the start, after getting used to his sudden change in employers, Captain O'Malley began to fit neatly into our little gang. He was from Texas, a fact that changed our perceptions about the Lone Star state in a good way. As we got to know him a little better, he turned out to be an adventurer by nature, quick on his feet and in his mind. He took things at their face value and he was skillful, able to fix old plumbing, repair recalcitrant electronic navigational equipment, and could use an arc-welder. Most of all, he was something of a rebel and nothing made him happier than to side with an underdog. "Which is what you are," he said, when we had fully explained our Fordlandia project. We never thought of ourselves in those terms, probably because we had some formidable help. We wondered how to introduce him to Leeram and tell him about Ubi's origins. We decided that we would wait a little while. It would be too much too soon.

In the meantime, we had to get our second crop of aguaje, much bigger than the first one and now ready for harvest, to the market. It was hard to believe that so much time had passed since that first day of planting, the day after Leeram's head had been thrown into the river. We had originally planned to call for the Dom Afonso but now we had our own little ship and would immediately save freight costs. I telephoned our wholesaler in Santarem that the shipment was going to be gathered and delivered. The Araci, tied to our dock, awaited her first green job.

It took a full day to pick and load the harvest of aguaje fruit. Over the last week or so, we had built hundreds of wooden boxes to pack it in. They were all stenciled in black with the words "Fordlandia Project," so many that by the end of the day, several hours after sunset, they made a stack six deep covering almost every inch of Araci's deck. Captain O'Malley, who preferred his cabin ashore over our cottages to live in, turned in. He was going to rise an hour before dawn and wanted to get underway as soon as there was enough light. Lisa and I went aboard, along with Pericles, to accompany our cargo to market. At the last moment, Dean Knotwell joined us. "I want to see Santarem," she said. "I've been in the boonies long enough!"

We cast off at daybreak and the Araci headed downstream. Captain O'Malley coached us all in the ways the little ship was navigated. Steering was easy enough, and before long we were competent enough to handle all the ordinary challenges of seamanship that could arise on a river. The hardest part was knowing where the shoals were, the shallow bits. "Keep a sharp eye on the depth sounder, throttle back, and always steer offshore if you see less than ten feet of water under you," he said. We were all under notice to call him immediately if anything seemed out of the ordinary, or if we had any questions at all. When my turn at the helm came up, my watch, I settled into the routine quickly. I amused myself by channeling Mark Twain. It was a very different thing I was learning, to actively navigate a vessel on the river than to be a passenger, idly watching the scenery go by. After about an hour, or about halfway through my watch, I thought about Leeram, whose coconut was in its usual place at my side. "You there?" I asked. To my surprise, he answered immediately.

"Hell, yes, I'm here. Where else would I be with you doing such a crazy thing as this?"

"Come on now, Leeram," I said. "It's easy. Just like driving a car, only a lot slower."

"Never drove a car myself, but a lot of people get killed behind the wheel. Watch out, damn it!"

The last thing I expected was a back seat driver on this trip. "Come on, I need to concentrate."

Leeram was quiet for a while, then: "Son, I apologize. You are a very different person than you were back in Boston and as much as it amazes me to say this, I am too. I've gotta admit that you surprised me and you keep doing it almost every day. Just don't blame me for getting a little nervous."

At that time, Leeram and I were alone in the pilothouse, but Lisa came in and put her arm around my waist. "How's it going, Gilly," she asked, and gave me a kiss on the cheek. I was a very happy man at that moment. I could even sense Leeram's concerns dissipate slightly. We were silent for a few minutes, watching the shore go by. The last time we did that, we were more interested in each other, and the time before was at night, so much of the view was new to us.

My watch ended at noon. I was relieved at the helm by Dean Knotwell, who came into the bridge eating a sandwich. "You won't believe it," she said, "but O'Malley is a pretty good cook. He's got a big spread down in the galley. Go for it!" She didn't have to tell us twice; Lisa and I were down there in an instant, suddenly realizing how hungry we were. When we entered, the Captain was in front of the stove, a big iron range fueled by diesel oil, stirring the contents of a big iron pot. The pot and the stove were obviously a matched pair. They had been together for a long time. They reminded me of the same combination aboard the Dom Afonso, only with a Texan hovering over it this time.

"I started to do this out of self-defense," he said when he saw us come in. "Sea cooks are usually hired because no decent restaurant will take them on ashore and I got tired of eating canned stew and peas. This here is my special recipe, but you can't eat it now. It's for supper." The galley smelled like the kitchen in the Four Seasons. Our stomachs roiled in hungry desire. "Sandwich fixin's are over there," he said, nodding his head toward a sideboard. "I made the bread this morning." Thus inspired, we layered up our lunch and left the galley.

Outside on deck, we went forward and found a place to sit on a hatchcover, away from the sound and smell of the diesel exhaust. Aside from being in view from the helm, where Dean Knotwell was now stationed, we were alone. We ate silently for a while, taking in the Tapajos River and the now familiar scenery along its edges. The sky was overcast but it didn't seem that rain was on the way; it felt as though the weather was in a kind of suspended state, not too hot or cold, just in stasis, almost as it was described in Leeram's world. Suddenly a large creature jumped across our bow wake. "Isn't that a river dolphin like the ones we saw before?" Lisa asked. It jumped again. This time we could see it clearly; it was about nine or ten feet long, with that strange, long, thin clothespin beak and a lumpy head. It startled me with its size and sudden appearance, almost like a river ghost.

"Did you see that?" Dean Knotwell shouted from the bridge. Pericles came running up, but it was gone by the time he arrived.

"Damn!" he said. "Inia geoffrensis—the Amazon River dolphin. They feed on the bottom, generally, on crabs and benthic fish. Tell me when you see another."

We waited for another half hour or so, our elbows on the rail, but the dolphin didn't return. We went back to the galley to talk to Captain O'Malley. "Yeah," he said, as he was wiping the stove and countertops clean, his cooking chores done for the moment, "They seem to come in bunches. You just have to be in the right place at the right time. Some of the locals seem to think they're good eating, although I couldn't say myself. Never tried it."

Lisa shuddered at the thought of eating a dolphin. Even though I am pretty omnivorous myself, the idea of eating the flesh of that strange creature left me without even a hint of an appetite. Maybe if I was starving, I said. "Well, we're a long way from that," she said. "I'd die before I had to eat one." I had noticed that in the last few months, Lisa had become a lot less particular about her choice in food and, although what she just said didn't surprise me, I couldn't resist a teasing comment.

"When we first met, you were such a vegan. What happened? You eat fish now, and soup made with meat stock. I'll bet you've even had bacon."

She looked at me, her arms folded. Like a queen, she was not amused. "Gilbert," she said using my full name with some effect, "What I eat is my own business." I changed the subject.

"Our cargo—aguaje—is supposed to taste like ice cream if it's frozen. Why don't we try some?" We retrieved a couple of them from a nearby crate; they had tough brownish-purple outer skins, which took some work to peel. Underneath was a tender lemon-colored fruit. We cut it into strips about the size of Popsicles and put them in the ship's freezer for dessert that evening.

"That stuff is supposed to give women big booties," the Captain said. "I'm not kidding," he said. "They advertise it. When you get to town, you'll see it in the pharmacies. It's a Brazilian thing."

I looked at Lisa. "You're just about right. Maybe we shouldn't mess with Mother Nature."

Chapter 20

The first crop we had shipped to market aboard the Dom Afonso a few weeks before was much smaller and accompanied only by Pericles. This time I was going to see how it was done myself. We reached Santarem in half the time it took in the old birdcage that Lisa and I had traveled aboard a few months earlier. The rattle of our anchor chain woke us abruptly at 4:00 a.m., and shortly after, Captain O'Malley's voice came over the PA system. "OK, folks," he said, "I'm going to need you for docking duty. On deck in ten minutes." Fortunately, he didn't tell us to rise and shine or make some other attempt at humor; we were groggy and in no mood to laugh. After we had the dock lines ready, he retrieved the anchor and we headed into a vacant space at the dock, already filling fast. Latecomers would have to wait their turn until another boat left. We could hear generators powering refrigeration units and a rickety collection of overhead lights. Old stake-bed trucks and even donkey carts were already gathering to collect the day's produce coming in from the river. Once we were tied up to his satisfaction, O'Malley called us all into the galley where he had a pot of coffee already made. "Figured you all would need this," he said. "Made it while you were getting your butts out of the sack." Now completely awake, we went back out on deck, mugs in hand, and saw that the sky was just a little lighter on the horizon. I thought of the old coffee shop in another life, and remembered the smell of my old apartment in the morning, so distant now.

As it grew lighter, buyers from the market wholesale companies began walking around inspecting the produce that had arrived overnight. Our own buyer came by eventually and began opening random boxes, taking an aguaje fruit from each one, usually well below the top layer. He opened them, tasting a bit of each, then after a minute or two said he would take the lot. "Give you twenty reals a kilo," he said. We looked at each other; it didn't sound like a lot. We had about three hundred kilos on board, and when we spoke to him on the phone a few weeks earlier, he said we should be able to get at least thirty, a promise that I reminded him of immediately. "That was for better fruit than this," he retorted.

"What do you think, Leeram?" I asked.

"Bullshit. Tell him you'll sell it to somebody else. He just thinks you are a gringo and don't know the ropes around here. The stuff is perfectly fine and a lot fresher than most of the crap around here."

"Look," I said to the buyer, who was rocking back and forth on his heels with his hands behind his back, looking down at us through a remarkably bushy mustache, "I'm going to go down this pier and find another buyer unless you give us forty reals." I put an edge into my voice.

"Impossible!" he said. "Go right ahead." A long moment of silence followed as he stood there. I silently implored Leeram's help—his nut was in his satchel by my side. Suddenly the buyer's disdainful expression softened into a look of faint concern, then he folded, saying "OK, thirty. It's a deal."

"Did you do anything?" I asked Leeram. No answer, then I had a mental image of Leeram shaking his head. I reminded myself to ask Pericles if he had run into this kind of thing the last time.

The buyer called his bank to transfer the sum, nine thousand reals, to our bank (which I verified on the phone). Then he turned to his crew and motioned them over to start unloading the cargo into his refrigerated trucks. I stood by with a clipboard, counting each one to make sure as many came off as went on the day before. The others all went back aboard to eat breakfast, while I had to make do munching on aguaje. We had made roughly the equivalent of $4,500 net for the trip, more than twice our profit last time. At this rate, we would be in the black a lot sooner than we had imagined. More than that, it was the first concrete justification of a whim that had started out in my mind as nothing but a ploy with an ulterior motive to get Leeram back. I felt quietly, but deeply, satisfied. My old life was so far in the past that it might have been lived by somebody else.

"Hope you don't get a big butt," said Leeram.

"Don't you wish you had a butt at all."

Finally, the Araci's deck was bare, save the scraps of dunnage and bits of aguaje, which we broomed over the side. It was time to explore the town. "I'll stay aboard. I've seen the place a million times," O'Malley said. "Take your time, I've got plenty to do."

We hailed a taxi and asked the driver to show us around. "Si, si," he said, getting out and opening the doors, "Por favor—get in." We folded ourselves into his battered Nissan and it was underway almost before our doors had completely closed. Lisa and I had been here before, but we didn't mind seeing it all again; it was even better the second time around, and we could point things out to the others.

Santarem was unlike Manaus in many ways. It was much smaller for one, but they are both river towns, and river towns have a completely different look during the dry season, the one we were in now. Lower river water levels leave spectacular sandy beaches, giving the shoreline an almost Caribbean feel. The conjoining streams of the Amazon and Tapajos rivers were so wide that they almost seem like an island-filled ocean at their junction. Our driver, Manuel, was a non-stop talker obviously calculating that sheer volume of words would inflate his tip. We learned that Santarem was the second largest city in the State of Para, and that farms growing soybeans and Brazil nuts were everywhere. Even the old staple, rubber, was still being harvested and sold. All that information was interesting enough but we told him that we especially wanted to take a look at the big soybean processing plant, owned by an American company, Soy Products International, Ltd. Soybean farming had made many fortunes for some people but was one of the causes of brutal deforestation in the Amazon, along with cattle ranching and mining. SPI's processing factory, gigantic and foreign-looking, stood like a vast, haphazard goiter on the landscape. "Just wait," the cabbie said excitedly, "they are finally going to build the highway from here right through to Cuiabra!" He was delighted that another wide road was going to slice through the rain forest and bring unimagined prosperity to his town.

Not so Pericles and Dean Knotwell. "Cuiabra is a big city in the exact center of Brazil," Pericles said. "They tried to do it in the 1970's, but they gave up partly due to objections from environmentalists even then, but mostly because it was just too costly. If they ever do built it, you can kiss the rain forest goodbye."

Manuel continued along the riverfront and up to a high point called the Mirante do Tapajos, where we could better see the knife-sharp delineation between the muddy Rio Amazon and the clear Rio Tapajos. It looked like cream was being poured on top of Kahlua in a clear glass, the demarcation lasting for miles, as though the two big rivers were repelled at the idea of blending with each other. The brown water contained organic remains from the vast floor of the Amazon basin and was almost alive itself. From there, we descended into the town itself, a sleepy place and lacking in many tourist attractions but quite pleasant, possibly due to that lack. We stopped for a few minutes at our bank to introduce ourselves and deposit the check, then went to the open-air market to buy groceries and things on Suxie's wish list for the trip home. Ben and Seth had asked for twenty 12-volt marine batteries, among other things. I arranged with a local boatyard for their delivery to the dock and with a farming supply business for the seeds and other supplies we needed. Not far away was the Centro Cultural Joao Fona, a small museum, which Lisa and I had been through earlier but this time found many things we hadn't seen before. Artifacts from thousands of years of human habitation were there, things left by Suxie and her grandfather's ancient ancestors. We all determined to get them to visit soon.

Finally, laden with supplies and gifts, we boarded Araci and prepared for our trip back upriver. Dean Knotwell had bought a selection of souvenirs, Lisa purchased a bowl carved out of jatoba, or Brazilian cherry, with a beautiful, deep mahogany color for Suxie, and she also found a very young blue and gold macaw in a bamboo cage. "It's only a baby," she said. "I don't even know if it's a boy or a girl."

I said that it would probably be better off with us than in some pet shop way up north. Pericles and I wandered around but didn't see anything that caught our eye and finally settled on a few cases of Brahma Chopp (the light but tasty Brazilian pilsner that I first had in the Casa Lugar Perfieto) and a case of decent champagne to be delivered dockside.

We cast off just at dusk and turned Araci's bow back upriver. Our ETA for landing in Fordlandia was in about twenty-four hours, since we were heading against the current this time and steaming slowly to save fuel. Our watches at the helm passed quickly, navigation aided at night by a powerful searchlight overhead, which we could control from the bridge, shining it on flotsam and sandbars near the riverbanks. I wondered how Samuel Clemens would feel about modern GPS systems and depth sounders giving him his constant and exact location. He was a practical man, I assumed, and after a short dismay at the loss of old skills and a diminishment of yet another challenge, he probably would have been happy to have those little blinking instruments. We also had a good moon that night, making it bright enough to see that the dolphins were still with us, playing in our wake.

The next morning they were still there with us as we stood at the bow, coffee in hand. They swam effortlessly, matching our speed. I had the feeling that they could easily accelerate ahead of us if they wanted to. It was odd, because none of us could remember such an escort when we first arrived. One of them had mottled skin almost like liver spots that set it apart and an abnormally large dome on its head. It kept a slight distance from the larger school, almost as though it was being shunned, yet not entirely excluded. Its ludicrously long, flesh-colored bill was kept tightly shut. By the next morning, it was the only one left. It followed us all the way to Fordlandia and only disappeared after we had tied up at the dock.

We were met by a crowd of waving Fordlandians, who had already heard the news of our successful voyage. Suxie and Ubi were waiting for us in front and took our dock lines, as Captain O'Malley gently eased Araci against the pier. "Sounds like you did all right," Suxie said when we stepped ashore. Ubi stood next to her, arms folded over his chest and a big smile on his face. Back in the crowd and making their way through it were Ben and Seth, also grinning. It had taken them a little longer to come down the hill from the lab.

After giving everyone their gifts and the batteries and seeds to Ben and Seth, we headed straight for the office, accompanied by the Mayor and Suxie. There, we distributed the cash proceeds and allocated payments to the farmers and a token sum to Suxie, who insisted that she didn't want it right now, but we felt that she should eventually be paid back for her investment. After much jocularity, we scotch-taped a ten real bill to the office wall. "That'll do for now," she said.

We had a big dinner that night to celebrate. Ubirajara

was at the head of the table, a place that he had assumed from the moment he appeared; it was his land and his table, we all agreed. He even taught our cook some tasty recipes of his own, some that he brought with him from the past. Even Captain O'Malley, a picky eater unless he had personally cooked the food, loved it. We opened the champagne, which had been on ice for the last hour or so, and toasted all around. "Saude!" we said and lifted the bubbly to our lips.

Ubirajara smiled broadly and said, "Nothing like this where I just came from. I think I had it once when I worked for Mr. Ford, though."

I asked Leeram whether anyone drank in his universe. "Not exactly," he said. "We don't get thirsty here, but I do miss an occasional slug of cachaca. When I was on your side, I only turned down a drink when I didn't trust the bastard who offered it." The conversation went on about our trip, the museum, and Lisa's parrot, whose cage now hung from the wall in a prominent place. We had a mascot, but what to call it? After naming Araci, we had great confidence in our abilities. Suggestions abounded: Beaky, Cosmo, Captain Sully (that one from O'Malley), Cracker, Lola (I kind of liked that one), Pink Floyd, Tin Tin, and so on for several minutes; the champagne had begun to work its magic and the names became more bizarre: Zolaster, Master of Disaster, Angry Bird, and so on.

Finally, Lisa said, "I bought the bird, so I get to name

it. I will call it Green Flash." We all looked at each other questioningly.

"I like it," said Captain O'Malley. "The green flash is what you see just as the evening sun sets below the horizon at sea. It's very rare because the conditions have to be just right, but it's spectacular when it happens."

Done! We all said. "How do you do, Flashy!" we said, raising our glasses in a toast to the bird. When we find out if it's a boy or a girl, the name will still fit, we agreed.

Chapter 21

During a lull in my work, soon after we got back from that trip to Santarem, I decided to go back across the river to revisit the Carvahlos in Urucubituba. I would have brought Lisa, but she was busy. "Next time," she said. "Give them my love." I put the book I bought for them in Santarem in the bag next to Leeram's coconut, climbed into the dugout, and set out across the river. I had come to prefer it over the aluminum skiff we had used before; it was much more appropriate for the Tapajos.

Suddenly, before I had gone more than a dozen yards, I saw a big, pink dolphin break the surface right next to me. It startled me. For an instant it seemed as though we would collide. It swam for a while almost within arm's reach and parallel to my course, rolling on its side just enough for its near eye to make contact with mine. I recognized it almost immediately—it was the one that had followed us all the way upriver from Santarem just a few days before, the one with the liver spots. Suddenly I heard Leeram in the closest thing to a shout that a coconut is capable of: "Hey, Greenbush, I don't know if I can believe this myself, but hang onto your hat!" At first I thought that the big creature was going to try to attack us and I took an oar to defend myself, jabbing at the dolphin's head.

"Ow!" the dolphin said. "Put that thing back, you're hurting me! I just want to talk with you." Its beak was scissoring open and shut and I was astounded; at first it seemed stranger that he was mouthing words with a long, pink beak than it was that he was talking at all. It wasn't unlike an LSD trip that I took when I was a lot younger, and I knew I hadn't dropped acid for years.

"Who are you?" I asked.

"Henry Ford," he replied. "I understand you wanted to meet me."

Perhaps it was because I had become a little more used to the bizarre in this place, or because just spending time in the Amazon basin itself unhinges the mind, but I was not so shocked as to fall overboard. I pulled in the oar, gathered my wits, and croaked "W-w-what?"

"I've been following you ever since I heard you took over my plantation," he said, in a squeaky but audible way, his lower beak splashing the water everywhere.

"But...but you're a dolphin!" I said, stating the obvious, still about as gobsmacked as I could be. Leeram was one thing, and even Ubi's resurrection was barely comprehensible but I could accept it. A big, pink river dolphin with a large sensory organ on top of its head, claiming to be Henry Ford was another, well, kettle of fish altogether. I had to try to make sense of things.

"But you died in Michigan sixty or seventy years ago and I know you never came here when you were alive," I said. "Why now?" In order to keep what was left of my sanity, I had to accept what he had just said.

"I know this might appear to be a little unusual," Henry Ford said. "But I can explain. Bear with me for a while." I had a crazy thought of taking my clothes off, but he said, "No, bear with me, stay where you are. Just listen. After my death, I found myself in a world that wasn't all that different from the old one, but with one big difference. It is infinite. We all go to it. Problem is that they haven't really found a way to deal with boredom, and boredom is my bugaboo." Not a bad bumper sticker, I thought, my mind wobbling like a dreidel running out of momentum. I turned to the coconut.

"Leeram," I said, "can you tell me what in the hell is going on?" I asked, realizing that I was having a conversation with two dead people. It was giving me a headache.

"I haven't really told you everything about what happened on my side. Your fishy friend over there is, in fact, Henry Ford. I have to say he was not a friend of mine when he was here; we had a couple of run-ins. He can be pretty stubborn and was told by the authorities that he could never be allowed to cross back over the way

Ubirajara did. He is a pretty inventive guy, though, and I guess he managed to find a way despite it all."

"Damned right I did," Ford said, when I told him what Leeram had just said to me. "Don't let your jungle friend give you the wrong impression," said Ford. "I like to finish what I start, even if I can't finish looking like a human. I always liked a challenge and this is exactly what I needed. That other place was driving me crazy. I found a good lawyer over there, and he turned up a loophole, so here I am in Fordlandia at last. Don't worry, or as you moderns might say, don't freak out; I want to work with you."

So there I was, sitting in a boat in the middle of the Rio Tapajos, talking to a coconut and a dolphin that didn't like each other. "I get it," I said to the dolphin, "but I don't see how much help we can give you right here in the middle of the Tapajos."

"Easy," Henry Ford replied. "Just build a tank for me ashore. I'll tell you where. Connect it to a canal lock so I can get back and forth."

"Easy?" I said.

"Indeed. Once you put your mind to it, anything is possible," said the marine mammal who invented mass production.

Leeram was silent while Henry went on, but finally he couldn't control himself any longer. "What's he saying? That's the wackiest thing I ever heard!" A thought teased me. Wacky? Perhaps not so much.

"You know," I said to both of them, "we could do such

a thing. The Araci has a fully equipped machine shop and we can get supplies we need from downriver or even in Fordlandia itself. First, though, I've got to figure out a way to introduce you without causing permanent mental damage to my friends ashore."

The dolphin agreed, clapping its forefins for emphasis and even Leeram went along with it, grudgingly. "They're used to me," he said. "I can help, even if I have to hold my nose." I told Ford to stay close, then turned the boat around, and headed back to the dock. I would have to visit the Carvahlos later. "Can you hear me if I called you?" I asked. He nodded, throwing water everywhere again.

After I landed, I called an emergency meeting and when we were all gathered in the Araci's paneled conference room, I turned to Captain O'Malley and said, "We haven't told you this yet, because the time just didn't seem right, but all along we have had some, ah, help from unusual sources. We were going to mention it sooner but we didn't want to startle you."

"Are you going to tell me how you bamboozled Calhoon?" he asked, getting right to the point.

"That's part of it," I said. "I think you'll find that we've had some assistance that will benefit you as much as it has us. There is something very special about this location," I went on. "As you probably already know, the Amazon forest, this entire place, is not what it appears to be. We have been getting advice from some very unusual sources;

I'd like to introduce one of them." I took Leeram's coconut from its valise. O'Malley burst out laughing.

"I get it!" he whooped, tears running down his cheek. "Just be happy and everything will go your way!"

"Not exactly," I said. "Leeram, tell him about yourself."

"I think you are forgetting something," Leeram said. "I can only talk to you; it's not like the old days when you had my actual head." I had gotten so used to the coconut that I momentarily forgot.

"Ubi," I said next, beginning to worry that I might have stumbled hugely. I would have to pull something out of my hat or look like an idiot. "Ubi, can you tell the Captain who you are?"

Ubirajara stood up to his full, impressive height, walked over to O'Malley and put his hand on the Captain's shoulder. O'Malley jumped as though stung by static electricity and he stopped laughing. "I was born in your year 1865," Ubirajara said. "Don't worry, I won't harm you, but I watch out for my granddaughter and her friends. I want to be here when what they are doing comes about." His voice was underlayed by frequencies inaudible to human hearing and it carried absolute conviction. O'Malley looked around the cabin as though he was trying to escape, but then Ubi smiled. "Don't be afraid," he said. "These people will become rich and so will you if you stand by us."

When he wanted to, Ubi could sell ice to an Eskimo.

I explained the relationship between Suxie and

Ubirajara, and then went on to more fully describe what was going on. "Ubi isn't the only one who is helping us. How do you think I won this boat in the poker game?" I held up Leeram's coconut and explained its provenance. O'Malley seemed dubious, which I reminded him was a natural reaction for anyone, but urged him to withhold judgment until I gave him information he could trust absolutely. "For now," I said, "Give me the benefit of the doubt." Then I turned to the rest of them and said, "I have something to tell you that you don't know, either. Come out on the deck."

Henry Ford was already there, swimming in circles and looking up at us. Even Ubi was impressed. He had a way of grasping things immediately and recognized who the dolphin was. Now we had three from the other side, counting Leeram. "By the time I left your company," Ubi said to Henry Ford, "I began to realize that it was not altogether a good thing for our people. Nothing did so much damage to this land than your American business landing among us like a bomb. I didn't know this at the start, and while I worked for you, the money and the new world deluded me. I learned to read and educated myself, which never would have happened if I stayed with my tribe in the forest. I owed you that debt, but I have paid it in full." The others all looked at him as though he had lost his marbles.

Ford peered up at him. "I think I remember your name in the reports," he said. "Nice to meet you in the flesh.

Especially in the flesh." Ubi nodded reservedly. Henry paused for a moment, then continued: "I can understand how you feel about me. I learned a great deal after I passed on, and know now all too well where I went off the road. I was too cocksure, too dependent on my own ideas to imagine that others could be right and me wrong, but you can't grow that way, can you?

"I always knew," he continued, "I had let Pandora out of the box when I built that factory on the River Rouge," he said. "I thought I could somehow limit the damage by building an ideal city for people and I tried many times. The last one was right here, and now and then I thought that if I had come down personally in those days, I might have made it work. Well, here I am, even if it has to be in the body of a dolphin. The other choices I had were a lot worse, believe me. I want to work with you in any way I can."

We were all quiet for a long moment. I took what he just said at face value, as did Lisa, Suxie, and Pericles. Dean Knotwell, Ben, and Seth were a little more questioning. Captain O'Malley, not having had as long an exposure to our little cabal, sat down heavily on a nearby crate and said, "I need a drink."

It was Ubi who broke the silence. "We have made the same journey," he said to Ford, "and I can hear the truth in your voice because of that. You have a chance to put things back together that your company tore apart, and I will work with you." We all started to talk to each other at once. Suxie went into the galley and emerged with a big glass of rum, handing it to O'Malley.

"Take this," she said. "I can imagine that it must be a shock for you, but we are used to the twilight zone by now. You aren't, but you will be." The captain emptied it without lowering the glass.

He coughed, wiped a tear from his eye with his sleeve, and said, "I have always been sane. I will always be sane in the future, but right now I am not too sure about that. I've gotten to know you all and like you. To be sane I have to believe you, so I will, even if it kills me." He rose, walked to the rail, and said, "Good morning, Mister...err...Ford, it's a pleasure to meet you."

"Likewise," said the dolphin. "Now let's build that tank."

Chapter 22

That evening our conversation at the table was all about wormholes. Captain O'Malley, still blinking his eyes at the revelations we presented him with earlier, needed to be brought up to speed. He was teeter-tottering between belief and absolute rejection of us. We knew we had to convince him soon or we would lose him.

"Everyone knows about the wormholes," I said, then realized that most people didn't at all. "They are anomalies in space and time," I explained to O'Malley, and also for Ben's and Seth's hearing, "that some think of as just theoretical, but here, we know the truth. They are very tiny flaws in the *brane* — the membrane — between parallel universes. In this case it's the one between this one and the one we pass over to when we die. It's like the way an osmotic barrier keeps salt on one side but allows water to flow to the other. Here, our physical bodies are the salt, but the most important part of us is the water." I nodded toward Ubirajara. "Wormholes, or traversable wormholes," I said, "are very scarce. My friend Leeram, who you see here in the form of a coconut, lives in a parallel universe and communicates with me frequently through a kind of wormhole that only allows the passage of thought, but there is another kind that allows a physical being to pass through. That kind is the kind Ubirajara and the dolphin came through. Ubi, can you tell the Captain a little more about it?"

Ubirajara put his hands on the table and looked straight into O'Malley's eyes. "You are still alive, or as I think of it now, in your first existence, so you have no way to completely understand what I will try to explain. I will use analogies. Once you go through it, from your existence to the second one, the chances of getting back are almost impossible without a lot of help," he said. "What I did took a lot of help, not only from Leeram, who is especially talented, but from others too. I took a big chance, but coming back here to Fordlandia and being with my granddaughter Araci made it worthwhile. It is impossible to describe exactly, but it was somehow like crossing a long rope bridge over a steep canyon—so steep you can't see the bottom. The rope is frayed and keeps breaking underfoot and I only just saved myself by grabbing pieces that still held. When I finally made it to this side, it all seemed to fall away in back of me and I knew I could never retrace my steps.

"When I had a chance to rest and recover, I had a new

body, or should I say it was my old body in its prime. I think it is most likely indestructible," he said.

"But you are a human being," O'Malley said. "What about Ford?"

"I crossed a bridge. He swam and was put back together differently. You'll have to ask him about that. One thing I'm pretty sure about," he added, "he's probably indestructible too. You've got to be bulletproof to go through a wormhole."

O'Malley tilted back in his chair and put his hands in back of his head, eyes closed. Then he straightened up and put them back on the table with a slap. "OK," he said. "People have called me a little nuts at times, and maybe they're right. But I believe you. I'm in."

The next day we went to work building an "office" for the dolphin not far from our own, but a little closer to the river. The tank was sided with three heavily braced wooden walls about six by twenty by thirty feet, over a concrete slab. Before we filled it with water, Lisa painted rustic scenes on it of nineteenth century farms and fields, oxen and wagons. She was a pretty decent artist and the painting looked good underwater. The tank side facing toward the river had a heavy glass panel letting in a nice vista of the river to counter the rural depiction behind it. We arranged chairs and a table outside the glass for us and, thanks to Ben and Seth, had a jury-rigged two-way speaker system installed for meetings. To allow the dolphin free passage back and forth from the Tapajos, we dug a canal with a couple of locks that he could operate with his beak, letting himself in and out of the river when he wanted to in order to catch food. "It would help a lot," he said, "if you could get someone to build fish traps nearby so I don't have to hunt so far." Water came from a well we dug, using a drill we scrounged in the village. Ben, Seth, and Pericles had it running in no time. The water was pumped from the well into the tank and the overflow filled the locks sufficiently for them to be used two or three times a day. When we were finished, Henry swam into his new office, eager to look around. He explored every corner, pausing appreciatively in front of Lisa's painting. "Reminds me of my youth, although I hated that old farm," he said. We asked him how he liked his new office. "It'll do," he said. "It'll do." He swam for another minute or two and then said, "The water is a bit minerally, but it has a nice herbaceous finish."

At the table one evening, Ben started the conversation. "I know you haven't heard a report from us for a long while. We didn't want to talk about our experiments until we felt we had something to talk about, but I think we have discovered something important." Seth added that it might be premature even now, and we shouldn't jump to conclusions, "But what it is," said Ben, "is that we think we can produce electricity in commercially viable amounts from plants. Reed grass, to be precise." We had long known that they were working in that general direction. They mentioned it to us months ago, but everyone assumed that, even if it was possible, they were talking about the distant future. We were all silent for a moment.

"I knew you were going to use those batteries for that," I said. "I didn't want to ask you anything until you felt ready to tell us."

"Yeah, we had been using a few old car batteries from around here, but we needed an array of big, deep-cycle batteries to really make a practical demonstration. We plan to set them up tomorrow. If it works, we will hook this house up to the growing area and use it in our experiment."

We were quiet for a moment, thinking of what the two young men had just said. We had all known about their project for months, but somehow it seemed unreal, not frivolous, but just one of those pure research things scientists do.

"Haven't people tried this before?" I asked.

"They have, but never here in the Amazon," Seth replied. "There is something about this place that makes it work. Ubirajara has shown us techniques that no one else knows anything about. He also recommended that we use this kind of grass, which proved to be the best producer." Ubi sat, smiling, at his place at the head of the table. "We managed to charge a 12-volt automotive battery with current from an array of grasses aligned in rows of connected trays. We've known about the potential for this for a couple of years," Seth continued. "Ben and I read the literature on it back in grad school. The research that others have done was positive, but the electricity that they generated then was much too weak for any commercial use." What he and Ben had done, he said, was to essentially hack the photosynthesis process. "Normally," he explained, "plants convert photons from the sun into electrons, which then are used to create sugars that nourish the plant. In a natural state, 100 percent of those electrons are used in this conversion process with the help of thylakoids in the plant. They are kind of the heart and lungs of the plant," he added. "We developed a strain of reed grass that doubles the amount of electrons captured, making enough to nourish the plant but leaving enough surplus to bleed off into a storage device—the batteries. Without the availability of batteries to collect the excess electrons, the plants become very unstable, which is why they don't exist in nature."

They had to use an inverter, when they hooked up our house, to convert DC to AC, which was a necessary evil as it wasted some of the plant-generated power, but all our appliances were designed for 110-volt alternating current. The plants produced enough during daylight hours to keep the batteries fully charged by nightfall, so they generated more than enough power to last day and night.

"But they are very hardy when they are connected to the batteries," Ben added. "Essentially, they are about fifty times as efficient as a standard solar panel and a lot cheaper to put together."

"And this is just the beginning," Seth added. "If we were

to use all the land that is now used to grow soybeans, we could power all of Latin America."

The next step was to plant the grass on a larger scale, but we needed more. This time, leaving just Pericles to keep Henry Ford company, the rest of us took the Araci upriver to the little tributary that Ubirajara and I found a few months earlier. The water there was still too thin for the big boat to enter, so we dropped anchor and launched the skiff and the dugout, loaded with buckets and shovels. We made dozens of trips back and forth from the clearing, each time bringing back more grass until we had about as much as we could handle safely. Back in Fordlandia we re-ploughed the field we had used to grow the aguaje—the first field we had cultivated after we arrived, and transplanted the shoots we had collected. The Fordlandian farmers were perplexed, to say the least. "Grass?" they said. "Tu estas loco!" when they learned what we were doing. We tried to explain that it was an experiment, but all we succeeded in doing was making things worse. We realized that their estimation of us had been lowered by a notch or two.

It would take three or four months, at least, for the plants to mature to a point where they could produce anything; we would just have to wait. In the meantime, other crops were getting ready to harvest, and the Araci would make several more trips downriver to market, returning with cash. One trip was all the way to Manaus. That one was especially profitable and helped a little to repair the damage our reputation suffered with the locals. They still shook their heads about the grass, though.

When weather permitted, we had taken to eating our evening meal at the table outside of the tank, where we could more easily talk to Ford. One of us, I think it was Pericles, suggested that we could sell electricity if we had an excess of it. We could become an Amazonian power plant. "Aren't we getting ahead of ourselves?" Suxie said. "This is a communal farm. We are here to help the indigenous tribes, in case anyone has forgotten."

"No doubt," said Henry Ford. "But the genie is about to fly out of the lamp you crafted here. If you want to protect your people, you are going to have to control it."

"Mr. Ford is right," said Ben. "Seth and I have a proprietary interest in this process. We've already talked about protecting it." They wouldn't be the first academics to take financial advantage from their discoveries, I thought.

"I agree with Ford," I said. "We don't have to let this take over Fordlandia, but we can certainly use the process elsewhere. How about all those soybean fields in Belterra?"

"The forest has already been cut down there, and in a lot of other places too. We wouldn't have to compound the damage," said Pericles.

Lisa thought for a moment, then said: "Well, we could always let some of it grow back."

"Put first things first," said Ford. "In this case, you have to control the process. You need to own it. Once you have complete control, you can either license it out or run a power plant yourselves. I recommend the former. I also recommend a good patent attorney." A long silence followed.

"You're probably right," I said, when his words became clear. Looking at Ben and Seth, I asked how far along they were in putting their discovery down in writing.

"Give us a couple of weeks and we will have something you can use," they said.

"When you do, and if our bank account can justify it, I'll make a trip back home and get the legal protection Mr. Ford is recommending. We can figure out where to go from there." As soon as I said that, the coconut became fully awake.

"We'll come too," the two scientists said together. The fleeting thought occurred to me that until that moment, I had mentally referred to them as the "two young graduate students." No longer.

"It's really up to what we can afford right now," I said, looking at Suxie, who for obvious reasons had assumed the job of project treasurer. She said she would take a look and tell us how much travel expense we could manage, if any. She was still a little dubious of the direction things were taking.

It only took them a week to do the paperwork. They wrote it up as part of their larger article to be sent to the Journal of Agricultural Science for peer review. "We'll hold off on sending it until we get the green light from a patent attorney," they said. "It will be the basis for our PhD thesis."

Back in the mundane world of ordinary farming, the Araci arrived after her last market trip with a healthy profit and Suxie decided, reluctantly, that enough could be spared to send two of us back to the United States to retain a good patent attorney. "But you'll need us if he has any questions," Ben said. I replied that we had good telephone and online connections and that would have to do for now. Lisa wanted to go also. Suxie finally stepped in.

"Maybe in a few months," she said, "but right now all we can afford is one round-trip ticket. You can't be staying at very expensive hotels, either," she added, looking at me. Since the Araci wouldn't be going downriver for another month, I booked passage on the next river ferry, along with my hammock and backpack. Needless to say, Leeram was excited.

"I'm used to things taking forever over on my side," he said, "but I thought you would never get out of this dump."

"You can thank Mr. Ford for it," I said. "Him and the two kids. And hold your water, I've got a lot to do."

Chapter 23

My decision to go back to the states alone, and with a certain coconut, was not popular, especially with Lisa. Suxie's insistence on the bottom line was the only defense I had against rebellion. "When this is over, we'll go on a vacation that you will never forget," I said to her. I didn't want to leave her behind any more than she wanted to go with me, but at that time we just didn't have the money. Leeram didn't cost a cent; as far as the airlines went, he was a snack I brought aboard for the flight. Ben and Seth put the best face on their disappointment at being left behind, despite the unarguable fact that they knew more than any of us about the technicalities I was going to have to present to our patent attorney, whoever he or she might be. We had, after all, the Internet to communicate through. I knew I was the best generalist in our little group and could lean on them for the details.

"What the hell," Seth said, "We have a lot to do here. Might even have some surprises for you when you get back. They both admitted that they were reluctant to leave the most fascinating place they had ever been, and right in the middle of the most fascinating discovery in their lives. Suxie doubted that she would ever leave Fordlandia, so she was the least affected. Pericles, though, was beginning to think about returning to academia; I asked him to hang in just a little longer.

As for Dean Knotwell, it was all about Ubirajara. "I could spend a lifetime learning from him." We had all noticed how she acted around Ubi. She would jump to her feet whenever he came into the room and sometimes was at a loss for words when he spoke to her. "I don't really know what it is," she said to Suxie once. "There is an old song, 'Bewitched, Bothered, and Bewildered,' which pretty well describes the way I feel around him." She, too, had no desire to leave Fordlandia very soon.

I made flight reservations from Santarem to Brasilia and booked a connection directly to Dulles International, as well as a room in a hotel nearby. I boarded the first passing riverboat rather than taking the Araci, which would have burned more fuel than it was worth without a load of produce to pay for it. When it came into view, everyone came down to the dock to say goodbye. Earlier I had a chat with the dolphin, who said he was glad he didn't have to go as he hated flying. "I only went up a few times in my company's tri-motor. It was noisy and it made me sick."

I was used to the river trip by now and it was uneventful, if mildly annoying. I had no one to share a hammock space with. The flight to Brasilia was like the one up, bumpy and sleepless, but when I boarded the big air-conditioned Boeing to Washington, DC, with its endless rows of seats, I got my first taste of the life I had left so long ago. I realized, as the attendant came down the aisle, how vast the gap was between my new and old lives. It was exciting and sad at the same time. My emotions were unsorted and I couldn't quite get them to fit together. My musing was interrupted by Leeram, who wanted to know if the stewardess was good-looking. "They are called flight attendants," I told him, "but don't worry, I'm not going to put you in the overhead luggage compartment."

"You forget that it's just a coconut," he said testily. "I don't give a shit where you put it."

We landed in Dulles in the late afternoon, and as I waited for the flight crew to let us out, I watched the passengers as they slowly unraveled from their seats in front of me and slowly, slowly inched toward the doors. My mind was still in the Amazon and the artificial air in the plane seemed monochromatic, lifeless compared to the rain forest. I couldn't wait to get out. The crowd at the baggage carousel seemed somnambulistic, or maybe it was merely the world of the living.

After my backpack was finally disgorged and clicked its rocking way to me, I climbed on a shuttle bus and checked in at the hotel. I decided to splurge and opened the minibar, popped open two little bottles of scotch, added some ice, then sat down at the desk in front of the Yellow

Pages, looking for patent attorneys. It didn't take long to realize that that was a foolish way to find one. I might as well just throw a dart at the book. I needed advice; I knew that whoever I picked had to have a good knowledge of electrical engineering, but would it be even possible to find one who also knew something about agriculture?

Since I knew I was going to have to visit the US Department of Agriculture anyway, to hand-deliver our latest grant progress report (written by Dean Knotwell, who normally mailed them in), I decided to start there in the morning. I finished the drink and went downstairs to the bar for a nightcap, only realizing how tired I was after I got there. She had written ATTN: Mr. Llewellian Bean, Assistant Deputy of Grant Administration, Agricultural Research Service, Division of Sustainable Agricultural Systems, USFDA, the pinpointed source of our grant money. I would call him in the morning. I barely remembered falling into bed.

I walked into his office at 10:00 a.m. to find a smallish man, in a wash-and-wear shirt and repp tie behind a cluttered desk. He had a haggard, pallid look, almost like a prisoner. I couldn't see it, but I was sure he had a brown paper bag with lunch in it somewhere. He rose and shook my hand. "Dean Knotwell has very good things to say about you," he said, smiling faintly. His ancient Windows 98 desktop computer took up half the available space in front of him and papers covered the rest of it. I handed him our report and he tossed it onto a pile of other reports that looked unread. "I have to apologize," he said, "We are terribly understaffed here and we are all a little behind because of that." I told him the report listed the crops we had been growing and the income that the local farmers had earned from them. The reed grass was mentioned as an aside, in just a sentence or two.

"We are making a small but growing impact on the local population," I said, lapsing into bureaucratese. It must have been the building.

"Impact is an understatement," he said. "We have been hearing from the Brazilian government about you. You seem to have stirred something up down there." I had almost forgotten about the visit we were paid many months ago from the big agribusiness, Chefe Agro, S.A., but it all came back. Mr. Bean continued, "We have been contacted by several major corporations with questions about what you are doing, and just last week we got a letter from the Brazilian government, the Ministerio da Agricultura, inquiring about you." He swiveled to a filing cabinet and pulled out a folder, backhanded a clearing on his desk, and opened it. I felt the approach of an ominous cloud.

"But we have a legal right to be there," I said. "You guys have supported us right down the line."

"Look," he said, "I know you're in the right, but apparently there are a few higher-ups down there who have a lot of clout in Washington. I would advise you to be very careful from now on. You might as well assume that nothing you do in Brazil is not observed." I was silent for a moment, taking it all in. Our little moonlight kingdom suddenly seemed ever so slightly less serene.

"I appreciate your advice," I said. "We will stay in touch." I turned to leave, but just before I opened the door, I turned back and said, "You might be able to help in another matter. Please keep this confidential, but I need the help of a patent attorney with special areas of expertise, but he or she must be an engineer, preferably an electrical engineer, and have a background in agriculture as well. It's a long shot, I know, but if you know anyone like that...."

Llewellian ("call me Lew"), who I was beginning to like, said he would get back to me. He was as good as his word. About an hour later, as I was having lunch, my cell phone rang.

"I might have someone for you," he said. "We deal with a lot of lawyers outside of government here. I asked around, and a friend came up with someone who might be what you're looking for. She works for an intellectual property protection firm that specializes in engineering patents. She grew up on a farm in the Midwest, according to my friend. She has an MS in electrical engineering and a law degree from the University of Missouri. Actually my friend dates her, so he should know."

I had her on the phone a half hour later. "Jillian Roberts speaking." After I told her how I got her number, I gave her the briefest of outlines, not even mentioning Fordlandia.

She was noncommittal, though I thought I could detect some interest in her voice. She agreed to meet me in her office the next day. I spent that afternoon in the Smithsonian's Botany Department looking up reed grass. There was a huge number of varieties. I had Ben and Seth's paperwork in hand to guide me but I quickly got confused. They were using a variant of Reed mannagrass (Glyceria maxima), which is generally abundant in the Americas, Europe, and Asia, although their particular kind, or subset, grew only in the rain forest. When I left the Smithsonian, I was even more befuddled than I was when I went in. I needed to talk with Leeram but it would have to wait, as I didn't dare bring his coconut in with me, afraid that a guard would take it away thinking I found it there.

Back at the hotel, with another drink from the minibar in my hand, I put the coconut on the table and made contact. The first thing he wanted to know was how it felt to be back in civilization. "You've gotta be my eyes," he reminded me. "Tell me what you see." It was a little touching, as if Leeram needed a cane with a red tip.

"We got you to see for that poker game," I reminded him. "How can I do it now?"

"Yeah, that was a pretty good trick, but you could only do it with Ubi's badge, and even then I could only see what was in front of me. In the old days, I could see whatever you did."

"If I could kill that son-of-a-bitch Edson all over again,
I'd do it," I said.

"My, we really are getting red in the tooth, aren't we?"
Every now and then, Leeram could switch from his New
York cabdriver persona to a strange kind of metrosexual
one. It threw me off a bit. I let it pass. Quantum physics is
strange.

The next morning I was in the offices of Cheswick,
Barnum, and Zapinski, Ms. Robbin's firm. A gigantic
photograph of the Grand Coulee Dam met the visitor,
the first thing he or she would encounter coming into the
reception room. It covered most of the wall in back of the
receptionist's desk. An attractive young woman dressed in
a formal, yet perfectly tailored business dress came into
the room and, smiling, held out her hand. "Hi, I'm Jill.
Come into my office." She turned and I followed, feeling
a little out of place in my own suit, which I had tried to
unwrinkle as best I could with the iron in my hotel room.
I had not worn it since I left Boston and almost left it
behind until Lisa said I might need it when we met with
authorities in Brazil.

She waved at a comfortable chair next to her desk, in
front of a window with a great view of the Potomac River.
Rather than sit behind the desk, she perched in an
identical chair in front of it so we both faced each other
equally. She started the conversation. "After you called I
spoke with Lew. He said you were involved in a fascinating
project. Tell me more about it."

I took Ben and Seth's papers out of my briefcase. "Then you must have some idea of where we are and what we're doing, but that doesn't have much to do with why I'm here. In the process of our work on the grant project, we have stumbled, accidentally, onto something pretty strange." I decided to go for broke. "What do you think of producing cheap electricity from plants? We have discovered a way and we want to protect our rights with a patent."

She didn't say anything for a moment, then slowly answered, "People have been working on it for years. I read a research paper about that back in 2008. The problem is that while it's possible, plants just don't make enough of it. No one has been able to get enough juice, so to speak, out of a plant to make it worthwhile." She made a small grin.

"Well," I said, "we have." She sat upright; the grin was gone.

A half hour later, Ben and Seth's paperwork was scattered all over her desk. She was reading them, stopping now and then to scribble notes and going online to look something up. Finally she looked up at me. "I am going to have to talk with the authors of this paper, but if it actually works, it could be huge. The world would be a very different place." She called in a paralegal and asked for a sample contract. "Are you authorized to sign for your partners?" she asked. I said that I was, and read the document carefully. It had been written in an uncharacteristically straightforward manner. It essentially bound us to appoint the law firm as our sole legal representative and stated a fixed fee for their services. It would become final when they received a retainer from us.

I signed it, saying that our bank in Santarem would transfer the funds directly. She walked to the door with me and shook my hand once more. "I just wanted to say that you might be onto something that you can't imagine. Please stay in close touch."

Back at the hotel, I took the coconut out and told Leeram everything. He took it all in. "I told you once that I can't see the future," he said. "But now I'm finally beginning to think I'm going to like this. Keep me tuned. Let's go out and get drunk."

"I hope you mean some kind of metaphysical bender."

"No, that's all I can do on my side. You can actually do the real thing."

I thought about it. "Can I get drunk and give you the hangover?"

"You could try."

"Sorry, I don't take chances anymore." I had a couple of glasses of wine with dinner at the hotel that night and went to bed early; I had to get up well before dawn to catch a 6:00 a.m. flight back to Brazil. Leeram was a bit grumpy when I said goodnight.

Chapter 24

Returning to Fordlandia was pretty much of a blur—planes, crazy cabs, sleeping rough in a hammock were all in a day's work to me by then. My equilibrium had been thrown into a cocktail shaker right after I had finally adjusted to the smooth flow of life along the river. I was exhausted by the time the riverboat (this one with truly inedible food) pulled up to the dock in Fordlandia shortly after daybreak. In the forty-nine hours since I took off from Dulles, about eight of them had been spent in scattered sleep. I called Lisa right after I landed in Santarem and bought a ticket for the river trip home, so I was expected. Suxie, Lisa, and Pericles met me and we went inside for a good breakfast. I was starving. "We've had several long phone talks with the lawyers you hired," Suxie said. "So have Dean Knotwell and the guys. This really changes things on the ground, here." I asked if Henry Ford had been kept informed; they replied that they were waiting for me to talk to him since they felt I knew him best. I related everything about my trip to them, including the meeting with Lew Bean and his help finding Jillian Roberts, who was the proverbial needle in a haystack. I could only believe the gods of the Amazon were looking over me there, helping me find someone who had such an unlikely set of skills.

After breakfast, and feeling like a new Gilbert Greenbush, I went over to Henry's tank. He had just returned from his own breakfast in the Tapajos and was just settling in. Ubirajara was sitting in a chair by the glass partition, talking with him. They both looked up when I approached.

"That didn't take long," Henry bubbled. "You just left." He seemed perplexed until I told him about modern transportation systems and even then was doubtful that I could have pulled off such a quick trip. "Well, I'll take your word for it, then. I think you had better get cracking."

"Cracking?" I said. "Cracking about what?"

"First, let's get to business," he said. I thought for a moment, and then had to admit that I had no idea what he was talking about. "Look," he went on, his big cranial sensory organ pulsating slightly, "I may be guilty of a lot of things—I was anti-sematic, I was a strikebreaker, I was a lousy father, I know, I know. Believe me I had a lot of time to reflect on these things, but there was one thing I was, and still am: very good at making money. We are going to create an empire—an energy empire!" I stepped back a little mentally. I was hovering slightly above everything like a thought cloud, more than a little amused by the scene below. There was a Brazilian native guy, arms crossed in front of him, talking to a big, blobby river dolphin through a glass wall about world domination or something. At this point, the most likely reason for my vision was stark, raving insanity, but if I was insane it felt perfectly fine to me. Actually, I rather liked it. "You and your friends have been very lucky so far," Ford went on, "But you are up against powerful forces that can squash you like bugs. You don't have a minute to waste."

"Let me see if I follow you on this," I said. "Are you saying we are in some kind of danger? Why do we have to protect ourselves?" A warning from a voluble freshwater dolphin is cause for concern, but somehow the source diluted its intent.

Ubirajara had been watching the entire time, a serious look in his eyes. "Mr. Ford can be a little dramatic," he said, "but I think you should pay some attention."

"Didn't you learn anything from that Texan?" Ford asked. "Or from those people from the big agricultural company, or even the local banditos?"

I turned to the dolphin and said: "I don't get it. What goes on in the place you just came from? What made it worthwhile for you to come back like this just to help us?"

"It's a long story and I'll get to it in time," Ford said, with a little annoyance. "We have to make sure your ducks are in a row first." I sat down next to Ubirajara.

"Sorry," I said, "Please continue."

"Once those patents are filed, you are going to need them, sooner than you think." I looked at Ubi and he nodded.

"Listen to him carefully," Ubirajara said. "When I was first here, I worked for this man and worshipped his company. All those years it treated me well and I gave it everything I had. If it hadn't been for the Ford Motor Company, my granddaughter would have never gotten the education she has; she would never have been able to bring prosperity to my people."

"But, Ubi, you're with us!" I said, suddenly wondering what was going on. Ford swam back and forth complacently.

"Of course I'm with you," Ubirajara said. "Don't worry. We're all together here. We have the same ita, the same devils to face here. Mr. Ford is on our side."

"I thought you were mad at him for disrupting your people so," I said, still a little perplexed.

"While you were gone, we came to a better understanding of each other," Ubi said. "He's not the same person he was back then; he wants to repair the damage that he was responsible for back then, and I will work with him on that. My granddaughter feels exactly the same way. There's another thing, too," Ubi continued. "I know what's deep inside the rain forest. We have to protect it. It retreats every time the bulldozers come, but it's still there."

I turned to the dolphin, who had been silent while Ubirajara and I talked. "OK," I said, "so tell me how electricity from plants fits into all this? Won't they have to cut down even more rain forest to grow them?"

"If you take all of the land that has already been cleared to grow soybeans, you would have more than enough to power half the world," he replied. "The income from that will give the indigenous population a standard of living they never had before, and will protect against further clear-cutting." Henry Ford may have been a lot of things, but once he had a goal, he was relentless. His cranial dome gave everything he said a flat, direct logic and believability. I began, slowly at first, then with growing conviction, to give him the benefit of the doubt. Was he just one flipper over the line, or not? I decided not.

"So, what you're saying is, we have to get control of the farmland. How in the hell do we do that?"

"I'm working on a plan," he said. "In the meantime, we have to secure our position here. That's why the patents were so important."

I needed a place to think quietly and decided that the best place to do that would be aboard Ubi's dugout on the broad waters of the Rio Tapajos. After excusing myself, I walked down to the river, the coconut in a backpack, and climbed aboard. Five minutes later, when I was far enough offshore so that all I could see of Fordlandia was the water tower, I opened the backpack and pulled Leeram's simulacrum out. "On the damn water again," Leeram said. I admitted that it was so. "Every time you get in a boat, you get into trouble," he said.

"Leeram, you left a message saying you were out hunting when I tried to reach you earlier, but I had a long talk with Henry Ford and was trying to decide if he has lost his marbles." I then filled him in on the conversation. "I don't have any idea of what to say to him," I said.

I had begun to notice that the coconut's face was starting to show signs of wear and tear, having been stuffed into various containers so many times that its expression had become scratched and blurred. "I don't think I ever told you exactly why Ford and I didn't get along together," Leeram said. "We had a run-in once. Why I would even get within a hundred miles of him in a world that contains every single person who ever lived on earth is hard to understand, but I did."

"Miles? Is that how you measure things in your universe?"

"OK, OK, it's a little different, but I have to use language you can relate to. Actually, distance isn't measured in miles or meters, it's measured in moments of time. If you froze time, we would all be totally isolated from each other."

I didn't quite get it, I told him, and I didn't know if I ever could.

"Don't worry," Leeram said, "you will, one of these days. Over here, time is all at once, we just move around on it—not in it, on it." I always knew when Leeram was getting serious; his language changed. I guess it's hard to be sarcastic talking about the metaphysical. "Anyway, as

I was starting to say, Mr. Henry Ford brought a lot of his ideas with him when he arrived in my universe. First thing he wanted to do was build rows and rows of houses just like the ones in Fordlandia. It was like he just couldn't stop being himself. The next thing he wanted to do was find his son, Edsel, which he eventually did, only because he was Henry Ford and was so used to having his way that it carried over with him. He brought that attitude with him when he passed over here."

"But he wants me to be Edsel," I said. "What gives?"

"Edsel wouldn't go back if you paid him. Maybe you're his second choice."

I thought for a minute about those cars from the late 1950's with their funny looking noses. "I guess I don't blame him," I said. "But I want to know more about his dad. What happened between you and him?"

"I got into a big fight with Henry Ford when he wanted to build those houses next to me. You saw where I lived, it's pretty much like right here in the Amazon, where I was born. Even though I like to go into civilization, I hate it when civilization comes to me, so I burned them down."

"Despite all that mojo he had?"

"Well, I have some myself, don't forget." I had to admit, Leeram wasn't lacking in that department.

"So what did he do when you burned his settlement down?"

"He tried to kill me, of course," Leeram said. "That was before he realized he couldn't. He would build some more houses and I would burn them down as soon as he put them up. He even tried to build a fleet of what he called 'Model T's', but every time he did, I'd slash their tires. I drove him crazy. It was the only thing that really amused me. Finally, he agreed to stop building anywhere near me and to keep those rattletraps where I couldn't see, hear, or even smell them. That's why I didn't want to help you get him back here, but I guess he found his own way, the bastard."

"You fight over there?" I asked.

"Of course we do. It's something to do when we get bored more than usual. We obviously can't kill each other since we're already dead, but some people really have sharp elbows."

"Well," I said, "he's here now and it looks like we're all going to be working together, whether we want to or not." The coconut, in response, somehow relayed a sense of resignation, edged with annoyance. "Look," I said, "while we are out here, we might as well go visit the Carvahlos." Leeram was noncommittal. I pointed the dugout toward the other side of the river. Once ashore there, I walked up the street, passed the Casa Lugar Perfieto, turned right on their road and found them as usual, rocking on the porch. They rose, glad to see me.

"My dear Mr. Greenbush," Gabriela said, "it has been too long since you stopped by. And where is the lovely Lisa?" I said she was busy but would come by soon and that she wanted me to carry her greetings.

Gustavio smiled and held out his hand. "We were wondering if you were all right," he said. I assured them that I was fine, but had been very busy.

"So we have heard," Gabriela said, clasping my hands between hers. "There has been much talk here about Fordlandia, but nobody really knows what's going on."

Gustavio pointed to a telescope on a tripod. "We thought that the Texans had taken over when we saw that big ship tied to your dock, but then the name changed and we didn't know what was happening." I told them that we had bought the vessel from Mr. Calhoon and that it had been very handy for taking our produce to market. We chatted for a while after Gabriela brought out some coffee, then I took my leave. "Just one last question," he said. "We've heard rumors that you are planting grass now. How are you going to make money with that?" I replied that it was an experiment, but we thought it was going to be very worthwhile.

"It is just the beginning," I said, then changed the subject. "I see many people from Urucubituba working with us over there. You would be most welcome if you would like to come over for a visit. I've told my friends about you and they would like to meet you."

When I turned back to wave, they had worried looks on their faces. "Be careful," they called.

It was hot; I was thirsty and was tempted to go into the Casa when it came into view. The thought of a cold Brahma was tempting, but I decided to keep going.

Dragons be there, I said to myself. An afternoon beer would just make me sleepy, I knew. The sound of many voices gushed out of the open door, mixed with the smell of stale rum and disinfectant as I walked by with a quick glance at the dim interior, and I was glad I was not inside.

"Good choice," Leeram muttered. "I'm not around to get your sorry ass out of trouble." I knew well that chance, as well as otherworldly intervention, were equally important. I would need my own instincts if we were to get through this.

Chapter 25

That evening Seth and Ben were missing, just at dusk as we were sitting down to dinner. Suddenly the sound of the generator faltered and then went silent. The lights dimmed and died. We started to rise to see what was the matter and the illumination suddenly came back. The new light was different, brighter than it had been before, and it was quiet! "Surprise, folks!" Seth said as he came into the room with Ben at his heels. "We finished the hookup this afternoon." He and his partner had been puttering around for the last few days with spools of electrical conduit leading back to a shed nearby, so we weren't entirely clueless, but it still startled us.

"Congratulations!" we all said, impressed by the brilliant silence.

"Awesome," Lisa said. Awesome it was indeed, even in the old sense of the word. Impossibly, the light even had a curiously invigorating glint, faint but genuine. It seemed to clarify our thinking in an indefinable way, as though the vision it provided was slightly more crystalline.

"It's not fairy dust," Ben said, "We aren't entirely sure why it seems that way. It's got something to do with this place we are in. It'll take people with very different training than we have to find out what is really happening, but for now we should just enjoy it." He and Seth then gave us all a guided tour of their work. We already knew that they had planted shoots from the buckets of grass Ubi and I had brought back from the trip upriver. When they had been separated from the clumps, they numbered in the several hundreds and, individually planted, stretched out in four long rows, their roots all connected to copper wires leading back into the shed. Inside were the batteries we had brought back from Santarem, which in turn were connected to an inverter the men had salvaged from the old Ford generating building. From the inverter, 110-volt AC power flowed into our house. "It's pretty simple," Seth said. "We have more than enough shoots from your expedition to power this house. You could even put in an electric stove and air-conditioning, as well as your refrigerator with the juice we've got already."

"The inverter changes DC to AC," Ben added. "Maybe one day we can develop plants that will produce AC, but for now we have to use the inverter, which is too bad because it wastes about a third of the power the grass makes."

"On the other hand," Pericles said, "That power is free

to begin with, so who cares? Maybe what we should be doing down the road is getting appliances that work on DC."

We celebrated that evening, toasting our new electrons and their creators. I went outside and told Ford about it. "I already know," he said. "Don't drink too much; tomorrow you're going to have to go to work." The eye that faced me had a disapproving look; Henry had been a strict teetotaler in the old days. Back inside, the conversation had turned to the next day as well. We decided to meet with the Mayor and demonstrate what we were going to do next: electrify Fordlandia. The grasses we had planted all those months ago were now ready to "harvest."

I asked Lisa if she wanted to go for a walk after we finished dinner that night. The air was cool and refreshing. Instead of our usual route down toward the river, we went up the hill in the direction of the graveyard. "I don't quite know how to say this," I said, "but there is another person in there, and I'm glad he is." She looked at me.

"I think I know what you mean," she said. "It's the old Gilbert Greenbush." We had become so close that she could read my mind, even better than Leeram could. I took her hand. "Sorry about the analogy," I said, "but I hardly even recognize myself sometimes."

She smiled. "If you hadn't changed, I think I would have eventually gotten bored with the former Gilly. You were so laid back, so passive in a funny way. Now you are much more interesting. You challenge me in a way that I like."

So much had happened since we arrived in Brazil that I hadn't really had much time to indulge in introspection, but she was right. We didn't return to the house for another hour and when we did, our clothes were covered with grass stains. My grin was even wider than hers.

The next morning, after breakfast, we all went to the village and I knocked on Mayor Inocencio's door. His wife opened it and ushered us inside, where we found him reading a week-old newspaper from Belterra. "Not much in here," he said, "except a lot of stuff from the Soy Products International company about how well they are paying their local employees and how much better their lives are than they were in the old days. My uncle lives there and he told me that's all mentira—bullshit; he'd rather be here with us." He tossed the paper on the table and smiled. "I'd rather be here too," he said. "You people are worth ten SPI's."

We invited the Mayor and his wife to our house, waiting until Ford had left through the canal for his morning feed in the river. Some things, we agreed, were just too weird to explain away lightly.

"Ahh!" they said when they saw our project working. The Mayor knew instantly what the implications of our discovery were. "The Fordlandia Light and Power Company!" he said.

"You may be right," I said. "With your permission, you

and this village are going to be part of this from the beginning. Someday, maybe, SPI will be buying electricity from Fordlandia! But first we need to make this work on a larger scale than this house, so we will hook up as much of Fordlandia as possible. This way we can work out any problems before we really expand."

"When do we start?" asked the Mayor. I told him just as soon as we could get supplies and equipment, especially electrical wiring, storage batteries, and DC to AC inverters. I asked the Mayor to gather everyone who had experience in municipal services and even those who didn't, but who he though could learn. Later, Suxie calculated that our budget would justify taking the Araci downriver to Manaus, where most of the supplies we needed would be available. We set a date for the trip that would coincide with the next delivery of produce to Santarem, which we could drop off on the way.

When I told Henry about it, he smiled with that beak, almost making it ripple. "I'm going with you," he said. "The last thing I want to do is sit around here while you people have all the fun."

"Are you sure?" I asked. He nodded.

In the meantime, before we left, we worked with the Mayor, who was organizing his volunteers into work crews. Much could be done right away; there were some utility poles already in place, but more were needed. In order to avoid cutting any more trees down, we salvaged poles from the stash that Ubi found earlier. A large shed was built for electrical storage near the field planted with the now mature reed grass. Pericles, the Mayor, Lisa, and I all worked on the plans, with occasional help from Ben and Seth.

It took a couple of weeks before we had a full load of produce aboard the Araci. Finally, with our little ship loaded to her marks, her decks piled high with our latest harvest, Lisa, Dean Knotwell, Pericles, Ubi, and I left, bound for Santarem—first to sell the produce and collect our profits, then on to Manaus for the electrical equipment. Ubi wanted to see what the modern world looked like, while Suxie had long since decided that she was where she wanted to be for the rest of her life. Ben and Seth had plenty to do directing the work in Fordlandia, so they elected to stay, too. The villagers had agreed to invest their share of the proceeds into the purchases; the Mayor had done a good job of convincing them of the even more profitable use of their money. "And," he told them, "it means you are a part of it; you're not just workers, you are also owners!"

By now, the trip north, downriver, was routine. I told Ford when we were ready to leave and he was eagerly swimming in circles near the dock when Captain O'Malley cast off. It had taken O'Malley a little longer than the rest of us, but he had finally gotten used to "the pink guy." When we were fully underway, the big dolphin swam playfully in our wake, sometimes in the bow wave and sometimes alongside. "Tell him to watch the hell out for the propellers," the Captain said nervously when Ford got too close for O'Malley's comfort, but Ford apparently knew what he was doing. He stayed out of sight when we were in Santarem unloading our cargo, but quickly rejoined us when we turned into the Amazon proper and made a course to Manaus. He gave us a wider berth in the now muddy river water.

"Visibility," he said. "My sensory dome pretty much takes over when I can't see anything, but I'm a bit rusty. It takes a little getting used to."

We were in radio contact with Fordlandia, and had our satellite phone, so we were not exactly isolated on the river. Once we were underway toward Manaus, we began to see much more river traffic, from tugs and barges to passenger vessels, brightly lit at night. The riverbanks were generally dark then, so the "birdcages" were almost welcome, usually preceded by thumping salsa music that grew louder, then softer as they passed us going the other way. They broke up the long night watches. Ford hated them. "They make my dome hurt."

It is exactly 345 miles west from Santarem to Manaus on the river, or just a little over one hour in a modern aircraft. Since the Amazon River drains the largest river basin in the world, providing about one-fifth of all fresh water on earth that flows into the ocean, the current, especially during the rainy season, is strong. We were making slow headway against a flow of almost eight statute miles per hour, forcing us to make good just six over the bottom.

This meant over two days of steaming day and night. Finally, Ford came alongside and squealed loudly at the Captain, "Slow down. Either you slow down or give me a lift." All we could do, Captain O'Malley said, was to tow a big cargo net astern, so he could swim inside and rest, which he did immediately. "You have no idea how exhausting this is," he said. "Next time I'll have you build a tank on deck for me."

The riverbanks rose as we approached Manaus; we were leaving the relatively flat terrain as we proceeded westward. The frequency of little settlements grew as well. Manaus is the largest city in Amazonia and we were all looking forward to spending some time ashore in it. The last time we were in "the Paris of the rain forest" as the natives called it, we were far too busy for sightseeing. We would do so this time. Since our time was limited, I called ahead to locate electrical supply houses, getting prices on the various components that Seth and Ben suggested they would need. After we arrived, Ford found a nice little cove a mile or two downriver with a gentle back eddy to hang out in while we were ashore. "Be back in four days," we said, "but keep an eye out anyway."

After the hassle of finding a suitable dock space where the Araci could be secure for a few days, we went ashore, leaving Captain O'Malley in charge. Our little ship with her businesslike appearance contrasted distinctly with the gaudy fleet of riverboats jammed together so closely that it seemed impossible to add even one more, but our captain managed to shoulder the steel Araci into an opening just inches wider than her beam, coming up to the dock stern first. It was a pretty impressive display of boat handling. Once ashore, we took a cab directly to a hotel recommended by O'Malley, the Hotel Saint Paul, located in the center of town within easy reach of the best restaurants, shopping districts and, most importantly, the industrial section. We were tempted to book rooms in the gorgeous Tropical Manaus Hotel, but it was too far away on the banks of the Rio Negro and surrounded by the rain forest. Hell, we said, we are already surrounded by the rain forest in Fordlandia. We wanted city life.

Manaus is an old city but it has been so completely rebuilt in the modern architectural vocabulary that we were a little disappointed. Ubirajara was bewildered. But there were a few old survivors of the rubber boom days: elegant European buildings such as the Justice Palace, which now housed a cultural center, and the Province Palace, home to a museum, still stood. Even though Pericles, Lisa, and I had passed through here on the way down (it seemed like eons ago), we didn't really have time to go sightseeing, an omission we wanted to rectify. Our hotel rooms were quite pleasant with decks giving a view of the fantastic Theatro Amazonas and the Rio Negro in the background. We settled into our rooms and then met in the hotel restaurant to make plans over lunch. That afternoon we visited several of the supply houses in the industrial district and ordered great coils of copper wire, insulators, crates full of inverters, big industrial storage batteries, and everything else we needed to re-electrify Fordlandia. What we needed was relatively low-tech: mostly batteries and wires.

Once we had made arrangements for the equipment to be delivered and loaded aboard the Araci, we went exploring. Ubi led the way. "I was here last back in the 1930's," he said. "I saw the old opera house, I recognized that, but I might as well be in your New York City when it comes to everything else here." We were walking down a street toward the gigantic domed opera house, which was so enticing from our hotel balcony, past blocks of new construction. Dean Knotwell was walking next to him, occasionally brushing her arm, accidentally, against his.

"It's beautiful," she said. "The past isn't all gone! What was it like when you were here last?"

Ubirajara looked down at her, almost surprised to see her there so close. He smiled. "In those days, there weren't so many automobiles and when you saw one, it was always a Ford." He went on, pointing out landmarks here and there that he recognized. We went into the Pinacoteca, a museum featuring contemporary Amazonian artists and were charmed and amazed. "My granddaughter should see this," Ubi said.

"I feel so privileged to be here," Dean Knotwell said. "I will get her to come here, I promise."

We left only when the museum closed down for the day and, using the tour guide map from the hotel, found an excellent restaurant nearby where we ate a civilized meal for the first time in months. Ubi liked it immensely, telling Dean Knotwell, who was sitting next to him: "The food in this universe is the best!" We lingered for a long time in the tropical evening with cups of Kahlua-laced coffee, looking up at the stars in a clear sky. When we finally left for our hotel, we all agreed that we would come back as soon as possible.

We woke late the next morning, slipping seamlessly into a new Brazilian circadian rhythm, one that we had been denied by our work schedule in Fordlandia. Over a plate of croissants that might have been served in the real Paris, and coffee that tasted as though it came from the very freshest of all coffee beans, we languidly made plans for the day. Suddenly the maître d' came up to our table and, with excuses for interrupting, said "You have a message from your Captain O'Malley. He says he needs you down at the dock. He needs you right now."

"Get us a cab," Pericles said, and we all left for the lobby. By the time we got there, the taxi was waiting right outside and we piled aboard. As we neared the Araci, we could see a crowd on the dock. O'Malley was gesticulating but we were too far away to hear what he was saying. Someone threw some reals, probably more than was necessary, at the driver and we ran toward the scene, shouldering our way through the crowd. When we were close enough, we saw a net with a big pink dolphin inside, thrashing from side to side.

"Put it back in the water! Put it back now!" I shouted.

"Hey, buddy," said a burly fisherman, holding the net, "I caught it and it's mine." Ubirajara, after bulling his way through the crowd, approached the fisherman and put his hand on the man's shoulder. Ubi was even bigger and his baritone voice took on the timbre of a ship's foghorn, if not the decibels.

"Put. It. Back," he said in a deadly, even cadence. The man's expression morphed almost instantly from defiance to astonishment to acquiescence.

"OK, OK," he said and dragged the net to the water's edge, opened it, and rolled the big creature back into the river. Henry landed with a walloping splash and resurfaced right away. "I owe you a big one," he said. I looked around to see how the crowd would react to a talking dolphin, but apparently we were the only ones who heard him. I walked over to the fisherman and gave him fifty reals.

"He is tame," I said. "He is our pet; this should compensate you." The fisherman took the money and frowned. Apparently it wasn't enough, but it would have to be. I was running out of cash.

"I think we should leave as soon as possible," O'Malley said. "I don't trust these people." We all agreed that it was a good idea. Most of the equipment and supplies we ordered had been delivered and were stacked on deck. A last delivery was on the way, so Pericles and Ubi went back to the hotel to get our baggage and check out while Lisa,

Dean Knotwell, and I stood guard with Captain O'Malley. In a half hour it arrived and we were ready to cast off, not a moment too soon as the crowd, mostly very poor people from the settlement of waterfront shacks on stilts all around us, wasn't disbanding, but getting larger. As we hauled in our dock lines and moved forward, literally scraping the sides of the boats next to us, the crowd started throwing stones at us. Once we were clear and were back on course to the Amazon River, we saw Mr. Ford back in his usual place in our wake. He looked a little chastened.

"I must have been dozing," he said. "I drifted too close to a fish trap and couldn't get out." Then, after a while, he came up to the Araci again and said: "Listen. Do you think you could let me hang out in your net again? I feel safer in it."

There he remained, only leaving to eat until we pulled up once more in Fordlandia. He was in his tank before we had even unloaded our bags.

Chapter 26

We unloaded spool after spool of cable and other gear until the docks and nearby shore looked like D-Day had just occurred. Electrification was a big project. Even though we had done some planning earlier, its scope didn't become apparent until we actually began to unspool the big rolls of conduit and string it on poles. Quite a few of them had been set up in the weeks before we returned from Manaus, but now we really needed manpower.

Lisa and I went across to Urucubituba on a recruiting mission, but before we started putting up signs, we paid another visit to the Carvahlos. They were at home and came to the door when I knocked. "Gilbert!" they said, smiling, "And your beautiful Lisa." They invited us to sit down on the veranda. Gabriela went inside to fetch iced tea and returned in a few moments with tall, cool glasses already condensed with the humidity. We chatted for a while about our relationship, and then I brought up our project.

"Assombroso!" they said. "Amazing!"

"We could do it here, too," I told them, "if you would like us to."

At first they shook their heads. "We already have electricity. Look, where do you think this ice came from? What about those lines overhead?"

"I know, I know," I said, "but what are you paying for it?" That gave them pause.

"Too much," Gustavio said. I described what we were doing in greater detail, not forgetting to mention that the grasses we were using had been identified by a native, indigenous Brazilian.

"What we need now," I said, "is open land. We don't want any more clear-cutting, so we need land that is already available. Right now most of it is planted with soybeans, from here to Belterra, not to mention open land just about everywhere else in the Amazon basin that isn't being grazed on by cattle or used for other crops."

The Carvahlos were quiet for a while, then Gabriela said, "I don't remember whether or not we told you this before, but I am descended from the Franco family, the ones who originally sold the Boa Vista land to the Ford Company." I had heard something like that, I replied, but didn't give it much thought. "We still have title to some of it in Belterra," she said. "We have leased it for years to businesses as farmland. One of our tenants is the soy products company." That explains a lot, I thought to myself. As I had noticed the first time I saw it, their casa was large and well appointed compared to most of the dwellings in town.

"Why didn't they just buy it, or take it over? I thought that was the way they worked," I said.

"They don't pay us a lot of money," Gustavio said, "so it's probably a lot cheaper for them to leave old arrangements alone."

I thought for a minute. "Would you rent it to us?" I asked. Gustavio and Gabriela looked at each other.

"It may not be a simple thing to do," she said. "They more or less dictate the terms of the lease as they have for years. It is as though they were the landlords and we were the tenants, even though they are the ones giving us the money. It is probably to keep up appearances, but they choose to do it this way."

"I would never do anything to put you in harm's way," I said. "Please know I won't do anything unless I have your permission, but I have some resources, some people, who might be able to help. May I ask their advice?"

"Go ahead," Gustavio said.

"It is our land, even though we sometimes forget that," Gabriela added. "But be careful."

A surprisingly large number of Fordlandians and some from across the river had skills to contribute to the project. There were even more than a few who had earlier twirled their fingers next to their heads as they described us as "loco" for planting all that grass.

The assembly of our new electrical network was made

much easier, perhaps even made possible at all, because of a political skein that wound everyone together during the decades before we had arrived. It had developed largely under the Mayor's influence over many years. Differences between the villagers were worked out, face-to-face, almost immediately and grudges rarely festered. Any doubts among the population that our grass project was too crazy were limited to a small number, growing smaller as the days and the lights went on. Before long, Fordlandia could be seen all the way across the Tapajos at night.

Now it was beginning to resemble a real town, which created some new problems. It needed a professional manager to guide it through the complexities that real towns have to deal with. I knew that most of us would eventually leave, but a few would not—Suxie and Ubirajara in particular. I was getting worried that Fordlandia's future as a community organized around its citizens was not all that certain, given its new access to money. Would it be an attractive prize for the next freewheeling invader? Running a modern municipality was much more than Mayor Inocencio had either the time or inclination to do, as he freely admitted. I told him we would help locate someone, but his decision would be given much weight as to whom it would be. One day I ran into him walking along the riverside, fishing pole in his hand. "Just who would you like to run things here one of these days?" I asked.

His answer didn't surprise me. "Suxie. Araci," he said

immediately. I take that back, it did actually surprise me a little. I thought he might have chosen Ubirajara, but I instinctively knew that he probably wouldn't want the job. He had not come through the wormhole just to be a mayor. That evening I mentioned our conversation to her.

"I've had the same thoughts," she said. "It would make a lot of sense if I did it. At first I came here to be myself; I followed my ancestry, my blood. When we first came here, that was enough, just to be here physically, to breathe this air, but I can give back to the people I came from."

Over the next few weeks, while work went on electrifying Fordlandia, Suxie, the Mayor, and I held several meetings to work out the transition. There would have to be an election, of course, but with the Mayor's popularity and the ability it gave him to shape public opinion, we didn't think there would be much of a problem. They both agreed to do everything they could to maintain the sense of community, the human network that had been developed over so many years.

Chapter 27

After I came back from the meeting, I went to the tank where Ford was recuperating from his recent travails. He was slowly yet gracefully doing barrel rolls in his tank, but leveled out when I came up. "Exercises," he said.

"I need your opinion," I said. "I'm not going to be here forever, nor will most of us. This place has reached a point where it has to have some kind of permanent leadership after we go. Suxie will take over and Ubirajara will stay too, but they'll need help."

He floated quietly for a minute, then his beak parted: "Am I not here?" he asked, calmly.

"Um, yes, you definitely are," I said, "but don't you think that there may be, well, some practical impediments?"

"Rubbish."

"But how do you think people will do what you want them to do? We had to get you out of trouble just a few days ago."

"Gilbert, my young friend," Ford said, "I made myself known to you for the simple reason that I knew you were capable of doing anything. This is up to you to figure out. Now, if you will excuse me, I am going down to the river for a little snack." He rolled over like a big pink fighter plane, an old one to be sure, and swam out through a portal into his canal. I watched his tail flip once in a dismissive way and he disappeared. After he left, I went looking for Lisa, finding her in the private vegetable garden we had planted next to our house. I was trying to organize my thoughts and inadvertently came up so quietly that she didn't hear me.

"Lisa," I said and she jumped. "Sorry," I said, "I didn't mean to startle you."

"Not your fault," she said. "I was just daydreaming and you woke me up." She gave me a warm smile. I told her about Ford's comments. "I think he knows you better than you know yourself," she said.

But what to do next? I thought to myself. I had, I knew, taken charge of the Fordlandia project almost by default. It wasn't because I had set out to do that in the beginning, but I had unconsciously put myself in a leadership role. Even Suxie had gradually ceded many important decisions to me. Yet I had gradually begun to realize that there was a hole in me, a place that once was filled with a reassuring presence. I suddenly knew what it was. I needed Leeram. I needed him as much as I needed Lisa. For very different reasons, of course, but his absence was almost as heartbreaking as hers would be. I hadn't talked with him since I came back from Washington and things had been so busy after that, I just forgot. Since that time over a year ago when his head had been thrown into the river, and despite the fact that I could still contact him, he had slowly drifted out of my life, almost in direct proportion to the ascent of my leadership here. The distance between his universe and mine had grown. The string between our worlds attenuated until I sometimes went days, even weeks, without even thinking about him. In his place I had a big, occasionally repulsive, freshwater dolphin. I wondered, at times, if I was losing it. I had even stopped carrying the coconut around with me. I went back to my room and took it out of my dresser drawer.

"Hello? Hello, Leeram, are you there?" I asked.

There was a long pause, and then when I was just about to put it back, I heard, "I was wondering about you, buddy. What's up?"

"I'm sorry for not keeping you up to speed," I said, "but things have been happening pretty quickly around here and I..."

"Don't worry about it," he said. "I know how it happens, out of sight, out of mind and all that stuff. Don't mind me." He was trying to sound as though it didn't matter, but I thought I could hear a little note of melancholy in his voice. I spent the next half hour talking to him, trying to reassure him that I still missed him a lot and by the end of the conversation, it was almost like the old days in

Brookline. I was, I tried to tell him several times, feeling really guilty about my inattention. Things were happening so fast lately, I told him, that I had just forgot.

"I wish I had your head back," I said.

"Me too."

"What are we going to do about Henry Ford?" I asked, after a long pause.

"Now you know, buddy," Leeram said. "Are you surprised I didn't want to deal with him when you were asking me about him every five seconds? When that guy wants his way, he gets it for damn sure," Leeram said. "Sometimes I think he had something to do with those bastards who killed me and shrunk my head."

"That's hard to imagine," I said. "He was living in Michigan at the time, so his alibi would probably stand up in court. But that was a long time ago, and he is here, high, wide, and not very handsome."

"Did you know I ran into his son, Edsel," Leeram asked casually, "when I was dealing with the old man trying to set up an ideal New England village in my rain forest?" I said I thought people were too scattered around his universe for such a coincidence to be possible. "That old man is so single-minded that he actually managed to pull it off, don't ask me how. Anyway, I kind of liked that kid, got to know him when I was fighting with his father; he actually helped me."

"I read that Henry was mean as hell to Edsel when he

was alive," I said. "Did he keep it up even on the other side?"

"Did he ever," Leeram said. "Listen, let me think about your situation for a while. I'll get back to you."

That evening, around our table talking about the events of the day, I told everyone of my conversation with Ford. "Suxie will be in charge after we leave one of these days," I said, "but she'll need advice from time to time. Eventually, most of us are not going to be around."

"Wait a minute," Suxie interrupted. "Things are working pretty well now. Why rock the boat?"

Ubirajara replied: "Boats are meant to rock, Araci. Gilbert's got a point—if we don't prepare now, we might get swamped down the river. I'll tell you what, let me talk to Mr. Ford; he and I have more in common than you might think."

Suxie looked at him sharply. "Grandfather," she said, "whose side are you on?"

"Yours, of course, but bear with me, trust me."

It was true, I said, that Ford had become one of us, oddly, but was that our doing or his? Right after we had returned from Manaus, Captain O'Malley, on his own initiative, welded up a steel tank on Araci's deck, with Plexiglas windows. "With this thing," he said, "the dolphin can be easily lifted on board and off with the ship's hydraulic cargo crane, and the whole rig can be left ashore to make room for more market produce if we needed it."

Ford, who was swimming nearby when O'Malley was showing it to us a few days earlier, added, "You are never too old to learn something. Don't get me wrong, I like being a marine mammal, but I know better now than to try to keep up with a two thousand horsepower diesel engine for days at a time. From now on, I'll use it for long trips."

At the dinner table that night, we agreed that we wouldn't go anywhere until our project in Fordlandia was stable and permanent. In the meantime, we needed more skilled labor; we would spread out and advertise. The Araci, a very well equipped little ship, had a small office with a simple but effective copying machine, sealed against the humidity, which we used occasionally to print Help Wanted posters. Each of us took a few and spread out over the following days, hanging them in places where they would most likely be seen. Not all that easy a task, since everyone in Fordlandia already knew about us and was either working for us or didn't want to. We had to go farther afield. Nailing posters to trees in the rain forest did not seem exactly like a good use of our time and we were surrounded by little else.

I told them that I would put up posters in Urucubituba, since I had been there so often and knew the place pretty well. The others would go to Boa Vista and downriver to Belterra. I knew exactly where I would go—the Casa Lugar Perfieto. It had always drawn me for reasons I did not exactly understand; I generally steer clear of dives that exude an unmistakable smell of stale beer and dull menace. Why did I keep coming back, drawn like a fly to, well, unpleasant things? The Casa had a queer draw on me, like a sink drain around which I was swirling. I could only hope it had a strainer. Early the next afternoon, after slinging a knapsack with Leeram's coconut and a half-dozen recruitment flyers inside it over my shoulder, I climbed into the dugout and headed across the river. As usual, my arrival at the little tin-sided bar was announced by squeaky door hinges that drew everyone's attention. As my eyes, pupils shrunk in the tropic sun, took their own sweet time to dilate again, I recognized the bartender and a couple of regulars, including the one who slept on his crossed arms. Even he raised his head to look at me, blinking.

"Ola, my friend," the bartender said. It looked as though he was wearing the same shirt he had on when I first saw him over a year ago, only the sweat stains under the arms were a little bigger. "Hey, we have a celebrity," he announced. "One Chopp coming up," he said, filling a scratched, cloudy mug from the tap. I reached in my pocket but he stopped me, raising his hand. "On the house, my friend!" I thanked him, a little warily. "Big news from your side of the river!" he said.

"Como é que?" I said. "How's that?"

"Maybe you're not so loco after all," he said. "My friends on the other side say you have something going on." As my eyes became used to the gloom, I noticed a man at the end of the bar. He looked a little odd, out of place. He was quite thin, obviously of northern European descent, and was strangely familiar. He was drinking a martini, or at least it was a clear liquid in a martini glass.

"I'm here to see if there is anyone with electrical skills who might want to get a job with us in Fordlandia," I said. I opened the knapsack and pulled out one of the flyers. "Wanted," it said, "people who have electrical skills for work in Fordlandia. Contact Mayor Inocencio for an interview." I handed it to the bartender: "Can you put this up somewhere?" I asked.

"Sure, of course," he said, grinning, and thumbtacked it next to the cash register. "You have been very good for us here," he said. "Muito obrigado." By the time I finished the beer, I could see everything in the room more clearly. The odd man at the end of the bar was well dressed in a rumpled, slightly stained linen suit and a tie. He didn't take his eyes off me. I nodded to him, put the empty mug back down on the bar, and went back out into the sunlight. It was now well into the afternoon and I wanted to make sure I was back at my dock before sundown, so I started to walk quickly down to the river.

"Leeram," I said, "did you hear any of that?"

"When you're in that place, the wall between your universe and mine is very thin. It's almost like I'm in the same room with you," Leeram said. "I'm pretty sure there is a wormhole in it or very near it."

We were nearly at the dock and suddenly I heard a voice in back of me; it was not Leeram's. "Mr. Greenbush?"

I turned, and the thin man was standing a couple of feet away; he seemed hesitant. "Yes," I said.

"Do you have room for one more in your boat?"

"I do, but I need to leave right away," I said. I was mildly annoyed, mildly apprehensive and—curious.

"That's fine," he said. "I want to see my father."

Chapter 28

"Leeram!" I shouted, clutching the valise.

"I'm sorry if I startled you," the man said. "Your friend Leeram has been very helpful to me."

"Well, son-of-a-bitch," Leeram chimed in. "Is that..."

"Edsel Ford. Pleased to make your acquaintance." The thin man held out his hand. "I know this is rather sudden and I apologize if I startled you."

"Tell Edsel he should have told me first," Leeram said. "I hate surprises."

"But you are...are...not a dolphin," I said. It was kind of a dumb observation.

"No, I'm definitely not. I have no idea why my father would have chosen to do that. I know he was under blocking orders from the authorities. He got by them somehow—maybe that was the only way he could."

"But—and I think I believe you—why didn't you just show up in Fordlandia?"

"The portal, or wormhole, as your friend Leeram calls

it, is in the back of the Casa Lugar Perfieto, near the outhouse. Thank God it's not in the actual outhouse, but in some trees behind it."

"Is that bartender in on the deal?" I asked.

"I doubt it. These things don't last very long. This one comes and goes, so I had to time it closely."

"Did you know about this, Leeram?" I asked. "Have you been keeping something from me?"

"You said you wanted to know what to do about Ford....well, I arranged for his son to take him off your hands. I know when those wormholes are quiet, kind of like when they're asleep, and I shot him through. Thought it was worth a try; if he wound up on Pluto, it was no skin off my back and I knew he wanted to do it."

I turned to Edsel. "Your chances of getting back are next to nothing. Do you realize you are here for good?" I was so used to talking to the formerly departed by now that it was almost routine.

"Why do you think I want to go back?" he said. "While I was around before, up in Michigan, this place always intrigued me. Father would never allow me to travel down here; he said he needed me in Dearborn, which was pretty amusing. He really just wanted to keep me around to torture. When your friend here told me he had come back as a porpoise, I saw my chance to turn the tables on him. I lived my entire previous life trying to please him. Now, he is going to find out that he really does need me."

As we motored back across the Tapajos, Edsel was full

of questions about Fordlandia. He listened, fascinated, as I gave him an outline of what we had done over the past year. "Your Leeram, as you call him, only gave me the faintest idea of what you have accomplished," he said. "I can't wait to talk to Ubirajara and the rest of your crew." As he went on, my apprehension lessened. I had to admit, after having met four dead guys who had transitioned from death back to life—OK, one had not exactly come back as a homo sapien and another was still over yonder—that they were far from being scary monsters. "If you will accept my offer," he said, "I would like to help in your work here." I assured him that he would be welcome.

After we tied up at the dock, Edsel wanted to go right to his father's tank, but I thought it would be best to introduce him to the others first. It would help, I said, if he first had a better idea of our project. After all of us gathered in the office, Ubi was the first to shake his hand. "It is a little strange at first," Ubi said, "but you'll get used to being back on this side pretty soon. The food is better, for one thing." When I told him where Edsel had appeared, Ubi nodded; "I wanted to get as far away from it as I could. When I was here in the old days, I spent a lot of time pulling my workers out of that bar. I hated it." After much introductory chitchat, we found a spare bedroom for Edsel and some clothes to replace the tattered suit he was wearing. The fact that he was wearing anything at all was amazing. Going through that portal must have been a real milk run, I thought.

By then it was time for dinner, and we needed another plate. We managed to convince Edsel to postpone meeting his father until after we ate. He agreed, reluctantly, but then after a glass of cachaca (which he enjoyed), he brightened up. We had a fine meal of roast pork ribs, marinated in feijoada spices, and fried plantains on the side. Unfortunately, Brazil is outside of the "wine belt," being too tropical, so we didn't have that to go with everything, but cold alua, the drink we first encountered when we arrived, served perfectly well on the side. Ours had been made from lightly fermented pineapple juice and complemented everything beautifully.

Edsel stood up and raised a glass to us: "Your hospitality," he said, "is far more than I expected, or, I suppose, even deserve, but I thank you. I know that I am among friends." We all applauded (cachaca does that to you) and told him he was most welcome among us.

It was dark outside when we all pushed from the table and walked down to Henry Ford's tank. The night was tropically warm, as usual. We were all used to it, but Edsel was sweating profusely. We switched on the lights. The dolphin rolled toward us and Edsel said: "Hello, father." I thought he would jump out of the tank, jerking so fast that he threw a geyser of water down on all of us.

"Sorry to have startled you," Edsel said, startled himself.

"You could have warned me," Henry Ford said to all of us.

"Edsel is going to be staying here," I said to his father.

"He wants to work with us." Dolphins are normally expressionless, except for the one they are born with, which humans have anthropomorphized into one that emotes mild amusement. River dolphins just look weird. The Henry Ford dolphin, on the other hand, had a look that combined that with surprise and annoyance.

"Work with us?" he said. "I don't see a lot of polo ponies around here, or fancy restaurants. What on God's green earth do you think you can do here?" Such a touching pere-et-fils moment, I thought.

Ubirajara said, "I think, Mr. Ford, that you should give your son a chance." Not knowing what else to do, we all said goodnight and, after telling Edsel where and when we met for breakfast, went to bed, leaving him and his father alone to reacquaint themselves. My fingers were crossed.

The next morning we were all sitting at the table, almost finished eating when Edsel came into the room. "Sorry I'm late," he said. "Father and I had a long discussion after you left. We still have much to talk about, but there will be plenty of time to do that." He was smiling. I couldn't wait to hear more; it must have been an epochal discussion. When I asked about what happened, he looked at me and said, "It was interesting, very interesting, and I will tell you about it in time." I looked at Lisa, eyebrow raised.

"Maybe it's time for us to go," she said, sotto voce.

We spent the rest of that day showing Edsel everything, introducing him to the Mayor, and giving him a tractor ride around the fields. "It's one of ours," he said. "A

Fordson. I remember shipping them down." Ben and Seth showed him their grass laboratory, a thing that fascinated him. His questions were insightful and penetrating; he mentioned a few practical uses that they themselves hadn't thought of, such as planting on inner city rooftops to power buildings beneath them. He loved the Araci and laughed at the way we came to be her owners. "I used to know people like that," he said, chuckling. He was tireless, walking so quickly we had to work to keep pace. "And what is this?" he would ask, "and that?" By the time everyone met again at dinner, he was ebullient. "You have no idea," he said, "of how good it is to be finally back in this world."

I went back to the tank after dinner, to find the old dolphin looking a little down at the mouth. "So," he said, "the boy seems to have made a hit."

I replied that he had certainly liked what we were doing here, then said: "A while ago you said you wanted me to be your Edsel, but you have the real thing here. I really appreciate your confidence in me but I would feel much better if you let him do the job." Ford was quiet. "Well, nice to talk to you," I said, and turned to go.

"Wait!" the dolphin said. I stopped. "I want you to keep an eye on him."

"If you say so," I replied, "but I think you really should trust him. I do."

"Just make sure he doesn't try any tricks with me. Something's in the air."

I turned and left to go to bed. Lisa sat up and I told her about my conversation, getting almost through it before I was distracted by her mouth and her hands. In a few moments I forgot it entirely, only to have it come back much later when I realized the old fishy bastard had been prescient.

Chapter 29

The next day I received a letter from the Carvahlos, inviting me to their house. "We have thought much about your question about our land in Belterra," the letter read, "and we would like to talk with you." I was at their front door three hours later, midafternoon. After some small talk, sitting on their veranda, Gustavio said: "The lease we have had with Soy Products International, the company that rents our land in Belterra, will run out in a month. We've renewed the lease every year for decades without thinking much about it. The rent is always the same and since it is sufficient for us, we haven't changed it, even though we know it is much less than we could get if we wanted to. Gabriela and I have decided that you should have it, rather than our old tenants."

I should have seen that coming, but I hadn't. "Let me talk it over with my people," I said. "I like the idea very much, but you understand that I can't bind them to something like that without their support." The deep rain forest is no place for a cell tower and I had no way to simply call them or I would have done so right then. I thanked the Carvahlos and told them I would be back as soon as possible. I left for the docks, walking quickly past the Lugar Perfieto without a glance, getting a whiff of the odd odor that I now recognized as a combination of stale beer, old urine, and—yes—ozone! It was the ozone that took the edge of nastiness out of it. Back in Fordlandia, I called for a meeting around the table in front of Henry's tank so that he could participate also.

"It looks like you came here at just the right time, Edsel," I said, "We are going to need someone with a good head for business—in addition to yours, of course," I added with a nod toward the tank. "What do the rest of you say?" I asked. "Are we ready for this?"

"I had them move the rubber operation down to Belterra many years ago," Henry said. "That place is a lot flatter than this one. Don't know what we were thinking before!" he grumbled.

"I remember it, too," Edsel said. "You had so much invested in the village here that you were going to make it work no matter what." His father gave him an exasperated look, but kept his beak shut. I looked around the table.

"It means we'll be getting out of the Little Leagues," Pericles said

"It's time we expanded," Suxie said. "We've shown how it can be done. Nothing left to prove here, or soon there will be anyway. This stuff works."

Ubi spoke next. "I vote for Belterra."

Pericles and Lisa also raised their hands for it. Ben and Seth didn't need prompting. "As long as it doesn't get in the way of our research," Seth said. "Don't look to us for any business advice."

Finally, Henry Ford waved a flipper and said, "I'm for it. I like to finish things I start, and if it means planting something other than rubber trees down there, so be it."

"It is agreed, then. I think it is about time we invited the Carvahlos over for a visit."

This time we decided to take the Araci to Urucubituba. "You sure you want to burn all that fuel?" Captain O'Malley asked. I replied that this was an important, diplomatic trip and well worth a hundred gallons.

"We'll take it slow," I said. We all climbed aboard the next morning and, leaving Henry in his tank, at his request, headed across the river. It was only the second time the Araci had been there and, looking back on it from the hill on the way to the Carvahlos', our little ship had a very businesslike appearance. Ubirajara and Edsel walked past the Casa looking straight ahead, deliberately ignoring it. When we reached the house, I climbed to the veranda and knocked. Gabriela answered the door and smiled, calling her husband. After our introductions, Ubirajara invited them to come down to the Araci. When he wanted to, Ubi could sound almost like the voice of God.

"We are honored," said Gustavio, and we all walked

together back to the docks, where Captain O'Malley helped the elderly couple aboard. During the trip back to Fordlandia, they became excited: "The last time we were there," Gabriela said, "the jungle had begun to grow back everywhere and the only people who still lived there were squatters, too poor to leave. It was too dangerous to stay on." Once ashore, we gave them a tour. Much of the place, the structures that were too specific to the rubber business, and the buildings that were too far gone to repair, were obviously unrestored, but our efforts showed in other structures, notably the cottages and small houses that we occupied. We showed them the buildings that we used for our equipment, the laboratory just uphill, and our "office" when we weren't all sitting around the table next to the dolphin tank. The Carvahlos were very impressed with the electrical grid we had created and the source of all our electricity. Ben and Seth explained it with only occasional help in translating. We decided that we would wait for an opportune time to introduce them to Mr. Ford—it would have been too much too soon just then. Finally, we gathered around the table in our house and got down to business.

"We have gone as far as we can here," I said. "This is a pilot project. We have shown that it can work, but we need to ramp this whole process up. That's where Belterra comes in—and Urucubituba, of course," I added.

The Carvahlos were excited. "We are with you," she said, and Gustavio nodded. "Let's get to work." They stayed in Fordlandia as our guests that night and we had a memorable dinner to celebrate. By the time we took them back the next morning aboard the Araci, they were allies as well as friends. A week later, our new lease in hand, the Araci bore us downriver to Belterra to survey our new territory. Gustavio came with us to enforce our claim.

We had passed Belterra many times on our trips back and forth to the market and always said we would explore it when we could get away for a few days, but until this moment we had never found the time. Now we had the time, and moreover, a mission. At first glance, it looked almost like Fordlandia, but a Fordlandia that had not fallen on such hard times. The streets were cleaner and some new houses and buildings were signs that the final growth of the rubber industry had left it in better shape than its predecessor. We had brought our jeep, which was unloaded onto the dock with the ship's crane. "Let me show you your new land," Gustavio said. We climbed in and bounced along a dirt road for a few miles, then pulled to a stop next to a large field planted in soybeans. "This field and two more nearby have about two hundred fifty acres, or a little over one hundred hectares. You see, they are so sure of themselves that they went ahead and planted these fields without even asking us if their lease would be renewed!"

Nobody was in sight, so we drove back into town, to the local office of the SPI, a small nondescript structure with a tin roof and the company's initials painted on its side. The door opened into a spare reception area with a secretary on the phone and a crossword puzzle half-finished on her desk. We filled the room and she quickly ended her conversation, hung up and said "Posso ajudá-lo?"

"Yes, you can help us," Gustavio said. "I own the land you are growing soybeans on. Is the manager in?" Her eyes opened wide. Suxie and Ubirajara were standing there, arms crossed and taller than the rest of us. Edsel, Pericles, Lisa, and I left no space for anyone else. She jumped up and went through an inner door, returning in a minute with a short, sweating gentleman, face leathery from exposure to the tropical sun. "I am Abilio Guilherme. How can I help you?"

"I want you to inform your company that its lease on these fields has expired," Gustavio said, placing a copy on the desk. "These people are the new tenants and would like to begin planting their own crops in a month."

At first, the manager was speechless. "I...I have to talk with my boss," he said, bewildered. "He's in Manaus." The southern terminus of a telephone landline that connected all the larger cities in the Amazon River area was in Belterra, making communication there much simpler than from Fordlandia. Our satellite phone might have sufficed, but this particular trip had to be in person.

"Go ahead," I said. "We'll come back after lunch." We drove back to the Araci and, along with Captain O'Malley, enjoyed a meal in the air-conditioned main cabin. Ever since we had acquired the Araci, and her indispensable captain, his interest in our project had turned more and more into fascination.

"I thought you guys were nutty at first, nutty but interesting," he said. "I thought I would stick around for a while because I wanted to see where you all were going, then I would go back to the Gulf and get a job in the oil business. They're always looking for guys like me and the money's pretty good. I've gotta admit, you've got me hooked now with that dolphin that thinks he's Henry Ford. Him and Ubirajara." He turned to Edsel. "If you are who you say you are, I'm going to stick around as long as you'll have me."

Edsel smiled. "I am Edsel Ford. The dolphin is my father. And I'm about to have the time of my life."

Captain O'Malley nodded and shook his hand. "I'm ready to take everything here at its absolute face value. I'm Captain O'Malley, once a sane man," he said. "Pleased to meet you, Edsel."

After about an hour, the regional manager came aboard and knocked on our door. "I reached our property manager in Manaus and faxed him your new lease. He's on the phone; he wants to talk with you." We all followed him back to his office.

"Who the hell are you?" were the first words I heard when I picked up the phone. I told him who Suxie, Pericles, Lisa, the Carvahlos, and I were.

"And there are a few others," I added. "According to our lease, we can begin planting in a month, but we are willing to give you enough time to harvest your soybean crop. We will sublet the land to you until then." The property manager spluttered, saying he would turn the whole matter over to the legal department. "Don't take too long," I said. "It will only add to the rent you owe us, which, by the way, is twice what you were paying before, which makes it a fair value for once." I hung up the phone and turned to Abilio. "We are going to need someone here to look over things for us. When we begin our operations here, I would like you to stay on a provisional basis. If things work out, it'll be permanent." I gave him a letter that we had prepared earlier, listing our demands and deadlines, along with a copy of the new lease. "Please send these documents to your superiors in Manaus," I said.

We departed, leaving some not-so-small consternation in our wake. Back in Fordlandia, after dropping the Carvahlos off in Urucubituba, we got ready for expansion. I had left the coconut in my room, so as soon as we got back and I had a moment to myself, I contacted Leeram. After I told him of what happened in the last couple of days, he said: "I don't really know why I give a shit, maybe it's only because of you. Hey, I'm fine here, even if it is a little boring sometimes." Ah, the B word, I thought! The one thing he can't stand.

"Look, Leeram," I said, "Before, you used to complain all the time about being in the boondocks. When we were together in that dream, it looked pretty much like the rain forest. You kept telling me you wanted to go back to civilization, didn't you? Maybe this is the road back for both of us."

"Yeah, I know," he said, "but unless you can find my head again, I'm not sure just how much I can do for you." I told him that, given what we had all been through during the last couple of years, anything was possible. I didn't have much hope that his head would turn up anytime soon, though. Probably eaten by a river dolphin.

"Just keep doing what you have been ever since we got here," I said. "We did manage to make a visual link for that poker game, don't forget."

"That was lucky. You don't know how lucky."

"Lucky all around," I said. "Don't tell me you had nothing to do with it. We might need that luck again."

"Better keep your nut with you," he replied. I promised that I wouldn't leave the house without it.

Chapter 30

The next month passed quickly, although without a word from Soy Products International. We took the time planting reed grass in Urucubituba, starting with the Carvahlos' house, which had just enough land around it. Elsewhere, in areas that had been more densely built, we used land that was close enough to the houses to run wires from—each little field (or patch, in some cases) with its own junction box about the size of a doghouse. We had to make several trips upriver to harvest more of the grass with Ubi's help, in dense caches deep in the forest, well out of reach of outside developers. We could only imagine how much of it had been just plowed under thoughtlessly in the past by loggers intent on mahogany or farmers looking for soybean fields. We found enough not only to supply the Carvahlos' village but also to plant our land in Belterra, where we planned to grow enough to supply many more settlements. It would become the mother bed, freeing us from having to go so far to harvest it.

In fact, as it turned out, we needed the time before the Soy Products International lease ran out and even a little more. We knew the soybean crop growing on our land needed at least two months to mature, so we didn't press them overly hard on our deadline, but we meant it. After about six weeks, with still no response from SPI, we made another trip to Belterra. This time we had our tractor, plough, and harrow on board. We walked to the little office near the dock and found the manager. "I don't know if you are taking us seriously," I said, "but if your company is just going to ignore us, we will begin our own farming operations now. We will begin to prepare the ground even if your soybeans are still there. Tell them that if they want to salvage anything, they had better start immediately."

The manager looked as though he was going to have a heart attack. "Please, please," he said, "I have tried to get them to do something for weeks, but they keep saying their legal department has to respond." He wrung his hands and looked so distraught that I began to feel sorry for him.

"I'll tell you what," I said, "Get them on the phone; I'll talk to them." Fifteen minutes later, after the manager had been passed from desk to desk and finally to the company's vice president for the states of Para and Amazonia (who had to be called out of a meeting), we were finally connected to someone in authority. After telling the VP who we were, the manager wordlessly handed me the phone.

"This is the first time I have heard about this," he said in English. I reminded him that we had sent a copy of the new lease, signed by the landowners, and had been told that the legal department was handling things. I also said that I regretted that his organization had kept him in the dark, but we had every legal right, and every intention, to plough up his one hundred hectares of soybeans unless he was ready to make a decision right now. Leeram's lessons in hardball, taught to me over and over, came in handy at times. There was a pause, then the vice president said: "Look. How about this. Let the crop mature—I'm told it will be ready in a couple of months. When it's harvested, I will pay you one-quarter of its wholesale value and then relinquish any claim to the land, assuming you are correct about your legal claims."

I thought about it for a moment. If I agreed, it would mean a short delay in our plans, but if the transition was peaceful, it might be advantageous. "Check it with your lawyers, put it in writing," I said, "along with a check for the estimated sum you speak of to validate the agreement, and we will give you the time you need. Just remember," I added, "if I hear nothing from you in one week, we will begin to plough." I handed the phone back to the manager. "You know how to reach us," I said to him, and we steamed back to Fordlandia with Captain O'Malley grousing about the waste of fuel. "If this works out," I told him, "we'll be able to afford all the fuel we want."

We still had plenty to do in Fordlandia and

Urucubituba. The spring rainy season had caused all of the Amazonian river systems to rise, the Rio Tapajos was almost three miles wide in its lower reaches where it emptied into the Amazon River and that junction was so wide that it resembled an inland sea in places. The distance between Fordlandia and its neighbor across the river had tripled, making the trip across much longer. Our dock, which during the dry season stood fifteen feet above the water, was now only about eight or nine feet from the surface. One great advantage of the high water was that we could go much farther into the forest in the upper Tapajos estuaries. Sometimes little streams appeared that didn't exist at all when the water was low. Using the Araci as a mother ship, Ubirajara, Pericles, Edsel (and Henry), and I spent days exploring the jungle in our skiff and dugout, which we towed astern like dinghies to and from Fordlandia. We would occasionally run across native settlements and chat with them, with Leeram's help. As I had promised him, his coconut was with me at all times now. The natives were generally very friendly and generous, sharing their food and drink with us, as we did with them. By now, any fastidiousness we had at the beginning was long gone. Some of the things they ate and drank were actually very good, although they liked our rum better than theirs. Ubi finally told us to stop sharing so much of it. "They are in a natural balance with the forest," he said. "This liquor does not help."

Part of our mission, of course, was to find more reed

grass, but we also found much else. Either Ben or Seth or both sometimes would come along with us and they carefully extracted and transplanted specimens of strange plants into pots aboard the Araci for later study in their lab. The tribes were very helpful to our two biologists in their search for green secrets. Ben and Seth kept reminding us that the rain forest is so vast, even now after so much of it had been destroyed, that it still contained uncountable undiscovered life forms. Once, they returned in the dugout after two nights in the jungle, loaded with so many strange looking plants that only a couple of inches of freeboard were left. The stillness of the water was the only thing that kept them from swamping completely.

We finally got word via the satellite phone that SPI had harvested their soybean crop and we went back down to Belterra, tractor, grasses, and all the special equipment we needed. By now we had collected enough seeds to plant rather than merely transplant—an essential part of our plan. Ben, Seth, and Dean Knotwell had perfected growing techniques. We had enough to completely fill all the new land there. As we had promised, we kept the local manager, formerly employed by SPI, as our Belterra representative to look after our own interests there. "I am very happy and very grateful," he said, beaming. "Thank you so much. You do not have to worry about a thing down here. I already have my seed bins full of new soybeans and I will start fertilizing and getting your fields ready whenever you want me to start." I realized that we had not told him exactly what we were going to plant, but I couldn't put it off any longer.

"I don't think you want to do that now," I said. "You need to ship that stuff back to SPI, because we are going to grow a new, experimental product."

His eyes lit up and he grinned. "That sounds very interesting. What is it?" When I told him, his smile drooped. "Grass?" he said. "Grass?"

"Yes, grass. But it is very special grass and it will be worth a lot of money."

"If you say so, Boss. When do we start?"

By the time I finished describing the process, the manager was looking at me as if I had just described a way to grow Jack's beanstalk. "Don't worry," I said. "You are on salary, so just follow along and you'll see." We walked down to the dock, where O'Malley, Pericles, Ubirajara, and Edsel were unloading our equipment, including big spools of electrical cable. "We will need some help, so round up some of your farmers," I said. "This is not difficult, so once you see how it's done, you shouldn't have much of a problem to keep it going." By the end of the day, we had about an acre of good furrows prepared for planting. It was pretty straightforward and the manager had begun to cheer up again—a natural state for him, I decided. He rounded up some help, and they went at it the next morning, making sure that the wires and the root systems were in contact. Elsewhere we would just plant the seeds over the wires and let them grow into contact as the plants developed naturally.

Originally, when we first connected our own house to Ben and Seth's experimental garden, the process was pretty simple: grass patch to inverter to house. As we expanded into Fordlandia and later in Urucubituba, the grid was pretty simple, rudimentary. As the scale of our electrical farming grew, we were faced with the problem of simply moving our "product" over larger distances and greater volume, or amperage. Edsel was one of the first to bring this up, much earlier. He was a trained engineer himself, although his specialty wasn't directly in our field, but an engineer is an engineer. "We've got to solve this problem before we can go much farther," he said. "DC current just doesn't carry over long distances without a lot of loss, so either the grass has to be closer to the customer or we have to find a way to change it to AC cheaply and without too much loss."

We brought the problem to Henry, who contemplated it while lying on his back. "I'll ask Thomas," he said, finally. We waited for a while, but the Ford dolphin was not forthcoming with anything else.

"Thomas? Father, please be a little more specific," Edsel finally said.

"Edison."

"I thought everyone was so scattered about on your side that locating people is almost impossible?" I said.

"Some of us have our ways," the dolphin said. "We had

our ways on your end, and we have them now. It's only the little people, and Mormons, who haven't been able to navigate too well. I was in touch with many former people who made a considerable mark in this universe, although they are mostly my own contemporaries. We had a bond, you see."

"But you are here, not there," I said. "You can't talk with them now."

"True," he replied, "but you have Leeram."

Of course! I went back to my room and took the coconut out of my dresser. When the connection between his universe and mine formed into place (sometimes with a nearly audible snap, others only after a long, drizzly sound that reminded me of an old telephone modem), I relayed everything to him. "Yeah," Leeram said, "those types have a way of linking to each other, especially if they knew each other well in the past." He paused for a moment. "Thomas Edison? Ask Ford what he looks like and where he might be hanging out. Can't guarantee anything, you know, but for your sake, I'll give it a try."

A couple of hours later and a few more trips back and forth, I had Leeram back on the line again. "Short kind of guy—no neck?" he asked. I told him yes. "I've got him," Leeram said. "What do you want to ask him?"
I had a momentary mental image of Leeram holding Edison by the scruff of his little neck. "Tell him that his friend Henry Ford made it through back here all right, or mostly all right, and that he needs Edison's help in

designing a particular piece of electrical equipment." The line went silent for a while.

"Edison says there are too many relays, too many middlemen, and some of you have no training. He needs to talk to Ford directly."

"I don't know how that's possible," I said. "Doesn't one of them have to have something that belonged to the other to make a direct link, like you and I do?" I told Leeram to hang on for a little while. I needed to talk to Ford. When I found him, freshly returned from lunch in the Tapajos, I relayed my conversation, and our dilemma.

The dolphin pondered for a minute, then said, "Your friend Leeram gave you that coconut and that made a link. What if you lent it to me and he, in turn, lent it to Edison? Something like 'I'm lending you the coconut that I gave to Gilbert.'"

"But how can you lend something to someone else that you already gave away? It doesn't exactly sound like a deal you could take to the bank," I said.

"Just look at me, son" Ford said. "Improbable outcomes are not all that impossible in this world." I had to agree, and, sighing a little, tossed the coconut into his tank.

"Don't forget; give it back!" I said, feeling slightly nervous. I hoped that I hadn't done something irreversible.

The dolphin nosed the coconut into a corner of the tank, where it floated just out of my sight. I could only catch glimpses of it when it bounced against his beak. Then it was gone. Henry Ford had just eaten it! "What have you done?" I yelled. I had a horrible feeling that the link to my best friend had been lost forever. "I'm going to cut you open and take that coconut out of your fucking belly," I screamed.

"Calm down, son," the dolphin said. "It was the only way I could make a connection. Don't worry, you'll get it back." I was furious—as angry as I was when Edson stole Leeram's head.

I went off to find Edsel. "Your father just ate Leeram's coconut," I said, when I found him. "Help me."

We came back to the tank. "Father," Edsel said exasperatedly, "what the hell have you done?"

Ford turned toward us. "Calm down, hold your water," he said. "This is the only way I can make a connection with your aboriginal friend. If it doesn't work, you'll have the coconut back in due time. I don't digest coconuts very well and it is uncomfortable to pass them, but it will survive."

"Ewww!" I said. "You are going to defecate Leeram?"

"Well, I ate him, didn't I? How else are you going to get him back? Now just leave us alone for a while!"

Edsel turned to me: "Let's find Ubirajara. Maybe if we all concentrate, and if Leeram still has his knife, we can get up a critical mass." We found Ubi down at the dock, chatting with Dean Knotwell and told him what happened.

"If Leeram still has my knife, it will help," Ubi said. "Let's go!" We went back up the hill and found Henry

Ford swimming in a circle, his beak moving. He saw us come up to his tank and nodded.

"I have a connection," he said, "but I'm glad you're here. It gets clearer the closer you get to me." He paused, then, "Leeram? I need to talk to Tom. Tom Edison. You can find him at...." Something something something—it was garbled, and that was all I could make out. "Wait a minute," the dolphin said to us suddenly. Then to Leeram: "OK, yes, yes. I need to pick his brain for a minute."

"Stick around," he told us, then, "Tom, my good friend...How are you? What? You think I'm daft? Well, you may be right, but I'm having the time of my life." They went on like that for a while, then Ford began to describe our project, and, specifically, what we needed. "We need a kind of black box," he said. "A small, compact, inexpensive transformer to harvest the electricity from the grass, store it, and make it useful to people." Much back-and-forth ensued. Ben and Seth were brought in to answer specific questions from Edison about the nature of the green electricity they had discovered. Finally, Edison announced that he had a solution and, through Henry Ford, asked for someone to transcribe what he had in mind. By now all of us were gathered around the tank. Pericles and Dean Knotwell went off for pencils, paper, and a laptop. When everything was ready, the dolphin began to dictate. It went on for an hour or so, then after we read everything back and made corrections, according to Edison's instructions, it was time to sign off. We had a design for our transformer that looked simple, yet had some novel features none of us had seen before.

"Well, old friend," said Ford, "It's been very good talking to you, and you have our thanks. What? You say you want to thank me for giving you something interesting to do? Well, why do you think I wanted to come back so badly. You ought to try it yourself." He turned to Edsel and me and said, "Build that as soon as you can and get it patented."

Chapter 31

It took some elbow grease the next day to make Leeram's coconut presentable—not to mention odor-free—but eventually it looked and smelled pretty much the way it had before, although in my imagination the smile had lost some of its carefree lilt.

We had to go all the way to Santarem to find an old radio and TV repair shop that had the wire and fittings we needed, as well as a place to buy some sheet aluminum to case it in, but once we had everything together, we worked with the man who operated the little shop and pieced together a working model of the inverter according to our plans. We then contacted Jillian Roberts in Washington, and emailed scans of our diagrams to her, along with detailed descriptions of the grass-to-AC electrical device. Jillian was impressed and promised to get back to us via our satellite phone as soon as she could. We commissioned the shop to make another dozen to take them back and test them in the field. Lisa and Jillian had become good friends over the phone and chatted quite often. "I really admire her," she said to me. "I can't wait to meet her when we go home."

Back in Fordlandia, we tried it first on our own little group of cottages. When Ben and Seth threw the switch, the lights came on even more brilliantly than they had before, and instantaneously as well. It was an amazing difference. "According to our meters, this inverter has doubled the useable output from the grass," Edsel said. "It is exactly what we needed to make it work everywhere." In the next few days, after the rest had arrived, we hooked some of them up to our grass fields in Fordlandia and Urucubituba, saving the last six for Belterra when the fields we had planted there reached maturity.

"Naturally it works," the dolphin said, when we gave him the news. "Everything Tom does works!" Edsel shrugged and rolled his eyes.

"Please thank him for us," the ever-polite Ben and Seth said.

Our reed grass in Belterra grew rapidly—faster than it would in the wild, since the excess electricity, which would normally slow its growth, was being drained by the wires it was planted on. Our fields there were ready for "harvest" in a few months, and we set up our equipment. Before long, the entire town was so bright as to be visible from space, if any astronaut was interested in looking at it. The electricity cost a small fraction of the charge the local diesel-generated power company levied, and the town reveled in the quiet nights that followed. Our new manager, Abilio Guilherme, was ecstatic. He was now a man of some local influence. He had to hire two more people, who had worked for the old power company, to administer the project. Even at the new low rates, the income was more than enough to pay for everything and to put our project well into the black. We could now afford to keep the Araci in commission indefinitely and finally sleep well at night under our mosquito netting, dropping off without concerns about the next day. Guilherme's little office building that once displayed SPI's logo, now had a big sign saying, "Amazon Light and Power Co. Ltd." We would get to actual papers of incorporation later, but it looked pretty impressive.

By now, Ubirajara and Dean Knotwell were rarely seen apart. "I saw them holding hands!" Lisa said to me one afternoon, after they had returned from a long dugout ride on the Tapajos. For weeks they sat next to each other at the dinner table and usually left together. I had noticed, as had the others, that she was beginning to look younger. Even her hair, which had been mostly gray when I first met her, had darkened imperceptibly and had lost some of its brittleness. It became smoother and more supple, almost like the hair in shampoo ads. She had broken free, mentally and physically, from the ivory tower and become more like Suxie, breathing the rain forest air in deeply. Even the subcutaneous layers under her skin seemed to have firmed up, flattening out her wrinkles and softening her features. We all had become so used to her new persona that it almost came as a nonsurprise when Ubi called for our attention one night before we began dinner.

"Elizabeth and I have something to tell you," he said solemnly. Then he reached over and took her hand, smiled, and said: "We have decided to get married."

I said "almost came as a nonsurprise" but the word almost was the operative one. In fact, we were gobsmacked. Suxie looked at them with her mouth open, knife and fork dropping to the table. After a long pause, she was the first one to speak, and we all looked at her. She was as startled as we were at first, but then she broke into a wide smile and raised her glass. "To my grandfather and step-grandmother," she said. "I love you both and I am so happy for you."

Everyone stood and spoke all at once. "Congratulations," we said. "Bravo." We all laughed and cheered and raised our glasses, too.

"Ubi and I have taken a long time to come to this decision," Dean Knotwell said. "And I can understand how, well, unusual it may seem. I know that some people would think there is a small age difference between us, but it doesn't really matter. We are two halves of a whole. I bring my lifetime of knowledge in the modern world, and Ubi brings his overwhelming knowledge of the natural world; together we are greater than the sum of our parts." Our applause drowned out everything for a long time. It was several minutes before anyone could speak and be heard. "Captain O'Malley has agreed to preside over the nuptials aboard the Araci," Dean Knotwell said, nodding toward the Captain who was sitting at the other end of the table. Ubirajara, grinning like a teenager, rose to his feet.

"No woman I have ever met in both my lives has ever approached Elizabeth's intelligence, charm, and complete embrace of this place—my home. I never thought I would fall in love again, and to have it happen here and now is a gift beyond my ability to describe. I love you, Elizabeth." We all rose to our feet again and the sound of cheering applause was overwhelming.

O'Malley stood up, smiling from ear to ear, and said, "I'm very happy to marry you, I mean, perform the marriage. I've never done this before, but I'm your man," he said. He raised his glass and said: "To a long and fruitful life together." We all toasted with him while Ubirajara held Dean Knotwell with his arm around her waist.

"I'm sure you're going to do a great job," I said. "Maybe you'll become known as the Marrying Skipper of the Amazon."

He laughed. "I've been called a lot worse things!"

The wedding took place a few days later in the middle of the Rio Tapajos, accompanied by a small carimbo band playing traditional Amazonian marriage songs on flutes and guitars. Later, they switched to sambas while we all danced aboard the Araci's decks as the tropical evening slid into the cool of the night, the music drifting all the way across the river. The Carvahlos were there, as was the Mayor and his wife, and many other guests from Fordlandia, all bringing gifts and things to eat and drink. Henry Ford leaped and splashed around us to the beat. "He only needs a lampshade," Edsel said. The next morning, leaving the rest of us behind, the Araci went north with the newlyweds aboard for a short honeymoon in Santarem.

While they were away, a letter from our Washington attorney's office came with a copy of our patent for the "green box," as we called it. Earlier, we had made plans to have them built in Belterra because, unlike Fordlandia, it was accessible by ground telephone lines. We thought about manufacturing them in Manaus, but it was just a little too far for us. When the newlyweds came back in a few days, we got started. With the help of our new manager in Belterra, we bought a small building and equipped it with the necessary machinery to build the green boxes in quantity and before long, they started coming off the production line. Lights starting glowing in more and more little villages until the banks of not just the Tapajos, but the Amazon itself began to sparkle at night.

One day, a reporter from a big newspaper in Brasilia appeared in our office. He had heard about us from a number of people and was very curious. His article, complete with photos, came out in the paper's Sunday magazine edition about a week later, and our little cloistered world was soon visible to everyone. The article was reprinted, linked to, or otherwise referred to all over the world and our privacy became a thing of the past. Soon, reporters, politicians, grifters, and job-seekers began to arrive by the boatload. Inevitably they came across Ford's tank and we had to pass it (and the dolphin inside it) off as a curiosity, saying we just liked weird pets. Ford was savvy enough to keep his real identity secret when they were ogling him, although when they left, he would make a rude gesture at their backs. What he actually did is too complicated to describe here.

It was the first new house built in Fordlandia since the Ford Motor Company abandoned the place in 1945, but Ubirajara and Dean Knotwell decided that it was necessary. No existing structure could possibly contain this couple. They decided that it should be a home that could float with the seasonal rising of the water as the rainy season progressed, and settle back down when it got dry. Their address would change when the rains came and went, which gave them a sense of being woven into the forest. "Don't worry," Dean Knotwell said, when she described the new place, "we'll never be that far away."

Ubirajara held out his new smartphone. "When we get a cell tower built here, you'll always be able to call us."

It was the point at which we knew we really weren't in the rain forest anymore.

The Mayor was the one who insisted. "We need to be part of the grid," he explained. "How else can I call you when you're in Belterra? So the appropriate utility company was contacted and, at our expense, a cell phone antenna was built right next to the water tower. It was disguised to look like a rubber tree, a subterfuge that only fooled the occasional passing dog, who would usually pee on it.

We were now working seven days a week as we assembled our growing business and spread our product over a wider and wider area in Brazil and even neighboring countries. Before long we had to relocate our main office to Santarem and even bought a new freight boat after the Araci became overwhelmed with more cargo than she could carry. In addition to the grass, all the other agricultural produce the native Fordlandians and Urucubitubans were now producing needed to be shipped to market. We were so busy that even our evening get-together was skipped more often than not. We were getting professional business advice from both Fords; Edsel was moving to Santarem to take charge of things there. Henry's suggestions were invaluable; he had taken every bit of his business cunning through the wormhole with him, starting with his insistence that we patent everything. Also, with Edsel far enough downriver, there were fewer opportunities for them to clash.

And then one day, it all came to a sudden stop.

Chapter 32

The letter was from Washington, addressed to Dean Knotwell, the one officially in charge of our grant. With an unreadable expression, she silently gave it to Suxie, who was nearby. When she finished, she handed it to me.

"Dear Dr. Elizabeth Knotwell," it began. "This office is in receipt of an order by the US Department of State, enjoining any further activities on your part or the NGO that you represent in the State of Para, Brazil, until certain allegations by the Brazilian National Bank regarding proprietary agricultural rights have been settled.

"In accordance with the Order, the Department of Agriculture hereby suspends any further grant payments until this issue is resolved. In addition, you and your associates are ordered to vacate any property in Fordlandia that you currently occupy." The letter was signed by the Director of the Department.

I was stunned. "But we have permission from the

Brazilian government to be here. How can the USDA order us off the land?"

We called everyone to meet in our office. Our complacency had been shattered like a dropped egg. Ubirajara was confused. "What do they mean? How can they make us move out? This is our land!" We explained the intricacies of grants-in-aid and the blind corridors of bureaucracy, but he still couldn't understand our dilemma. "I do not accept this," he said and walked out the door.

"And the grant has nothing to do with Amazon Light and Power," Edsel, who had returned from Santarem for a periodic meeting with us, said. "Nor does it have anything to do with me or my father."

"How much time do we have?" I asked Dean Knotwell.

"Hard to say. I think I may have to go to Washington myself. I just can't believe this," she said. Using the satellite phone, we placed a call to Lew Bean at the US Department of Agriculture, the man I had met on my trip to DC, it seemed years ago now. When the connection was established, Dean Knotwell picked the phone up. "What is this letter all about?" she asked with incredulity. The speaker was on, so we could hear both sides of the conversation.

"I was hoping you would call earlier," he said, "and I wish I had a chance to warn you about it, but I was kind of blindsided myself. I think you guys have stirred up a hornet's nest down there."

"But we've followed the rules," she said. "We have made life much better for the indigenous population and are trying to motivate people to stop cutting into the rain forest! We have done a lot of original research here and it's just the tip of the iceberg. We can't leave now!"

"I know, I know...I've read all your reports. It's not my decision. Someone from the Administration got to my bosses, so whatever happened is a lot bigger than you and me. All I know is that you have to be out of there as soon as you can."

"We just can't shut the lab down like, like, snapping your fingers," Seth said, Ben next to him, nodding his head vigorously. "We have experiments underway that will take months and years to complete."

"I'm really, really sorry," Llewellian said. His voice was low and he obviously meant it. "I am out of the loop on this, and if I tried to stop it, I'd be out of a job." It was as though we had just walked through a weird osmotic barrier from a bright, sunny world full of promise into a void, a world of hurt. Shock, disappointment, anger, and grief rushed in to fill it.

"Who wants to tell Mr. Ford?" I asked. They all looked at me. I sighed and left for the tank, arriving just as he came in from the river. "I have some disturbing news," I said. "We are being evicted." That got the dolphin's attention.

"What are you talking about?"

"I think we have stepped on some toes."

He looked at me silently for a long moment, then: "It was SPI, wasn't it? I could have told you." I replied that our contact in Washington didn't name anybody or any corporation, but the circumstantial evidence was undeniable. Who else's nose could we have put out of joint? "Well, I feel sorry for you folks," Ford said, "but they will have a much harder time kicking me out. I'm going for a swim." He performed a rolling turn and disappeared into his canal.

At first, back in our meeting room, we were defiant. "We'll stay until they point guns at us," Dean Knotwell said.

Ubirajara, who by then had re-entered the room, said: "They might be able to force us out of Fordlandia and Belterra, but they cannot force us out of the rain forest. My people, my granddaughter's people, and now yours too," he said, smiling at Dean Knotwell, "live here. It's time for a strategic retreat. We can leave Fordlandia and go into the deep rain forest far enough to make them think we are gone. We can load everything we need on board the Araci, tow our house behind, go as far up the river and its tributaries as we need to, and live there indefinitely. Granddaughter, are you with me?" For some time now, Ubirajara had incrementally assumed a leadership role among us and now it became total. I knew I was leaving everything in good hands.

"You mean leave without putting up a fight?" the Dean said. Ever since she had fallen in love with Ubi, she had become quite fierce, as though her primitive inner core had been suppressed for all those years in the ivory tower and was just coming out with a vengeance.

Suxie, the one I thought might object, merely said, "We aren't really leaving, just going farther into the heart of my land. I want to do it. Yes, I am with you, Grandfather." She was as changed from her old towering, angry self as could possibly be imagined. Schwartzkopf had been replaced with a very different persona—Gandhi perhaps. "Grandfather," she said, "lead the way. We have done all we can here."

Edsel, who had been silent until now, said: "I took a chance to come here that was more difficult and more dangerous than anyone here except Ubirajara and my father could understand. I have no intention of going back to the United States now or anywhere else but the Amazon. My father and I like it here. We can run Amazon Light and Power and keep it as a base that the government knows nothing about. The river is my father's home now, and the SPI company has no idea of our existence. This is a wonderful opportunity and I vote for Ubi's—Ubirajara's—plan. In time, we will prevail."

In the end, even Ben and Seth agreed on the strategy. Pericles, Lisa, and I would leave for home while the rest would load everything aboard the Araci—their Ark now—and find a new home deep in the Amazon jungle while the water was still high enough for her to navigate that far. Araci's shallow draft meant that she could go hundreds of miles up tributaries that only existed during the rainy season; they could take her deep enough to make her disappear. They would have to wait for another year at the earliest to get back, during which the little ship would just rest in the mud while the water retreated. In the meantime, they would have time to regroup and plan their return. Ben and Seth's biological work could continue.

"But how can we communicate with you?" I asked. "Your satellite phone can be traced."

Lisa, who had been silent until then, said one word. "Flashy."

"Flashy the parrot?" I said.

"Yes, Flashy. Green Flash," Lisa said. "She's really remarkable. Sometimes I think she's as smart as we are. She can take messages back and forth from wherever you are to Santarem, and Edsel can contact us in Boston."

We discovered, by the way, that Flashy was a female when an egg showed up in her cage one morning.

"Flashy knows the forest and the rivers like the back of her hand, I mean claw, because she grew up here. But what about Captain O'Malley?" Lisa asked. "Does he want to do this?"

We found him aboard the vessel, working on some routine engine maintenance. It was pretty obvious that without him, our plan was a pipe dream.

We showed him the order from the State Department and then told him what we were thinking. "This isn't a defeat," I said. "We'll be back when we figure out a way."

At first O'Malley was undecided, and asked for some time to think about it. "Thanks to Henry Ford," I went on, "we have patents on file and some pending that nail down our financial interest in Amazon Light and Power. Pericles, Lisa, and I are going to follow through on them when we get back to the states. If you stay with us, we'll include you in that business."

Finally, his face went from frown to grin; he put out his hand and said: "You are the nuttiest bunch of weirdoes I have ever met. I don't know what the hell I would do with myself that would be half as interesting if I went home. You're on—it's a deal."

The next few days went by quickly. We sent a letter back to Washington acknowledging receipt of our eviction notice, and began packing the essentials for the Araci's retreat, including most of Ben and Seth's lab equipment. The Araci had a freshwater distillation plant, so that eliminated the need for water storage. Medical supplies were sufficient and already stocked aboard. Captain O'Malley topped off the fuel tanks in Belterra while we informed our manager there, Abilio Guilherme, that he would be reporting to our new headquarters in Santarem under the new president there, Edsel "Smith." I made a solo trip to Urucubituba to say goodbye to the Carvahlos, telling them that I would see them again someday. The hardest thing, though, was telling the Mayor in Fordlandia what had happened. He was going to have to pick up the traces himself again. "I don't really mind," he lied.

"We'll be back," I told them. The Mayor insisted on giving us a great send-off party. The villagers all gathered that evening and the cooking fires started. Cachaca and alua flowed, a pig was spitted and before long, the smell of roasting meat mixed with the delicious odors of frying plantains and other fruits began to surround us. The Mayor, standing at his usual place at the table, gave us a long, heartfelt farewell. Not a few air-conditioners were humming in cottages, powered by the cheap, plentiful electricity we had made possible.

The party lasted well into the evening. At one point, after coming back from talking to some villagers, I caught Lisa, grease on her chin, eating a chunk of roast pig. When I expressed surprise, she smiled at me. "It's really good," she said. "Try some."

Things went quickly over the next few days. Lisa, Pericles, Edsel, and I waved from the dock as the Araci backed off into the river and turned upstream, minus the dolphin tank which had been left ashore. We waved until the Araci and her tow were out of sight. We boarded the cargo vessel we had bought earlier to supplement the Araci and left for Belterra, steaming slowly so the dolphin could keep up. Edsel remained aboard, and Lisa and I took a riverboat to Santarem just down the river. We all had plenty of cash from the Amazon Light and Power Co., which would be administered by Edsel "Smith." He took up residence in a small house, while the dolphin found a snug cove nearby. Two days later, Lisa, Pericles, and I were at the Santarem airport, ready to board a plane to Manaus, then one to New York. We parted after a farewell drink at the Manaus airport bar. Pericles was bound for Illinois, and Lisa and I had tickets to Logan Airport in Boston. We arrived late on a cold, rainy May evening and stood in line to go through customs. When our turn came, the customs official looked at us a little longer than he should have, and asked me to open my backpack. Naturally I had packed Leeram last and he was the first thing the officer saw. The coconut's battered smile seemed to bother him and he said "Sorry, but you can't bring this into the country. Why didn't you declare it?" He picked it up and dropped it into a bin marked "contraband."

"But that's Leeram," I shouted.

"I don't care if it's the King of Siam," he said. "Didn't you read the rules? No vegetable products from Brazil." I had made such a scene that it attracted the attention of some heavily armed Homeland Security personnel nearby, and I immediately quieted down. "Son," he said, "that's a coconut and you can't take it into this country. Besides, that's a lousy job of carving. You can get a much better one on line." I couldn't think of anything to say. "Next," he said, motioning to the line in back of us. Lisa and I left, numbed by the loss and our inability to say or do anything. We took the shuttle to a nearby hotel, unable to do much more than look at each other. We tried to eat some dinner but finally fell into bed and curled up in misery. Leeram did not make an appearance in my dreams that night.

****

The next few weeks were so busy we didn't have much time to think about him, although when I did, I felt his loss almost as keenly as I did when Edson threw him into the Tapajos. We had the plans and documentation for the green boxes and enough money to get a start on a North American headquarters for ALP — Amazon Light and Power Ltd. — and as soon as we found a place to live, a small apartment on the north side of Beacon Hill, we immersed ourselves in the project. It helped our grief.

Then, one gorgeous Saturday on a June afternoon, Lisa and I decided to take a walk down Charles Street at the foot of Beacon Hill, stopping to look in the windows of antique stores along the way. We had just finished an ice cream cone while standing on the narrow sidewalk, making ourselves into a two-person island in a stream of tourists and other pedestrians. On a whim, we entered one of the stores, accompanied by the *ching* of the doorbell and smelled the fusty air within. I wasn't really concentrating on anything, just letting my eyes skip over the junk on the shelves—the oak-framed mirrors with their peeling silver in back, art glass in all its forms and variations, bronze garden statues, and cracked paintings. As I got deeper into the store, I hear Lisa call suddenly from another cranny: "Gilbert! Gilbert!"

When I found her, she was looking at a small object partly hidden behind some gourds and what seemed to be an African spear. I picked it up. It was a dog-chewed baseball, only this time the dog must have gnawed on it for a long time. Then I looked a little harder.

It was Leeram.

The stitches had come loose in a few places and the hair was no longer luxurious. "Where did this come from?" I asked the proprietor, trying my best to sound uninterested, just a little curious about its provenance. He told me that it was a fake shrunken head he got from a wholesaler in South America.

"He tried to tell me that it came up in a fisherman's net in the Amazon," the dealer said. "I could tell right away it was bogus, but I took it from him anyway because it was part of a large consignment of good stuff. If you want it, you can have it for ten bucks." I looked at Lisa. A few minutes later, we were back on Charles Street, holding a paper bag.

"Are you sure?" she asked.

"It is Leeram. I am sure." I had no doubt that it was him in spite of the strange sense of vacancy that surrounded it. When we got back to our apartment, I took it out of the bag and put it on the kitchen table. I poured a glass of rum (I had developed a taste for it in Brazil), added some tonic and ice, and filled a glass of wine for Lisa. When we were both seated, I picked up my glass and said, "Leeram, if you can hear us at all, we've got your old head." I have to admit, I felt almost embarrassed, sounding so stupidly. I hoped Lisa wouldn't think I was completely nuts.

Then I heard her say, "Hi Leeram, It's Lisa and we missed you." We looked at each other, both slightly embarrassed. A long moment went by. Suddenly, I was aware of a very familiar odor—ozone! Even though nothing at all changed physically about the head, everything was different. It was alive again!

"Is that you, son?"

"It is, you old bastard," I said. "It's me, and you're back! I don't believe it!"

"Where am I?" he asked, sounding a little dazed. I told him everything the antique dealer had said.

"Son-of-a-bitch," he said. "When that bastard threw me in the river, I thought that was it. I cut the connection because I had no interest in hanging around while a fish ate me and I never came back." Lisa and I shrieked and whooped. I couldn't keep from crying. We did a little dance around the living room. When we finally calmed down, Leeram told us that he had kept in touch with Ubi, and that the Araci had found a perfect hiding place so far up a seasonal tributary and under a solid canopy of tall trees. She was invisible from the air, and that her crew had settled in to their new home, getting ready for a comeback.

It was, I knew, the beginning. I reached out to take Lisa's hands in mine. "We're going to Washington."

CPSIA information can be obtained at www.ICGtesting.com
Printed in the USA
BVOW08s1114041015

420880BV00001B/57/P